THE GOVERNOR'S DAUGHTER

THE MYSTERIES OF COLONIAL CAMBODIA

SAMBATH MEAS

THE GOVERNOR'S DAUGHTER

The Mysteries of Colonial Cambodia

Sambath Meas

Published by Red Empress Publishing
www.redempresspublishing.com

Copyright © Sambath Meas 2017
www.sambathmeas.com

Cover by Cherith Vaughan
www.empressauthorsolutions.com

All rights reserved. No part of this publication may be reproduced, stored in a retrieval system, or transmitted in any form or by any means, electronic, mechanical, photocopying, recoding, or otherwise, without the prior written consent of the author.

To Mom and Dad

ACKNOWLEDGMENTS

Thanks to two candid editors, Lisa Balthazar and Nowick Gray and my friend Sharon Moy for the final input as an avid reader.

1

BEING WOMEN

I took my first breath in 1903. The French were celebrating their fortieth year of colonizing Cambodge, which they called the French Protectorate. My country used to be known as Kambuja, Kambuja-desa, or the Khmer Empire when it dominated almost the entire region of Southeast Asia. Tragically for us, by the 15th century, two new groups of people—the Siamese and Annamese—emerged and gradually pushed our people aside. They started out by seizing control of the lower Mekong basin—the economic ground and key to controlling Southeast Asia.

The French referred to the region as Indochina, an area between India and China. The ancient people of Southeast Asia were heavily influenced by India in terms of religion, philosophy, language, and culture. We identified more with India rather than China. According to our history, as relayed to me by my grandfather, Princess Soma was the first monarch and ruler of our Kingdom of Nokor Phnom or Nokor Korktlork. Her union with an Indian Brahmin named Kaundinya combined our language, religion, and culture. The kingdom flourished and came to be known as Kambuja. However, Chinese travelers who found an easy and profitable life in Cambodge reported back home about the country's richness in gold, so many Chinese migrated here and lived quietly among us, intermarrying and assimilating with the Khmers.

By the 19th century, European colonial powers, especially the British and the French, whose countries rivaled each other in many aspects—including their goals of world domination—set their sight on Indochina. Siam, as a buffer state between the French and the British, dodged colonialism. According to French historians, King Norodom requested the establishment of a French protectorate on our country. However, my grandfather, and others who witnessed the signing of the treaty, saw it differently. That year, my grandfather recounted in a sad and disappointed tone, Cochin China's governor Charles Thomson came from Prey Nokor to Phnom Penh on a steamboat to force the king to sign a treaty to the further detriment of the Khmer people and country. One hundred armed guards were at the ready to show him no mercy should the king refuse to sign. That was the French's injection of diplomacy in my small but resilient country.

By the time I was seventeen years old, we had lived under fifty-seven years of French "protection." I knew my place as a Khmer; I had seen, on several occasions, at royal functions or French diplomatic functions, the French president and ministers sitting in the middle and higher than our king and queen. We, the loyal subjects, bow and prostrate to our king and queen, but when I saw their Majesties bowing to the French president and ministers, I recognized the hierarchy within our own country.

Wealthy Khmers and peasants alike complain about how much more in taxes they have to pay in comparison to their Chinese and Annamese counterparts. People barely getting by find themselves eating one meal a day in order to raise the money they must pay to the French. Many poor peasants go into hiding whenever the French tax collectors and their Annamese assistants, who spoke broken Khmer, come by the villages to collect taxes. For those wealthy ones who are brave enough to question such unfairness, the French respond, "If it weren't for us, you would have ceased to exist as a people and as a nation a long time ago. We saved you from your belligerent neighbors, Annam and Siam. That doesn't come cheap. You must pay your dues." So much for saving us from our "belligerent" neighbor Annam, considering they held them above us. They built schools for them, educated them, and hired them to monopolize our civil service and professional positions. The French controlled our economy and allowed foreigners to dominate that as well. Meanwhile, they were reluctant to improve our literacy rates, and for those of us Khmers who found education on our own, the French did not create opportunities for us. As demonstrated by our ancient temples that were built to align with space and time, our cosmic architectural wonder, they saw our capability in using our brain, but they still believed us to be dark, ugly, and lazy people. I often overheard adult Khmers attending ceremonies at the pagoda complaining about how the French denigrated our people at the rubber plantation and exploited our labor by paying our people less than Chinese and Annamese immigrants, yet they turned around and forced us to pay higher taxes.

Devastatingly, Khmer leaders and people alike did not do enough to challenge the French's unfair treatment and their supremacy over us. Instead, our people complained but remained docile and accepted our "karma." Father said the majority of our people misinterpreted the meaning of karma and misunderstood the Buddha's teaching of it. "Karma represents cause and effect," he explained. "Action or inaction decides a person's fate in their future existence. Too many of our people believe God or a higher being had already shaped our destiny. They believe they're cursed and predestined to live the way they live. This inaccurate thinking causes them to be stuck in this paradigm of ignorance. They will not change and improve their lives with such superstition."

Father was right. I observed my fellow Khmers wherever I went out with my parents and relatives. Too many of them relied on the notion that we, as a people, were destined to live a life of enslavement. They became inactive and willingly accepted whatever treatment others bestowed upon them just to survive their life cycle on earth. Instead of living their lives now, they prayed their next life cycle would be better. At one of our attendances at the local pagoda, Father said to me, "See. Our people put too much stock on lavish ceremonies and prayers."

"What is wrong with prayers and religious ceremonies, Pouk?" I asked Father.

"They rely too much on 'boon' and 'merit' from religious ceremonies."

"I don't follow," I replied.

"Khmer people rely too much on prayers and religious ceremonies and not enough on personal initiative. Prayers will only work if they learn how to use their mind to receive guidance for their actions to get what they want in this life. They don't realize that they can have a good life here and now, not just in the next life. It's a shame that they save all their hard earned money to bestow lavish ceremonies at the temple when they should have invested in food for themselves, to give nutrients and strength to their brain, so that they can learn how to think for themselves."

He was right. They would do anything they could to contribute to the temple, even if they did not have any money, so that they would be born into a better life in their next life cycle. I greatly admired my grandfather and my father. They learned how to navigate through the system of colonialism and tried to help others along the way. Unfortunately, ignorant people tend to be stubborn. They did not see what Father was trying to show them, the path to happiness and peaceful existence. He did what he could. Father was one of those who did not complain but used what he was dealt to his advantage. I, like Father, liked the French language, customs, clothes, culture, food, vehicles, and technology they brought into our country, but I wished they saw us as human beings and did not treat us like we were third class citizens in our own land.

I should be thankful I lived a fairly comfortable life in comparison to the general population. I could not bear to see regular people fear the French and the authorities in general. I wanted to see them confident and brave, how the French portrayed themselves to us. I wanted them to see what I saw and learn what I learned. Father and his father greatly inspired me by what they had done for our country, and if the majority of people followed their way of thinking, we could break free from the iron claw of the French. Father and grandfather taught my brothers and me about the knowledge and truth that governed the universe and the people within it.

This is why I left home every morning, when I was not attending to my lessons, to apprentice under Father. My parents did not treat me any differently from my brothers when it came to education. They taught us what they knew and provided all of us a formal education. The only difference was that they were more protective of me because our society viewed women as delicate flowers or as prey.

My grandfather once told me when I was a little girl, "Matriarchy is the foundation of our country. A queen founded and ruled this land. Women ran the market. Notice how the beginning of most words consists of the word 'mother.'"

Unfortunately, under French colonialism, women and girls had no place anywhere, let alone in an office. But then again, working in an office was a fairly new concept in our corner of the world. That did not stop me from ranting and raving when Mother made it her morning ritual to delay and deter me from going to work.

It was Friday. I woke up to the glow of an orange, yellow, and purple sky. I quietly bathed and dressed in hopes of catching up with Father and riding with him to the office in our quaint town of Siem Reap. I could hear the engine of our car purr. Father's driver, Suon, was waiting up front. I could see Tony, my long-haired ridgeback dog, playfully running back and forth to him and barking. Unlike French and westerners, Khmer people do not allow dogs in the house, let alone let them sleep in and jump on our beds. We generally keep them as hunting and guard

The Governor's Daughter

dogs, but that doesn't mean we love and care for them any less.

As I tiptoed out of my bedroom door with my satchel across my body, Mother called from the kitchen, "Anjali, is that you, dear? I need your help."

I made my fists and struck the air in a fit of anger.

"I saw that," said Father good-naturedly as he walked out from the dining room. He must have finished his breakfast. Father was tall with salt and pepper hair. His eyes and demeanor often displayed calmness, like a monk. "I teach you not to be quick to give into anger."

"I'm not angry. I'm annoyed," I lied.

"It's still a negative emotion."

"Father, why must I go through this every morning? Why don't you say something to her?"

"Anjali," he said, putting his hand on my shoulder. "Do you know how hard it was to convince your mother to allow you to work with me? She's old fashioned. She's not used to a young woman—women in general—working at an office. Besides, the job you take an interest in is not easy on her mind and heart. To her, it's dangerous; you have no place in it. It's not helping when she hears from certain people in the community, women and men alike, that she is being liberal with you by letting you run around playing detective. They fill her head with negative thoughts."

"Do they say this around you?"

"No. They would not dare. They know my opinion differs from theirs."

"Why doesn't she put them in their place?"

"She can't."

"Why not?"

"Because she doesn't think differently from them."

"You have taught me martial arts and shooting."

"Shhh," said Father. "I have told you many times not to mention your self-defense lessons. Your mother doesn't know anything about them."

"Oh. Sorry, Father."

"Since I convinced her you'll be safe and will not do anything dangerous, she agreed to let you work with me. Now don't let this little thing called chores jeopardize your desire for something greater. If you have to go through them every morning, so be it."

"She's trying to run me down so that I will be too tired from my chores and not want to follow you to work."

"Are you going to let her run you down?"

"No," I said in a low voice.

"That's my girl."

"But what she's doing is mean." My voice started to rise again.

"Don't say that about your mother. She loves you. She means well."

"Doesn't she take into consideration what I want? How I feel?"

"She's your mother. A mother believes she knows what's best for her child."

"I don't like it. I have a mind of my own. I can certainly think for myself."

"Be kind to your mother. This is all she knows."

"Why don't you mentor her to know more, like you have been mentoring me all of my life."

"It takes longer to mentor her. It's the mentality that has been passed down from her parents to her. Like I said, this is all she knows. Give her more time. All you need to know is that she loves you. She cares for you. I have to go. I need to meet with Monsieur San Nuon before I go to the office."

"Okay, Father," I said.

"Now put on a smiling face and do as your mother asks. Once she sees how hard you work, she'll come around." He put on his bowler hat and descended the stairs.

I walked into the living room, left my satchel on the chair, and went to see what Mother wanted.

I walked into the kitchen to find my thin, curly haired mother sitting with both of her legs on either side of a small wooden bench that had a grater attached to one end. She vigorously shredded a half cracked coconut. She stopped when she saw me strolling in.

"Mother, you called me?"

She looked at me with her big, round, prominent eyes. "Yes, dear."

"What are you doing?" I asked.

"It's our turn to bring the food offering to the temple for the monks."

"What are you making?"

"Chicken curry. I'm also making chicken ginger."

"What can I help you with?" I asked, hoping she did not ask me to help her cook because the entire process would take hours.

"First, have yourself some breakfast."

"I'm not hungry."

"Oh, eat something, dear."

"Fine," I said, not trying to argue.

"After you're done can you clear up your father's dishes and clean them for me? And would you be a dear and harvest some potatoes, onions, ginger, basil leaves, and scallions for me?"

"Yes, Mother," I said, trying to control my annoyance.

By the time I was done washing and putting away the dishes, the mirage of the morning sun appeared. The cool morning changed to a sizzling heat. I descended the back staircase to the garden of fruits, vegetables, and flowers. After I had halfway filled my bamboo basket with produce, I saw my friend Jorani Sem, who stood as tall as me, riding my old bicycle my way. I had given it to her on an account that I received a new bicycle as a reward for doing well with my studies. She tied her stack of books on the cargo rack. She passed by my house every morning to get to the merchant's house some four kilometers away to teach his daughters how to read. When Jorani reached my house, she stopped and remained on the opposite side of my fence. "Good morning, Anjali. So here we are again," she said with smile on her face. She had been smiling a lot lately. She hummed and skipped about like she was floating on air. I wondered if being engaged to a twenty-year-old man named Kosal had anything to do with it.

"Good morning, Jorani," I said, giving her a quick glance before bending down to pull up scallions by the roots. I could hear the gravel under her feet as she walked over to the fence.

"Hmm. You don't sound so happy this beautiful morning."

I stood up and turned to her, seeing her resting her arms and chin on top of the flat surface of the fence. "How can I?" I said.

"Why is that?"

"It's terrible being a girl."

"Speak for yourself. I like being a girl," she said, tossing her hair back with her right hand.

I picked up my basket and walked over to where Jorani stood. I placed the basket on the ground next to the many lemongrass bushes flourishing nearly a meter tall by the fence. I lingered for a moment to face my friend. "That's not what I mean. I like being a girl too. But look! Look all around us. Look at our mothers, our grandmothers, our aunts, our neighbors. What do we all have in common?" I asked, turning to the left and the right of my backyard. Jorani displayed her pensive countenance, as if she did not want to give me the obvious answer—that I had expected something more intellectual. I did not intend for her answer anyway, just for her to listen. With my arms flailing about, I said, "We're bound by household chores. Here I am, trying to break away from domestic work, yet my dear mother keeps delaying me almost every morning with her endless chores just so that I will be too tired to work with Father. He told me community members had been filling her head with fear and negativity. Why does she care so much what other people say about me? 'Girls shouldn't be sleuthing,' they said. 'It's dangerous!' they said, Seriously. Why don't they say that about boys? Why can't I do all the things boys do? Why can't I be an explorer? Why can't I study abroad like my brothers? Why must I be tethered to household chores? How will I influence and change our people's mentality when I am stuck here? I want excitement. I want adventure. Why can't I choose my own destiny and venture far from here?" I moved back and forth in the garden as I pulled up green onions to put in the basket already containing basil leaves, potatoes, and other vegetables that I was sure Mother did not need, but since I was down there, I could not stop myself.

"Oh, Anjali. You're overly dramatic," said Jorani, waving her hand in dismissal. "Your mother asks you to pick some vegetables for her before you head out. You act like it's the end of the world. Even though we work outside the home, we still need to attend to our domestic duties. You're lucky you're working and not just bound to the house. You do have a sense of adventure. You get the best of both worlds. If anything, you're luckier than the rest of us. Look at me. I can't go any further than being a governess for a merchant's family. All I see are his wife, children, relatives, and a nice home. But your home is way nicer than his."

"Thanks."

"What I am saying is that you're luckier than women doing backbreaking labor in the rice fields, selling goods at the market or on the sides of the road, or being someone's indentured servant."

"I didn't look at it that way."

"I notice. That's why you need someone like me to put things in perspective for you."

"That's true. You, me, and Madame Montha are the lucky ones who get to leave our houses and go to work. Madame Montha and I get to interact with people of all professions," I said.

"In a way, you are right. I wish there were more of us in the workforce that mattered. We're such a small number that we're nearly invisible in comparison to men. Madame Montha and I work because...you know what? I can't believe I didn't realize it. You, me, and Madame Montha owe our opportunities to your father. Isn't that something? Your father allowed me to study with you. Lord knows my father and mother can't even afford an education for my brothers, let alone me. It's because of this education that the merchant hired me to teach his daughter how to read. As for Madame Montha, she lost her husband in the French battle and was forced to raise her three sons on her own. Your father gave her an opportunity to work and earn a living for her and her boys. Since you're his daughter, he has opened the path for you to do whatever you want."

"Not whatever," I said.

"Pretty much what you want. If only we had more men

like your father, then all of us women would have opportunities to contribute more to society than just raising children, performing domestic work, or working out in the fields."

"It's a good thing you're a teacher. You have influence over young minds."

"Hmm. Sadly, most of the people in our surrounding villages—in the entire country, for that matter—don't want their girls to learn. They're afraid the girls might read romance novels and write love notes to boys. To them, education is a corruption of the mind because, unlike boys or men, we don't know how to use it. They're afraid we might become rebellious, not conform to society. They might not listen to their parents' guidance. Parents believe they are responsible for picking and choosing their daughter's mate; hence, education would only turn their daughters against them. They equate education and knowledge to schemes and rebellion when it comes to educating girls and women. 'The less you know, the less trouble finds you,' is their mantra for us girls."

"That's sad, isn't it?" I said.

"It sure is! So, do you feel better about your situation?" Jorani asked.

"I do. Thanks for that." We looked at each and smiled our silly girl smiles.

Jorani blinked her lotus-petal shaped eyes and shook out her silky black hair. We have been best friends since we were five years old. We were born six months apart. I was the youngest of four brothers. She was the third oldest of seven siblings. She loved and valued education. Since her father could not afford to send her to school, I asked Father to have her study with me. He was more than happy to oblige, especially for a girl who loved learning as she did.

Sure, the female population generally did not attend school, but it was not an anomaly for girls in our town to attend a school taught by Catholic nuns or nuns from the local pagoda would teach girls how to read mantras to chant at the temple. If they had money they would hire private teachers like my friend Jorani.

Jorani had attained levels high enough in her studies to earn a living as a governess in the households of the elite of Siem Reap who wanted their girls to learn how to read and write while they sent off their sons to study abroad. Meanwhile, Jorani's brothers received their education at the Buddhist monastery. She also taught her sisters at home how to read and write in her spare time.

We stood similar in stature. Actually, our similarly tall physique prompted our neighbors to call us "coconut trees." We took it as a compliment. We shared the same peasant background, but her parents had to work much harder to feed their growing family. In western society, my family was considered an upper-class family, but since both my paternal and maternal families were rooted in peasantry, we still considered our family as such. We still had rice fields on which our relatives worked. My family may have lived as comfortably as the elite of Siem Reap, in a big and well-built home with big gardens of vegetables, fruits, and flowers, but we never forgot our peasant background.

"All right, I must get going. I don't want to be late. As your father said, 'Don't make others wait for you. It's a bad habit, not to mention rude.'" We said that last sentence in unison. We both flashed each other a pleasant smile and went on with our day.

Jorani left me and continued riding four kilometers to a merchant's home to teach his daughter reading and writing. I left the basket of vegetables for Mother, washed my hands, and ran out the door before she thought of something else to ask me to do. I hopped on my brand new bicycle.

Just when I pedaled away, I could hear Mother's voice calling out, "Be careful, Anjali. Don't stay too late. Come home soon, dear!" I waved her off. Mother—ever since she found out I wanted to follow in Father's footstep—tried to discourage me from it. It took some serious begging, pleading, and convincing from Father for Mother to allow me to work. *If I cannot make my own mother understand why I want to work and follow Father's footstep, then how can I influence others?* I could still feel Mother's bright eyes watching me from the encircled porch of our stilted wooden home. I pedaled hard. I did not dare to look back, as I was afraid she might call me back.

Once I turned from Phnom Meas Street onto Preah Khan Boulevard, I pedaled at a normal pace and enjoyed my morning ride. The warm wind blew my soft curly hair. Through my peripheral vision, I passed by random houses and buildings. It felt liberating to be traveling at my own leisure. I had time to think about things, to inhale the scent of the blooming tree flowers of chrey, plumeria rubra, roumdoul, and champei trees growing on both sides of the road. I was on my way to Father's office building in Siem Reap. Many thoughts rushed to my mind, one of which was the talk with Father. The time had come to approach him about moving up to something more challenging. As an apprentice under Father, the small cases he gave me such as missing jewelry, artifacts, and domesticated animals had become unchallenging. I wanted to investigate a homicide. I felt a bit nervous, as I anticipated he would shut me down due to Mother. Father was pulling me slowly into his life of mystery and adventure. I knew he had to tread lightly, as he loved Mother and respected her opinion. However, he had as much influence on her as she on him. Therefore, I hoped to speak to Father about my new position as soon as possible. I felt myself smiling as I thought about being promoted to do some serious sleuthing.

The sound of a horn woke me from my daydream. Someone yelled, "What's the matter? Do you want to die?" A red topless Citröen with four passengers screeched to a grinding halt right in front of me. Apparently, the car was coming from the east of Count of Vermandois Boulevard and I was heading north on Indara Devi Boulevard. We came at each other at the intersection of the two roads. My heart raced rapidly after nearly getting killed. Thankfully, the driver stopped in time, and in the process jerked himself and the passengers back and forth. I came in direct contact with the governor's stoic face. Two other western men who were sitting next to him gave me a look of disbelief at my carelessness.

"Hey, why don't you watch where you are going, little girl," shouted a red-faced plump man. The reed-like man sitting next to him did not say anything but maintained his displeasing facial expression at me. The governor gestured his driver to go, as if to not wanting to waste any more of his precious time.

I wondered who those two men were who were riding with the Provincial Governor of Siem Reap. Just then a loud and continuous honk came from behind me from the west of Count of Vermandois Boulevard. My heart leaped to my throat.

"If you want to die, go die somewhere else. Now get out of my way," a familiar voice roared at me. I turned around to find the portly Prince Phirun, the only son of Princess Nakry and the late Prince Dara Vong, who had passed away before I was even born.

I hated bowing to a person like him, but culture and custom demanded it, plus, I was blocking the road, so I moved out of the way, curtsied, and apologized. A young woman, adorned in the latest and flashy French dress who was sitting next to him, gave me a smile like she was on a wild ride, turned to the prince, and laughed like she found something utterly funny. He let out a belly laugh, hit the pedal, and roared off.

What a morning!

I finally made my way to Father's office at 777 Prey Nokor Boulevard with my ego a bit bruised. The morning sun greeted me with its hot rays. Indistinct voices echoed as Asian and European people alike hustled and bustled in our part of Siem Reap where colonial commercial buildings, shops, restaurants, and stores flanked next to each other on both sides of the tree-lined streets. I locked up my bicycle on the rail up front and made my way up the staircase to the third floor.

"Good morning, Madame Montha."

"Good morning, Anjali. You're bright and early," said the mature and gentle woman of twenty-eight.

"I finished my chores early," I said.

"Your mother is still at it, huh? Trying to get you to stop working here."

"You wouldn't believe what I have to go through every single morning," I said.

"I like having you here. You're about the only other female in the office. I wouldn't have anyone to talk about girl stuff if your mother decides to put a stop to your sleuthing job."

"That's not going to happen. My will is stronger than hers."

"Oh. So sure of yourself, eh?"

"You bet, but enough about my morning routine with my dear mother. I want to keep myself busy. What do you have for me today?" I rubbed my palms together in anticipation of something exciting.

"Nothing but these for you to file away." She handed me stacks of folders containing solved mysteries.

"Nothing? What? Again?"

"Sorry," she said.

"All I went through to be here and I have nothing again? What a disappointment!"

Just as I was about to turn away she said, "I'm leaving the office in a few minutes to deliver Monsieur Duong Chea's report. I have a few other errands to run too. Do you need anything?"

"No. Thank you. By the way, has Father returned from his meeting with Monsieur San Nuon yet?"

"No. Not yet. He should be back in another hour or so," she said.

2

MITH SOVANN

*I*dleness dominated my day. Nothing happened. "Nothingness is for the dead, not for the living," Father once said to my brothers and me. He was right. Something had to happen soon or I would lose my mind from boredom.

Dead silence. Well, except for the ticking clock, my beating heart, and my fingers drumming on the shiny oak table. No one had recently been killed, had mysteriously vanished, or had been cheated out of an inheritance. Father's business, Chinak & Associates, happened to be on the bizarre side. He and his men helped apprehend bad guys and solve mysteries like who murdered whom and why.

I apprenticed under Father. However, the cases he assigned me did not involve anything as serious as murder. He thought I was still too young to handle the grisly and gory aspects of homicide, but my time had come. "Soon," he told me. His definition of "soon" was vastly different from mine. He wanted to keep me as young and innocent for as long as he could while I wanted to grow up—and fast. I felt ready. I felt sure of myself. Besides, I had paid my dues of apprenticing with him and his associates for a few years now. Granted, I had worked only part-time during school and full-time only on breaks, but Father had been training me all my life. Almost every conversation we had became instructive, with him counseling me on how to be a good detective or about the cases he had solved. Plus, I had proven my talent and skill. Matters such as disappearances—unless they revealed themselves to involve foul play—and missing wills and heirlooms had become unchallenging. Yet, I had to admit, if one of these cases came my way, I would jump on it. Anything was better than sitting here with nothing to do.

I sat in what was essentially a file room. It housed thousands of records of our cases not related to murders. A few typewriters and a Photostat Machine kept me company. Father was proud of these human inventions. He liked to keep up with the latest 1920s gadgets. "What a great time for humans," he said. "With prolonged peace and stability, we are destined for greatness," he proclaimed.

A bigger room just across from this room housed murder records and mysteries related to sacred ancient artifacts—all of which Father barred me from accessing. Only he, his associates, and his secretary possessed copies of a special key to that room. I could not wait to handle such cases. The people of Siem Reap, including Mother, found it odd that I took an interest in such violent matters when I should be a prim and proper girl. The place for women for centuries had been relegated to the house, household matters, children, and the like. But based on the women's rights movement in Europe and the push for women's right to vote in the United States, we were destined for something great. Working women would no longer be an anomaly but the norm, like men. We would have regular chances for exciting work outside the house. At least I hoped so.

The silence broke. Muffled Khmer and French could be heard through my door, which was slightly ajar. I looked up at the clock on the wall: ten o'clock. It was April 1, 1920. I found myself pacing back and forth by the receptionist area and looking out the open door that led to the wide, bright corridor. Familiar voices greeted each other. When the postman made his way up to Father's office suite, I rushed to the threshold and greeted him excitedly.

The thin man, who stood as tall as I, smiled, understanding my exuberance. He handed me a stack of mail and said, "I hope there's something exciting waiting for you, Mademoiselle Chinak."

"Merci, monsieur. You are going to make my day if I should indeed find something interesting in this pile."

He let out a chuckle and shook his head in amusement. "À demain, till tomorrow," he said, waving and walking into the suite across from ours.

I rushed to Father's door, the last corner office on the right-hand side next to the forbidden room, which looked like a wall to the untrained eye. I knocked, turned the knob, and stepped forward into the room without waiting for his response. High spirits made me forget my manners. Father, clad in a dark two-piece suit with a blue *sampot chang kben* —a pant-like cloth wrap, his attempt at maintaining his traditional world and accepting a new one—looked up from his polished mahogany desk, which sat in front of two high arched windows. The wall-to-wall shelves held a panoply of scholarly books, scrolls, and ancient sculptures of Khmer heroes, philosophers, and astrologers. Father liked to furnish his office with books. Statues of world heroes and scholars were strategically placed between shelves of differing heights and widths. The library decor and artifacts imbued the room with warmth and calmness. An intricately woven red rug covered the middle of the room. The room almost mirrored his office at home, except he possessed more valuables at home.

"Look, Pouk! The mail is here. May I?"

While city and so-called educated folks called their mothers Mak and their fathers Papa or Pa, I used the Khmer words *Mae* and *Pouk*. The city folk who had taken to using foreign terminology now thought much of the Khmer vocabulary was unsophisticated, crude, or even "derogatory." Our peasant elders had a nickname for those people who forget their pasts: *puok chluok teuk machine.*

I ran to Father's side, hoping he would let me open the mail.

"Where's Madame Montha? Why are you bringing in the mail?" said my fifty-three-year-old father, in his rumbling baritone, his hair plastered in place with hair tonic.

"She is at *La Police Nationale*, delivering Detective Duong Chea's report to Lieutenant Sun Minh Tan." Detective Chea was one of Father's five associates. "Besides, I have not had anything to do for months now, Pouk. I'm completely bored. I'm hoping there is something here. Maybe a wire from La Police Nationale de Phnom Penh. They might need our help in solving crimes. You know that city is a cesspool of criminals who commit unthinkable crimes. The police and authorities there do not have the brain power, expertise, or efficiency we do, Pouk."

He chuckled from behind his desk, knowing that I would do anything to get put on a murder case, even resort to flattery, which he did not find so flattering. But I meant every word of it. No one possessed experience and expertise like Father did. He gestured for me to have at the mail while he returned to working on his own reports. When crimes did not occupy his time, Father liked to work on his journals. They were filled with stories and events he experienced.

I once saw a thick leather-bound book titled *The Scribes of Brahmadhan* in his library. Unfortunately, it had a mechanical keyless lock of a naga looping itself into each corner seven times before its tail met its head at the top. The sacred geometric shape consisted of three loops on the left, three loops on the right, one loop on the bottom, and a tail with an intricately shaped majestic head met side by side at the top with the corner of each loop bearing a beautifully etched ancient Khmer incantation. Just as I recited each word and felt my fingers against the corner of each of the Naga's looped body, Father caught me and snatched it away from me faster than lightning. He told me I was not to touch it—not until I reached the age of maturity.

"I thought I was already grown up, practically, anyway," I said to him then. I remembered his reprimanding look. I dropped the subject immediately.

I rummaged through the pile of mail. A package from Bangkok piqued my interest. I dropped the rest of the mail on Father's cluttered desk and walked to his left as I opened the package. I pulled out a cover letter addressed to Detective Oum Chum Chinak and handed it over to him. I took the first folder and perused through the first few pages. "Ah. Unsolved crimes. A challenge, finally!" I waved a blue dossier containing records of cases that had gone cold.

My pensive father looked up at me. "Hand it over, child. You are not supposed to be reading any of these files." He collected his pile and arranged it in front of him.

"But I haven't seen anything yet," I said, standing next to Father with my right hand grabbing my left arm that held one of the folders. At the same time, I was rocking back and forth on my heels.

"Nor will you ..." He put his hand out for the folder.

"Oh come on, Pouk. Why not?"

"The contents are too gruesome for a young woman," he said.

"But I am seventeen. I *am* a woman."

"Not quite," he said with his arm still extending out for the folder.

"You know, Pouk, there are parents who marry off their daughters at fourteen."

"They are idiots," he replied. "What do you know about young girls being married off, anyway?" He raised one of his eyebrows at me.

"Oh, nothing, Pouk." I shook my head profusely. I brought the subject back to the case file. "Is it not time for me to graduate to something more challenging?"

"You are not ready yet."

"I never will be if you do not allow me to prepare myself for it. Besides, do we not live in a brutal and violent world, being constantly surrounded by external and internal enemies? I hear about death, abuse, and violence every day."

"Hearing about it is not the same as experiencing it," he said.

"Which is why you should let me be in the thick of it like you and your associates. Pouk, I'm ready to take on the world. You taught me to fight and shoot—"

"To defend yourself. Like I said, it is not time for you to be thrust into this world yet. You will have plenty of that later. Right now, I would like to keep my daughter innocent of the cruelty of the world for as long as possible. Besides, we went over this just this morning. Your mother is wrapping her head around you working here, let alone thrusting you into the horror of crimes."

"I'm ready for the challenge, Pouk." I could hear the exuberance in my own voice.

"Your mother is not."

"But you are."

"No, not really." He shook his head.

"But I'm ready. Please give me a chance. I don't see why I can't start getting into the thick of it now. I am a tough girl. Physically, mentally, and emotionally." I playfully put up my right arm to show him my bicep. "Aren't you short on staff? Don't you think it's time for me to learn and do more around here?"

He gave me an impatient look and put his hand out again for the folder. As I was about to hand it over to him, we heard a playful knock at the door. We both turned our heads to the door as if we could see something. Then Father shot me a perplexed look.

"No."

"What is it, Pouk?"

"You know only two other people knock like that: your brothers. They're not due to come home from Paris until next season." His surprised yet happy face suggested he dearly missed my two crazy twin brothers. They were the last two to move out of the house after my two oldest brothers got married and built their own houses.

Meanwhile, as the baby of the Chinak family, I was used to being the only child around the house. Indeed, my twin brothers had been gone for a long time. We all missed them. I shrugged, indicating to him I did not know who was knocking.

"Come in," said Father.

A tall, spiffily dressed man walked into Father's office. I gazed upon him, rapt. This day was getting more interesting. His dark eyes, bright as Sirius, lit upon my pleasantly surprised father. The man looked twenty-five, eight years my senior. He gently removed his homburg, revealing his prominent eyebrows and a slicked-back hairstyle, and placed the black hat on the peg by the door, as if he knew it was there all along. His strong masculine face was a welcome distraction. With his toothy smile he raised his palms, the tips of his fingers touching his narrow nose.

I wondered who this handsome stranger was. How did he know how to knock like my twin brothers who, as far as we were concerned, were still studying in Paris?

"Chum reap sour, uncle," he said, greeting Father with a gentle bow as he clasped his hands together in a prayer-like gesture. Father was not his uncle in a biological sense, but in Khmer culture, young people were encouraged to use kinship terminology to address their elders. It was done out of respect that they saw the light of day before us, but most importantly, it kept us connected and familiar as a people.

"Bless you, my boy! Is this Mith Sovann—the scrawny boy who left us to study abroad in Paris?" Father sprang from his chair in a jolly way, nearly knocking it down. He put on his professorial horn-rimmed glasses to get a good look at his visitor, then walked excitedly around his desk to shake the young man's hand. They naturally fell into an embrace. The young man, dressed in a dark gray three-piece suit, towered a few inches over my thin father.

"My, my. Look at you." Father extended his thin arms and held the visitor in front of him to get a full view. "You have grown up to be an exceptionally handsome young man."

I did not recall how he had looked as a boy but I completely agreed. No one I had encountered in Siem Reap could be as handsome as he. But then again, I had not paid much mind to men before. Certainly not in *that* way.

"Come. Come. Take a seat," Father said. Mith sidled down to one of the two chairs across from Father's desk.

"I'm sorry about deceiving you earlier with that funny knock."

"My two sons put you up to it, did they not?" Father chuckled. "They're rascals."

"They send you and the family their love."

"How are they doing?"

"They're healthy and doing well."

"That's good to hear."

"They sent some packages to give to the family. I left them with your wife at home."

Father beamed with his proud smile. "They are good kids."

"Yes. Look who they have as a father, the great Oum Chum Chinak! You have not aged one bit, detective. You are as lean and fit as the day I left for Paris."

"I accept your flattery only because you have the tendency to speak the truth," said Father, chuckling in a good-natured manner. He rarely accepted people's flattery, not even mine. "Anjali, come and *chum reap sour* Mith Sovann." Father turned to me as if just realizing my presence.

I placed the dossier on Father's higgledy-piggledy heap of files, books, and maps. I smiled bashfully and raised my palms so the tips of my fingers gently touched my nose. I gave a slight bow and curtsy. Mith Sovann reciprocated with a flash of his pearly white smile. Suddenly, a rush of heat surged through my body like hot tea gulped accidentally.

Could he see a flush in my cheeks? I could not help but touch my cheek to feel its warmth. He smiled. I wondered if he noticed me like I noticed him. What was this tinkling sensation that poked and prodded at me?

The more he looked at me, the more I started to feel this uncontrollable bashfulness enveloping me. My mind, my heart, and my nerves churned like the ocean. This had never happened to me before. What was wrong with me? This was not normal. This strange feeling turned me into an awkward person. How embarrassing! My cheeks grew increasingly hotter by the moment. What was happening to me? I became self-conscious of my every move, reaction, and thought—so much so that I stood in silence. Could anyone blame me? Look at him. Mith Sovann. What a name! What a man! I felt embarrassed just thinking his name.

I had heard a lot about him. Actually, the greater area of Siem Reap had heard about him. At ten years old, I accidentally overheard my parents' private conversation about him.

Contrary to most husbands and wives of this town, Father and Mother shared almost everything. Well, he did not tell Mother about my self-defense training, but other than that, they consulted each other on family and social matters. He trusted her with sensitive information—that which he could share, anyway. She had given him great reason to trust her.

I had overheard how they wanted to find the right time and the right way to tell Mith about his parents, should he ask. The only people alive who knew the truth about his background were his maternal grandparents, Father, Mother, and—unbeknownst to them—me.

The gossip queens of Siem Reap knew about him, too, but they did not have any proof. They could only speculate.

The Governor's Daughter

If they saw him, now that he was back from studying abroad in Paris, they would surely whisper that he was the love child of Prince Dara Vong. Actually, the similarity seemed uncanny. Mother had not divulged such information to anyone, including her younger sister, who liked to gossip about trivial things.

I did not reveal such sensitive information to my best friend Jorani Sem either. Surely she would have appreciated it. After all, most girls and young women in this town, possibly in the entire country, romanticized about being charmed, rescued, and carried away by a courageous, intelligent, and handsome prince—even if he was a half-blooded prince. As a feminist once told me, "The problem with our twentieth-century society is that not all classes of people can find exceptional men and women outside the ranks of kings, queens, and courtesans." I thought I had become more evolved—that is, until my eyes met his.

Technically he came from a peasant background. He had known no other life but peasantry—a peasant who had an opportunity to travel the world and study abroad. Besides, he knew nothing about his royal blood. I liked to tell myself this so as to make myself feel better about falling into the social norm of a silly girl where he was concerned. I doubted his paternal grandparents would acknowledge his royalty status as an illegitimate child, especially not when they had that evil princess as their daughter-in-law.

My family knew too much of the business of the royal family.

3

THE OTHER WOMAN

As a descendant of a long line of peasant-warriors of the Royal Calvary, which was created by King Chey Chetta II back in 1618, Father was privy to firsthand information about the many royal families of different lineages and bloodlines, mainly the one under which he served. In fact, he could trace his family ancestry from the glorious Angkorian days to the dwindled Khmer Empire under the suzerainty of the Siamese and the Annamese in 1840. The Annamese people and their country were known as Yuan and Srok Yuan in Khmer since ancient times, just as Chen and Srok Chen were known as Chinese and China, respectively. I could not help but wonder if the first Annamese our Khmer ancestors encountered was named Yuan, or the first Chinese named Chen, which prompted them to use those names until now. Anyhow, even in the 1800s my grandfather remained the protector of the royal crown and Khmer wealth. In 1863, our kingdom became known as Cambodge, under the so-called French Protectorate. Father made his grand entrance four years later, kicking and screaming like he was ready to take on the cruel world into which he was born—so my grandfather told me, may his beautiful soul rest in the house of Nirvana!

The country coming under French control did not mean the people went quietly into submission. They rose against the colonization of our country. The French met the rebellions with swift action and repressed the people with deadly weapons. Khmer scholars and patriots left over from the assimilation or annihilation by the Siamese and Annamese were either in hiding or killed. Most ordinary people who just wanted to survive and get by became deaf, dumb, and mute, even to this day. Hence, their progeny was ill-informed and unaware of what truly constituted their world. According to my courageous grandfather, "The idea of colonialism is to whip people into mental and physical submission while the conqueror reaps the benefits of the exploitation of the natives and the country." Those who refused to be enslaved fought to the bitter end. Tragically, not enough of them existed, nor had they any sophisticated weapons to challenge our colonizers. Hatchets, swords, sticks, stones, and axes could not be counted as fair weapons against cannons and explosive firepower.

In 1884, under the Norodom monarchy, another one of the many rebellions against the French took place. Father, seventeen years old at the time, had already been trained and thrust into the life of duty, responsibility, and violence. He and his ancestors had always been the protectors of the crowned king, which was why it puzzled me that he worked under his Royal Highness Kambujasatra XVII, one of the many different royal bloodlines of the kingdom. Kambujasatra was not even the ruler. The chosen king since 1904 had been King Sisowath. I have no idea why. Regardless, Father's loyalty, bravery, hard work, and intellectual prowess earned him the title of the youngest captain of the Royal Calvary, thanks to training by his father, grandfather, and various gurus. His Majesty Kambujasatra XVII trusted him implicitly.

Through adversity or fortune, Father became the favorite of his majesty Kambujasatra XVII, who appointed him to accompany his oldest son, Prince Dara Vong, to Paris where the prince would study for nine years. They were of similar age. In France, the prince became engrossed in politics, economics, history, and the art and culture of Europe. Meanwhile, Father became fascinated with law, science, and the detective branch of La Sûreté Nationale. They returned improved with knowledge and experience, ready to pass on what they had learned for the betterment of their countrymen and country.

In addition to his family's riches from rice cultivation, Father came back to open a private detective agency, working with the armed forces to help solve mysteries, crimes, and murders in this thriving country. "With the competing and conflicting interests of the Khmer natives, the French, the Siamese, the Annamese, and other global presences, the country has become plagued with fear, greed, revenge, anger, hatred, jealousy, and superstition that drive them into unspeakable crimes against one another," said Father. He did whatever he could to solve the crimes that set our country on a path of destruction. All people in this country need justice. Most of the time, justice favored the rich, the powerful, and the French. Father said, "The universe has a way of evening things out." I wondered what he meant by that. He said I would understand one day. That was the thing with Father. He sometimes spoke to me in riddles.

Poor people could not afford his services. Hence, Father worked without compensation for peasants whose form of subsistence came from their labor, livestock, and rice fields. With the help of Prince Dara Vong, he also contributed to our society by building hospitals, temples, and schools.

Cambodge's neighbors and those previously in power had reduced Khmer natives to subhuman people described commonly as having "curly hair, flat noses, big lips" and being "slow-witted, dark, ugly, and lazy." The French authorities shared our neighbors' perception of us. They considered us inferior even to Annamese and Chinese immigrants whom they already considered beneath them. Our inferiority served as their rationale for our subjugation. They would use it to justify our not being worth education or lucrative positions in our own country. "Dehumanization and denigration aren't good for our self-esteem. They tell themselves they are superior. They tell us we are inferior. They tell themselves they are white and beautiful while we are dark and ugly. They are inventors and creators. We are primitive and will never amount to anything. Like the Buddha said, 'What you think, you become.' That's why we need to shun their negativities," said Father. It was easier said than done when the forces of negativity surrounded us from all fronts. I often wondered where Father's optimism came from.

My grandfather and father had hoped the younger generation would change our negative ways of thinking. Sadly, most Khmer people gave into oppression and accepted many stereotypes about themselves. Meanwhile, the French authorities built many schools in Annam and hired only Annamese and Chinese immigrants, their "honorary" Asians, to work in their administrations throughout Cambodge and Laos, thereby broadening the gaps, animosities, and inferiority complexes between the Asian groups. "We're all first and foremost human beings. Politics, religion, and our skin color divide us. And our egotistical and hierarchical nature will always be at variance with our struggle to get along with one another," said my mild-mannered father.

Following their sojourn in Europe, Father found the marriage arrangement by his parents was to his liking, while Prince Dara Vong was forced to wed an uppity woman of royal blood of the Ang lineage—Nakry Ang—whom he did not love. His heart belonged to another—a gentle woman of peasant background just like my family. He requested of his parents a second wife, but they refused because it would not please Princess Nakry. Even though kings and princes before him had mistresses, he was forced to demean his love by trying to bring her into their royal abode as his concubine. Since they were not the ruling family, different royal lineages had their own palaces, smaller than the Grand Palace of Siem Reap. Naturally, his wife abused her husband's lover and drove her out of the palace. She knew he wholeheartedly loved his mistress and would remain faithful to her. He would not allow anyone else in his heart. She took the matter to their parents once again. To appease the princess, his parents forced him to let the young peasant woman go. Sadly, it did not stop there.

The prince would not give up. He would arrange for a rendezvous to see his love every chance he could. He secretly wedded her in the presence of her parents and my father. Their secret love produced an adorable, bright-eyed boy. To care for her, their child, and her parents, he built a cottage for them in Beung Mealea, a village that was twenty kilometers away from the city of Siem Reap. He called it Sok San's Cottage. The princess heard about it from her busybody lady-in-waiting. She confronted him but understood her husband would not have eyes for her as long as this young peasant woman existed. Jealousy drove her nearly insane. Her madness taunted her day and night. It dominated her rational mind, and eventually drove her to a premeditated crime.

One day, this vicious-hearted Princess Nakry, named after a flower that lent its fragrance only to the night, ordered her most trusted lady-in-waiting on an excursion to the border to seek a ruffian to remove this poor young woman from this world. Unbeknownst to the Prince and the young woman's family, the ruffian lured her to an abandoned pagoda on a hill where he murdered her. It took her parents and their fellow villagers an entire day to search for her. Her body was dumped in a secluded forest known to be inhabited by lions and tigers, with ravens and vultures to pick clean the kill. The tragic news reached the prince.

Her death enraged him. He hired Father to investigate her murder. Father and his men caught the ruffian. He confessed to everything. The news plagued the modest Kambujasatra's palace when the death of the peasant woman was linked to Prince Dara Vong's wife, Princess Nakry Ang. To protect his family's name, he forced Father not to release his findings to the public.

The prince wanted to confront his evil-hearted wife, but he decided against it since he found himself to be in the wrong by precipitating the entire mess. He suffered in silence. He fell into a deep depression.

He died of an aortic aneurysm not long after the conclusion of the case. Before his passing he put aside some of his fortune and asked Father to see to it that his love child was well taken care of and provided with a first-rate education. The little boy's grandparents abandoned the cottage at Beung Mealea. The place haunted them. It reminded them too much of their daughter's tragic death. They moved about ten kilometers away to a small village called Golden Hill in Siem Reap to live closer to us. Father kept his promises. He hired the best governess, and as soon as the boy reached the tender age of fourteen, he sent him to study abroad with a trusted Frenchman. Father had not seen Mith until now. They had communicated only by telegram.

Knowing this history concerning Mith Sovann made my heart grow fonder, my compassion deeper. Their reunion was touching and meaningful. Father had no idea that I knew all this about them.

"Humans. We are intelligent. We are destructive. We are complex creatures," he once told me in one of his many lessons about life and nature. His fascination with humans —our minds and our thoughts—brought him to this business. He loved his job, and he loved to help people.

Like Father, I became fascinated with social science, law, and detective work. Though it was not a popular idea at the time, Father believed I deserved as much of an education as my two older twin brothers. He sent them to Paris while he hired governesses and professors to educate me at home. "It's a crime not to provide an education for a child, male or female," he said. "Education makes us move forward. It improves our minds and our hearts. It gives us courage, takes us places, and brings us good fortune. More importantly, education would be for nothing if it were not put to a purpose." He cited Princesses Soma, Indra Devi, Raja Devi, and Kossamak Sisowath as influential women of great minds who had definite goals. Mother protested. She thought sleuthing was a dangerous job. But I loved Father's work.

"When did you arrive?" Father asked Mith.

"I've been home since Monday."

"Your grandparents must be overcome with joy to see you safe and in good health."

"Yes. They could not stop crying the first few days."

"They could be shedding tears of joy for having a handsome grandson who graduated from medical school in Paris and worked as a physician."

"Actually, I apprenticed under a well-known doctor in Paris," said Mith.

"Well, any of the hospitals here will be happy to offer you a position as a physician. Or you can just open up your own practice," said Father.

"When I am good and ready and have enough experience," said Mith, with laughter in his voice.

"Right. Right." Father sighed. "Anyhow, I don't blame your grandparents one bit for crying upon seeing you. You gave them a good fright when you wrote home about joining the French army to fight in the Great War between the Allies and Germany and Austria-Hungary."

"My conscience would not be clear if I did not use my medical training to help those who were in need. This Great War was not our war, but the world got sucked into it like a vortex of evil. They brought in 47,000 colonial troops. As you know, some of them were our Khmer brothers. They were left to suffer and die from their wounds. I had to do something. It was tragic. You know how dark and depressing it is to see a grown man howling for his mother as he lay there in a pool of his own blood, urine, and feces."

"I understand. Yes, I remember those days. I do not miss them. Not one bit. However, to your grandparents, you are the only blood they have left. They told me they would not know what to do without you. You are the only reminder of the beautiful daughter they once had."

"My mother," he sighed. "My grandparents still refuse to tell me how she left this earth. They said you knew Father, that you were a close friend of his. I want to know who he was. It is well known you investigated my mother's death. It was foul play, they say. I should like to know more about my father and my mother's murder. My grandparents told me how beautiful she was, physically and spiritually. I feel like she is always with me."

Father's countenance shifted. The subject made him uneasy. He looked away from Mith and walked back to his desk chair. He rested his back against his chair with his hands in a steeple. He had known this day would come. "What brought this urge upon you?" he asked, looking into Mith Sovann's eyes.

Mith briefly glanced at me as if he did not want to discuss it in front of me. Sensing this, Father told him they should meet at another time and discuss the matter in private. "Right now, we must catch up. You must come and join my family for dinner tomorrow. There is a royal ballet at the Nagara Theater in the evening. Plus, I'd like to learn more about the war."

"Father is a war buff. His face is always buried in *La Khemarak Gazette*, looking for news of young Khmer soldiers fighting a world away. Did you know he trained the cavalry regional corps that participated in that war?" I managed to chime in, feeling proud of Father and of myself for knowing this bit of information.

Father smiled, reminiscing.

Mith flashed me his pearly whites. I turned to jelly. My knees weakened. My heart quickened. What was this fluttering thing in my stomach? Even my soul stirred in an awkward yet sensational way. Though Father did not do it for my sake, I felt grateful to him for inviting Mith to have dinner and attend a show with us. What a wonderful night we would have.

4

ESMÉ LAURENT

*D*inner went by quickly, but thank goodness our evening continued. I savored every moment. Our driver, Suon, took us from La Mekong Bistro to the Nagara Theater. He pulled our 1919 Citroën to the curb where other cars were lining up at the entrance. The vast, opulent building, which overlooked the basins of the Tonle Sap River and was encircled by extravagant gardens with a topiary layout, consisted of Khmer and French architectural designs. It reflected Kambuja-desa's imperial past and the French imperial present. The royalty, aristocrats, and the social elites frequented the Khmer ballet and other theatrical shows at the Nagara. It had become the place where the upper echelon caught up with one another and showed off their wealth and status. They mixed and mingled. Though my family came from a peasant background, we inherited and earned enough to enjoy luxuries similar to those of the royalty and the elite.

The French discriminated against us due to our "slow wit" and "dark skin," but thank goodness our Khmer society did not have a caste system where people are permanently placed in social stratification. Our language, culture, and religion may have been heavily influenced by India, but our forefathers rejected the caste system. Our society was comprised of the haves and the have-nots. The former consisted of royalty, aristocrats, and merchants; the latter consisted of peasants.

In keeping up with the latest cultural events, some of the people frequented the opera and Western ballet, though mostly only French and other Westerners attended these shows. I have never been to Europe, but I read a lot and have seen their silent movies. I believed Europeans tried to mirror our faraway land as closely as they could to their own countries—though they hated the heat and humidity here, especially during the time of the dry season.

Casually strolling side by side, I hooked my arm with that of my conservatively dressed mother. She wore a dark blue *sampot chang kben*—wrapped-cloth pants—and a long-sleeved, eggshell-white laced blouse sashed in a dark blue *peanear*. I wore a golden silk printed *sampot chang kben* with a fitted blouse of solid golden silk and quarter-length sleeves. My voluminous light blue silk *peanear* was sashed over my right shoulder. I could feel it flowing like a river when the hot, dry wind blew. I garlanded myself with the finest golden Khmer jewelry. I had teased my close friend Jorani Sem about dressing to impress the man who became her fiancé, but today I found myself as much occupied with my grooming and my garb as she. I had now developed a sense of consciousness of my own looks, demeanor, and manner much more than I had before I met the man of my dreams. Like a bird of paradise putting on a display for her mate, I tried to impress Mith with my own display. This must be what it means to try to attract the opposite sex—though I was not at all sure if men noticed these things.

My handsome father wore his finest Khmer gear of an eggshell-colored, high-collared jacket and his pearly red *kben* trousers, while Mith Sovann sported a black three-piece suit. His hair was pomaded and parted in the middle. We blended in with other Khmers and Europeans who dressed in their most fashionable Khmer and Western garb. Their voices and laughter filled the air and so did their flowery *parfums*. My focus was not really on those surrounding us, but on the dashing man walking shoulder to shoulder with Father ahead of us. My good-natured mother and I followed behind them. But the smell of freshly cut grass and the aromatic light scent of the many flowers in bloom could not compete with the intoxicating light cologne mixing deliciously with the body chemistry of Mith Sovann.

"Tell me," Father said, "by the end of the war, how many colonial troops had the French called up?"

"I'd say 475,000 men."

"My Lord Brahma!"

As Father and his young guest discussed politics and warfare, I lost myself in a fantasy world where Mith and I walked among picnickers and beachcombers. The wind gently blew our hair as we engaged in romantic talk. I envisioned myself being with him and having a family with him. Strangely, my feelings, emotions, and thoughts had changed considerably in one day. I seemed to have become a brand new person. I became entranced just by looking at him. The way he dressed, moved, and talked mesmerized me. His masculine yet soothing voice sounded like a thousand a cappella choirs singing in my ears. His presence made me feel like I was falling through a gaping sinkhole, but somehow I knew and felt that I would land safely at the other end. Strange. My mind used to be stimulated by crimes and mysteries, but now a new kind of stimulation gave me a boost of energy. I had discovered love. Suddenly everything appeared brighter. The world became a more meaningful place. I found myself constantly smiling and feeling as if I were floating on air, just like my friend, Jorani. Butterflies fluttered in my stomach at the thought or mention of his name.

We ascended the lavish marbled stairways with intricately carved balustrades, then made our way to the balcony to the right of the theater. We settled ourselves into seats on the right-hand side of the upper level, which we shared with another favorite family of the royal court. We had known the Nuons for many generations. Like us, they were among the oldest Khmers. Monsieur San Nuon, strong and husky, was a judge by royal appointment. All the men sat up front together while the ladies sat in the back, talking, smiling, and fanning themselves vigorously. After I showed my respect and greeted everyone, I sat to the far left in the second row while Mother, Madame Soriya Nuon, and her future daughter-in-law Mademoiselle Channy sat to my right behind Mith. I did not want to speak to anyone and just wanted to be one with my thoughts—thoughts of the good looking Mith Sovann. I had a perfect view of one side of his handsome face. It was good enough for me to steal a glance at him every moment I could. I found myself beaming like a silly girl.

All the young women in town dreamed of finding their Rama. I believed I had found mine, and he was sitting just a few seats away. He made my heart smile. Normally I was very observant of my surroundings, but tonight all my focus was on the half-blooded prince. I watched him lean over to

Father and ask him something as he looked over at the balcony across from us.

Father chuckled and said, "That's Princess Dhana and her husband Charles Laurent. He's the current provincial governor of Siem Reap. That young lady is Esmé Laurent. She is one of their two children. Their older son is studying in Paris like my two sons."

"Oh. He would not happen to be Alexandre Laurent, would he?"

"Yes. Yes, that is he," said Father. "You boys must have hung out in the same circle."

"I met him a few times through a friend of a friend."

"Ah. Of course," said Father.

Father frowned upon gossip about Princess Dhana, but she had an interesting past. She happened to be first cousins with Nakry Ang and she came from the Duong's royal bloodline, which used to rule the country back in the Oudong Era dating back to the seventeenth century. Everyone knew about her royal parents who wedded her to a Siamese Prince to unify the royal bloodline and the two countries, but the prince soon became ill and died. The Siamese royal palace and its people accused the princess of performing witchcraft and killing him. They treated her with contempt and hatred. Fortunately she met the future provincial governor, who was in Siam to attend to his rubber plantation business with his English partner. He saved her before they burned her at the stake.

"Who is that gentleman?" Mitt asked, narrowing his eyes to take in a tall, pale, hawk-like man.

"Monsieur Nuon here informed me earlier that he is Mr. Andre Thomas. He's a merchant who arrived from Bangkok over a month ago."

Andre Thomas! The man I saw riding in the topless car

the other morning with the governor and another Western man who spoke rudely to me.

"He is a merchant. He comes from a wealthy family. His mother is English and his father is French," Monsieur Nuon chimed in. "His family is in the ivory business. His parents are old. They are now retired in Europe. He is taking over the business. He has traveled across Asia and Africa to harvest various types of ivory. I hear a large part of it is for making piano keys. Apparently pianos are still in great demand in Europe. I guess ivory is a lucrative business."

"Lucrative but destructive," said Father. "These men will deplete our country and other countries of natural resources. They will destroy the ecological system, certainly not during our lifetime but in the time of our progeny. Hopefully by then they will have figured out a way to seek independence and lead this country into prosperity and greatness once again."

"Indeed. We must plant the seed of freedom and independence now," said Monsieur Nuon.

Paranoia emerged. Could Mith be asking about the Laurent family just to know who was who in this magnificent town? If so, why did he not inquire about any of the other attendants sitting in boxes next to ours or next to the Laurents? They were movers and shakers in this town too. He seemed not to know anyone yet. How peculiar. My stomach dropped upon catching his smoldering stare at Esmé. All of the fluttering butterflies and the tinkling sensation vanished without a trace. My head spun. My heart no longer smiled. It ached. I felt as if Mith had reached into my chest, grabbed ahold of my heart, pulled it out, and squeezed it until it burst before him. The hot blood that surged through my body sent a different signal—a signal of disappointment, anger, and jealousy. A spectrum of emotional extremes had consumed me in just one day. I lost interest in the Khmer ballet, one of my favorite entertainments in this world. I wanted to go home. I had an urge to run out of the balcony and down the stairs to find my driver to take me home so I could cry my eyes out. However, my mind told my heart that such behavior would be very unbecoming. Instead I sat there with a crushed heart and a demolished spirit while glancing at the half-blooded prince with his glowing smile and lingering gazes at another woman.

My mind wandered as we sat there for over two hours with the orchestra in the background, accompanying my terrible mood. Misery did not make for good company. I tried to calm myself in any way I could. I rationalized. Putting my hurt aside, I could see why men of all types found Esmé attractive. She epitomized a beauty that most European and Asian writers and poets—influenced by colonization, of course—took great pleasure describing in their literary works. I sat watching them steal glances at her and came up with my own poetry about her.

> *The governor's daughter, Esmé Laurent,*
> *The object of many men's love and attachment.*
> *She adorns herself in an off-white embroidered*
>   *dress,*
> *Which compliments her long, three-stranded*
>   *pearl necklace.*
> *Her skin shines as bright as the moon.*
> *Her chestnut hair and baby-blue eyes make them*
>   *swoon.*
> *She is of statuesque height,*
> *A person of ectomorphic type.*
> *Asian men find her exotic beauty alluring.*

European men find her soft features reassuring.
Everything about her is virtuous, sensitive,
    and ripe.
"She belongs with us, not them," they gripe.
She's a woman of heavenly beauty and birth,
Personifying the most attractive and virtuous
    people on earth.

Confusion ran through me. I should be angry with her. I should be jealous of her. But such negative emotions took aim at something else. I blamed it on the universe. It had not done right by me. Not that I wanted to be like the governor's daughter nor look like her, I only wanted Mith to love me like I loved him. Was it love that I was feeling? How did I even know if what I felt was love? Maybe it was a crush—or rather, a soul-crushing moment of my life—and I had to sit there and endure it. The moment had changed so quickly. I was head over heels one moment and sad and depressed the next as his bright eyes constantly gazed at the governor's daughter.

The show finally ended two and a half hours later. Normally I could not get enough of the ballet, but this time it was the longest night of my life. It appeared we could not get home fast enough, especially considering my parents had to make their rounds, mingling with the politicians and elite society of Siem Reap. I wanted to get home to drown myself in misery. Since we were not heading home anytime soon, I excused myself to the lady's room and then to wait in the car. I made my way to the parking lot when a soft-spoken voice called out to me, "Anjali."

I turned around to find Esmé. Her light blue eyes, looking as if they were gray from afar, twinkled as they met mine. I put my palms together so that the tip touched my nose to *sompheas* and greet her, as the younger person was always the one to initiate the greeting to show good manners and respect—especially since the woman standing before me came from a royal family. "Greetings, your royal highness," I said, bowing. She reciprocated so that her palms rested at her heart.

"You do not have to refer to me as your royal highness. Esmé will be fine," she said.

"I shall not refer to you by your name in front of the elders, for they consider it rude. After all, you are older and of royal blood." She was three years older than I.

"Custom and culture, huh?" She let out a gentle laugh. "We are born into a world that has been laid out for us. I wish we could be free to be ourselves, not restrained by boundaries and customs."

She sounded more interesting than I cared to give her credit for. I flashed her a half-hearted smile.

"So, how are you?" she asked, as we walked slowly, shoulder to shoulder, to our cars. I had the feeling she did not approach me to talk about my wellbeing. Even though we had known each other since we were young girls, we had never spoken to one another.

"I'm doing fine," I lied. Just to be polite, I asked, "And how are you feeling this evening?"

"Wonderful," she said, as if she had worked out our conversation in her head and her every word came out as she planned it. She paused for a moment, even seemed thoughtful. "Well, my parents are in good health. My brother Alexandre is safe and doing well abroad. I could not ask for more."

Sure you can, I thought.

"But enough about me."

Oh, I doubt that, I thought.

"Your parents seem happy and in good health too."

"Yes, they are," I responded.

"Your father—he is a great hero of the kingdom. People at the royal palace often talk about him."

"Do they?"

"Oh yes. They talk about how brave and smart he is. They say he's very good at his job."

"That is so kind of them."

"He deserves such praise. You should be proud. I only hear good things about him."

"I am. Thank you."

"And you," said the governor's daughter. "You are not so bad yourself. Most of the female elite and elders are grateful for your work. They say you are skillful, clever, and detail-oriented. They claim they would not know where to go and what to do if it were not for you. They can always depend on you. What is that Khmer saying? That the leaves do not fall far from the tree?"

"They would if the wind blew hard enough," I said.

She let out a gentle laugh. "I love your sense of humor."

I'm sure you do. "That is awfully nice of them to say and kind of you to repeat. Thank you." Through my peripheral vision I could see her pleasant smile. The woman sure knew how to butter me up. Unfortunately, I had nothing to say about her father other than that he was part of the French authority that oppressed and burdened the Khmer people with heavy taxes and other hindrances to freedom. Since I had nothing nice to say about her father, I said nothing at all. Thus, a long awkward pause occurred. I could feel she wanted to say more. She fidgeted with her three-stranded pearl necklace. Actually, I did have nice things to say about her and her mother, but my unhappy mood drove away any pleasant words I had in my mind.

Esmé cleared her throat and broke the awkward silence. "You know. I have been meaning to get together with you ever since we moved to your area. But the time was never right. I am glad we ran into each other this wonderful evening."

I take it the time is currently right, is it not, Esmé? I thought. To avoid letting fly some caustic remark about her timing, I remained quiet.

"You know, we have a few things in common. For one, we both have brothers studying in Paris."

"True. So do other well-to-do families in this country." I just could not help myself.

"Oh. Yes. I suppose. I did not think about that." Instead of being offended, she sounded giddy, laughing a little. "You know, I believe I know all of your—well, know of your family members and relatives, except...um...except for the han...young man who is with your family tonight. I do not know who he is," she said. Her face revealed a flush of embarrassment.

Here it comes, I thought.

"Who is he? What is his name?" She stopped herself just then, probably at the thought that such outright curiosity was less than ladylike.

I tried to make things easier for her. I offered her the information she wanted. "His name is Mith Sovann. He is Father's godson. He has been studying in Paris for the past decade or so. He's currently living with his grandparents not too far from us."

"Hmm. I wonder if he knows my brother."

"Possibly."

"Yes. Possibly." She nodded her head in agreement. "Anjali, I hope you don't mind if I ask you some personal questions."

"Sure."

"I do not like gossip. And I do not like people who do it. That is why I came to you. You are about facts and honesty. I...I am wondering if you could tell me the truth about something?"

"Sure, if I know the answer."

"Is it true what they say about his mother?"

"I am not sure what you are asking. What have you heard?"

"Well. You know...that his mother was a mistress of Prince Dara Vong..."

She knew more about him than I thought. She was digging up information about Mith. This was not a conversation to be had in a short stroll from the theater to the parking lot.

"It's complicated," I told her, acting as if I knew his whole life story, which was not far from the truth. Before I could confirm or deny the rumors spread by the gossipy women of Siem Reap, a gaunt and hawk-faced Andre Thomas made his way through the crowd and approached us.

"There you are," he said in French to Esmé without looking at me or acknowledging my presence. Esmé introduced us. I curtsied. As if out of habit he was about to bow but stopped himself and instead flashed me a cold stare. He looked annoyed. This was par for the course, but we, the Khmer, never got used to it.

His attention returned to Esmé. "Your parents are looking for you. A beautiful and fair maiden like you should not be wandering off alone. We must go before they worry."

Geez. What am I? Garbage? I stared at him with curiosity. He continued to act protectively toward her. The more he talked, the more of a buffoon he made of himself. I believe men become inarticulate in the presence of a beautiful woman. Something about that man sure gave me the creeps though. I sensed Esmé did not like him either, but, as someone raised to be polite, she maintained her civility. The way he carried on like a lovesick man made me want to hurl. Just then I realized I was no different than he. We both went gaga over someone who did not even notice us. Too bad I could not tell him how useless it felt to be on the unrequited side of a love affair.

Esmé grabbed me by the hand and kissed me gently on the cheek. "We have so much to talk about. I will call on you," she said in Khmer, which he would not understand.

Esmé walked away with Andre, light on her feet. Though I could see only her back, I sensed she was smiling like a girl with many wonderful secrets.

My heart sank further into darkness upon realizing her mutual feelings for Mith. I do not remember when my parents caught up with me or where I sat on our car ride home. The next thing I knew, I was ascending the buffed wooden stairs of our five-cornered *Sethei*-style home, which faced east. I made my way to my room on the right-hand side.

A mixture of feelings whirled in me. Who would have thought that I would fall head over heels for a man one day only to have him break my heart by falling for someone else by the next day? It was not his fault. It certainly was not Esmé's fault. I only wished the girl Mith fell in love with was me.

*E*smé visited me at work on Monday. She stood by Madame Montha, engaging in a conversation about the woman's children. That was the thing about mothers. They loved to talk about their kids. The governor's daughter seemed natural socializing with common people like us. Madame Montha giggled like a schoolgirl, absolutely taken by Esmé, who was kind enough to show her the time of day. After all, most elites and royal persons did not like to make small talk with those who were not their equals, except to point their fingers at their indentured servants and order them around. Though I had never talked to Esmé before the previous night, I was impressed that she conducted herself in a sweet but ladylike manner.

I only made it halfway to the reception area when the two turned to look at me. I stopped short.

"Mademoiselle Anjali, Mademoiselle Esmé is here to see you. I offered her a seat but she wanted to talk to me and keep me company. Is she not the kindest and most gentle human being?"

"Thank you," I said to Madame Montha and turned to greet the governor's daughter. She gracefully moved to grab my hands and *faire la bise*—kiss on the cheeks—as if we had been best friends forever.

"Please have a seat here, your royal—um...Esmé," I said softly. I gestured her to one of the seats in the waiting area. She smiled at my dilemma of how to properly address her. She sat down. I remained standing, feeling completely taken by surprise at her unexpected visit. "Would you like something to drink?" I offered.

"Oh. No. No. Actually...well...there is a French cafe

down the street. I would like to give it a try. It would please me if you joined me."

"I...I do not think it is such a good idea."

"I know as young women we are not allowed to be at places like that without an adult chaperone, but Monsieur Bin is waiting there for us. He will be sitting at another table so we can have our privacy."

"It is just that I have a lot to do. May it be some other time?" I looked at Madame Montha, hoping she could corroborate my story and bail me out.

"We can afford to spare you an hour or so, if Monsieur Bin's there to chaperone," said a baritone voice. I turned around to find Father smiling and bowing at the governor's daughter. I consciously moved to be near Father in case I needed to say something to him without being heard by a third party. Esmé gently stood up and raised her clasped palms so the tips touched her nose and bowed to greet Father. Though she was of royal blood and the governor's daughter, she still had to show him respect as the elder and as a revered man in our society.

"Bless you, Mademoiselle Esmé," he said in response to her good manners.

"With all the new cases coming in, would you not be overwhelmed and in need of my assistance?" I was suggesting obliquely to Father that I did not really want to go, but he did not bite.

"We will manage, Anjali."

I gave Father a thanks-a-lot look. I turned to the governor's daughter and hesitantly said, "Sure. I guess I can go."

"Perfect," she said with enthusiasm.

"Anjali has plenty of free time these days," Father added. I turned to give him the stink eye. He smiled at her and whispered to me, "Go on, Anjali. Be neighborly. It is hard to find nice and honest people in this world. She certainly seems to fit that category. Be a good friend to her." I told him I already had a friend named Jorani Sem. He insisted, "It's good to have more than one friend." Then he began to speak loudly so everyone could hear. "It is an honor for Mademoiselle Esmé to call upon you and count you among her good friends." Then he whispered, "Be a good sport."

"Yes. Sure. If you only knew why she wants to be my friend, Pouk. She has an agenda," I hissed into his ear.

"Do not be negative," he whispered. Father. He constantly tried to make me more social. How convenient that she was right here.

"Let me grab my purse," I said.

It was a hot and sunny morning. The streets had already been hustling and bustling with pedestrians, workers, buggies, and modern vehicles. Though it was the beginning of April, the people of Cambodge were sweeping, decorating, and preparing the town to usher in the Khmer New Year, which officially began on April 13th and lasted until the 15th. Actually, people had been planning it for months now. Our Khmer New Year celebration had always been the biggest, most lavish and festive of all the holidays, rivaled only by Pchum Ben, the Light and Boat Racing Holiday. I often looked forward to it, but not this year. I felt a little off.

Seeing us coming his way, the traffic cop, Monsieur Din —whose hair curled like Father's and who stood at my height—stopped bikes, carts, and all other vehicles for us to pass through. He bowed to the governor's daughter. She nodded and smiled in approval.

"How are you this morning, Monsieur Din?" I said.

"I am ecstatic, Mademoiselle Anjali. It looks like we are going to outdo ourselves compared to last year," he said looking at the decorations for the New Year. "Everything seems grander and more festive every year. I cannot wait to ring in the New Year with my family and friends."

"We cannot wait either. Isn't that right, Anjali?" chimed in the governor's daughter. She and I exchanged pleasant smiles with the traffic cop as we crossed the gravel road to the nice cafe that had just been opened a few years ago by an owner whose son was educated in Paris. In fact, the strip consisted of shops that mimicked those of Paris and other European countries that either Khmer, Chinese immigrants, or European investors had opened. Beautiful trees lined both sides of the road. As the sun in Cambodge could get scalding, especially during this time of year, circle benches were built around random trees for pedestrians to rest from the scorching sun.

All eyes gazed at us at the cafe. They seldom saw the beautiful Esmé up close, out and about without her guards and entourage. "It is so good to finally catch up with you," Esmé said as she took a slow and gentle sip of her creamy coffee. While she gushed about how happy she was to know my family and me, my mind was somewhere else. It was as if my spirit had wandered away from my body. I slipped in and out of my melancholy as she described how everything appeared so bright. "It seems the flowers smell more delightful than before. The birds suddenly appear to be singing happily and free. Everything feels so perfect, so wonderful," she said. "I never knew such feelings existed. I wish I could describe it to you, Anjali."

You don't have to. I know the feelings. I had them for a day. I now feel a whole new kind of emotion. Thanks to you. Such were my unspoken thoughts. Though she never revealed the source of her happiness, I knew. I tried not to be rude. Once in a while I chimed in on the conversation. She seemed to be genuinely appreciative of me spending time with her. For a daughter of a Khmer princess and a French provincial governor, she sure did not act uppity and let her family's power go to her head like most of the princes and princesses, aristocrats, and wealthy merchants of this country. She acted very polite to everyone around her, young and old, men, women, and children. Poor or rich, she acknowledged them with a gentle smile. Father was right, I needed a good friend.

That first cafe outing turned into an almost daily visit from her. I hardly spent time in the office, instead finding myself entertaining her either at my house, my relative's house, the Nuons' house, or the garden at the Palace of Siem Reap with her mother and other royal and aristocratic ladies.

Mith often visited Father when he was home, so she ran into him conveniently enough. The first time I saw their eyes meet, I could tell how much they had been waiting for that moment. Her eyes revealed her love for the handsome young man standing before her. Father and mother introduced them to each other. Esmé later confessed to me that she and Mith had first locked eyes on each other at the main dock of the Tonle Sap basin when he first arrived at Siem Reap that Monday when he had returned home. She and her maid had gone to receive her parents, who were arriving from Prey Nokor. The lovebirds had met four days before he visited Father's office. If we were to consider the time, she saw him before I did. I had nothing. I could not beat their mutual love for each other. Sadness and disappointment came over me again.

My home had become a semi-private place where Esmé and Mith could see each other under the guise of the supervision of a notable family of Siem Reap. Mother would make lavish lunches, which I helped prepare whenever the two came over. We would go out to the flower garden and have tea. We also kept ourselves entertained by either listening to Khmer and French music on the phonograph or by playing chess. They laughed, flirted, and teased each other. I became a third wheel as the two became comfortable with each other. They did not notice anyone or anything when they were together.

Mith visited my house often, and so did Esmé. She even tried to display her domestic and spiritual side by showing up early in the morning to help Mother and me prepare food and desserts for the monks who went on their daily alms round between eight and nine. Monks could only *chann*—eat—twice a day before noon. They fasted the rest of the day.

The day Mith confessed to Father how much he loved Esmé and wanted to marry her, it broke my heart.

"I figured as much," said Father. "I see the way you two gaze at each other."

A flush of embarrassment on Mith's face showed his vulnerable side. A man of confidence suddenly felt shy. He cleared his throat. "That first day I saw her, I could not stop thinking about her. Then I thought about my situation...my family. I have no idea what happened to my mother. I do not even know who Father was. I want to find out more about my parents because I have reached that age where I would like to form my own family. It would be nice to know more about them so that I could tell my beautiful future wife and children that I did have parents—that they loved each other very much and they loved me. If they were alive they would love the people I love too."

Mith and Esmè now spent more time with each other, especially during the three-day New Year festivities. During the day, they welcomed the Khmer New Year together at

Wat Mahapanchasila—the temple known for its well-learned monks—where they went to wash and bathe the Buddha statues with fragrant water with flower petals. They made sand dunes and burned gentle aromatic incense to wish for wealth, health, and happiness for all. Then during the night, the handsome couple let fly their sky lantern in front of the lily-filled moat of the great and sacred Angkor Wat. There must have been thousands of people there, chattering, laughing, and launching their own unique and beautiful shapes of square, octagon, and flowery lanterns, but all Mith and Esmé saw were each other. As they gazed at each other, I overheard them wishing their love would last forever. Their brightly lit lantern flew higher and higher into the black starry sky among thousands of others. He reached for her hand, and she reached for his. They stood side by side, holding hands and staring into each other's luminous eyes before watching their lantern slowly soar away into the black starry sky. On this occasion, I was the fifth wheel, since Jorani and her fiancé Kosal were there as well. Jorani and Kosal were laughing and giggling as they floated their pink lotus lantern on the cool water surrounding the majestic and sacred temple of Angkor Wat. It appeared everyone but me was partnered up on one of the most lavish and festive holidays in Cambodge. Khmer New Year was all a blur to me.

I drowned myself in work at the office and did other things to keep myself busy. I needed to return to my first passion, but Father still rejected my request to be put on more dangerous cases. Instead, he asked me to investigate missing valuable items at the temple, pagoda, and museum. I had no appetite for social functions, thus, I seldom saw anyone. I did not feel like talking to anyone outside of my work either. I became a young woman of a few words. Jorani called upon me a few times, but I told my parents to tell her that I was exhausted and just wanted to rest. It was a good thing because she was busy herself.

I just wanted to be left alone. It was bad enough I had my heart and my head contending with each other, I did not need other voices whirling around me.

One evening I heard the voices of Father and Mother. This was followed by the sound of a soft knock on my wooden door. "Anjali, may I come in?" Mother asked. It was bad manners to not answer a mother's call. No matter how much I desired to be left alone, I had to open the door for her. I got out of bed to unlock the door and let her in. I returned to lying down on my bed, pretending to read one of the books I had recently purchased from a new bookstore next to Father's office. I realized I was just staring at words. I understood and retained nothing. Mother sat on the edge of my bed, looking at me with love and sympathy.

"How are you feeling?"

"I'm feeling fine."

"*Preah Neang* Esmé has been at our home a few times to call on you. As with our messages to Jorani, your father and I told her you had a long day at work and were not feeling well. That as soon as you felt better you would call upon her."

I did not say anything. I continued to flip through the pages of a novel called *A Thousand Miseries*.

She took a deep breath. "Anjali, we must talk."

I understood now that she needed my full attention. I sat up, closed the book, and put it down on my lap. I sat in silence. I wanted so much to tell someone about my feelings. I could not talk to my best friend or mother about it. I felt very embarrassed that I liked someone who did not like me in return. These feelings were very personal.

"My dearest Anjali, it doesn't take a detective to know what is bothering you. You have been sulking at home and at work. At least that is what your father has been telling me. Madame Montha confirmed it. It has been over a month now since you found out about Mith and Esmé's mutual feelings for one another. Since the welcoming of the New Year, you haven't been acting like your energetic self. Sure, you're around physically, but your mind and spirit have left you. You hardly say anything to anyone. Your sulky silence is deafening. Child…" She paused, as if she was struggling to find the right words. "Love is happiness. Love is beautiful. It is much more beautiful and rewarding if it is reciprocated. Mith and Esmé are obviously in love. He has spoken with your father to discuss requesting her hand in marriage." My heart throbbed and ached. I knew this day would come, but I did not expect it so soon. I understood I needed to get over it, but I did not yet know how to control my emotions. Mother moved closer to me. She reached for my face and gently stroked my hair. I wrapped my arms around her waist and put my head against her chest.

"I'm sorry, Mae. I'm extremely embarrassed. I made a fool of myself, didn't I?"

"That's normal, my child. Sometimes we fall in love with someone who does not feel the same way. We have to respect their decision. Let it go. Do not dwell on it too long. It will get better, I promise. Love has to be mutual. It cannot be forced. A forced love will only lead to…" She stopped herself. She was probably thinking about the tragic love between Prince Dara Vong and Mademoiselle Kolthida Sovann—that their love was disrupted by the woman whom he did not love. She probably thought I did not know about their love story, but I knew very well.

"Forced?"

"You know what I mean."

"The sad part is, he knows nothing of how I feel about him. I wonder if he would have given me the chance if he only knew."

"No. No ifs, ands, or buts about it. He has chosen the person he loves. No one else would have mattered. Dwelling on it will..."

"I know, Mae. It will only lead to misery and wretchedness," I said, saving her from divulging the bitter truth.

She smiled with a sigh of relief. "See. That's why you are my daughter. You are wise beyond your years. Besides, he's way too old for you." I was surprised to hear my mother say that. For centuries, men had often taken much younger wives. "Your father said to give you time—that you will come to your senses. He said, 'It's just a silly crush, that's all.'" She gently stroked my hair. "You will be much happier when you find someone who loves you back. There's a match for everyone. I'm not saying this because I'm your mother, but you have grown up to be a very attractive young woman. You are no longer the little tomboyish girl who ran after your father to work, loved to fight, duel, and shoot at things with slingshots. You can take your pick of any eligible young man in this town."

Maybe so, but I felt no young man in this world could compare to Mith Sovann. Still, I had to learn to let my romantic feelings for him go. After all, his heart had already been given to Esmè Laurent.

5

LOVE DENIED

The next morning I showed up to work to find the office empty with only Madame Montha sitting at her desk. She wore her wavy hair bobbed in the flapper style at ear length. Like many Khmers, she adorned herself in a Western blouse and shoes with a Khmer silk *sampot*. At twenty-eight years old, she had seen and experienced it all, the bittersweet life. Her husband was a soldier who got killed in the line of duty. She had three children—all of whom were boys. She was one of those women who was down on her luck when the French authorities seized her land, along with that of other poor farmers, and leased it to wealthy plantation owners. She lived on a small stipend of her husband's before she met my father, who hired her to be his receptionist. Mostly only men worked, but to help this brave young woman help herself and her family, Father created another position for his male receptionist and gave her this position. She worked hard for the betterment of herself and her children. In spite of it all, she showed up to work with a smiling and pleasant personality every day. She also showed the same kind of spirit to her children and neighbors.

"Good morning, Anjali. You look well rested and bright. You must be feeling better."

"What do you mean?"

"You have been looking tired and haggard lately. You father said you were not feeling well."

"Oh. I was just exhausted."

"I understand. And this heat wave sure does not help. Well, I am glad to see you in a better mood."

"Yes. I'm fine now. Thank you. Where's everyone?" I asked, looking into the empty offices of Father and his associates. It was unusual for everyone to be out at the same time.

Father owned this detective agency. He rented the office from his French landlord. Just as with taxes and other restrictions, the authorities wanted to force him to pay more for it than his Chinese and Annamese counterparts, whom the French favored. None of us knew how he did it, but he worked it out with the French owner to pay practically nothing. His business continued to thrive. Father had done well for himself. He could even build his own building, if he so chose. He employed five associates. At this moment, none of them were at the office except for Madame Montha and me.

"Your father was summoned to the headquarters of La Police Provinciale. He took the others with him."

"It must be serious. I wonder if it has something to do with those unsolved murders from Bangkok." I knew Father had been communicating with the officials in Bangkok about some unsolved cases. Father and his team had just got back to working on them full time now that the New Year's festivities were over.

"Not just Bangkok."

"Is that true?"

"Yes. Police chiefs from Burma, Siam, Laos, and other Asian countries are all here. They're meeting at the police headquarters. They said this person was not only a killer, but a rapist too."

"They know for sure one person committed these atrocities?"

"Yes. That is all they have to go on. And the fact that..."

"Yes?"

"I'm not supposed to talk about any of this to you," she said as if suddenly realizing the secrecy of the matter.

"Oh, come on. You were so close to revealing something intriguing. Don't stop now. Please, pretty please, Madame Montha. This is all I have. If my mind is not active and challenged, it will revert back to that melancholy verging on a maudlin state of..."

She eyed me intently. I stopped myself before I revealed my foolishness with Mith. Besides, I wanted to forget the whole ordeal.

"I'm sorry, but no is no. I like my job and I want to keep it, dear."

"This is big," I said with excitement. "I mean for all the police chiefs from so many countries to be here, this must be the case of the century. How often do you see these forces come together?"

"Never."

"Right. Never. Asians are distrustful and hateful of each other."

"True. Our relationships are strained by animosity and territorial issues."

"And for such cases to move higher up on the authorities' priority list, these victims must be important."

"Anjali, I see that crazed look in your eyes. You should not even think about it, you hear? You know your father promised your mother to let you work here only to accompany me in the office and only if you are not exposed to gruesome and dangerous cases."

"That's what she thinks," I said, looking at her mischievously.

"Oh?" She raised one of her eyebrows.

"Anyway, what's the point of stepping foot outside of the house if you are not going to explore and venture out as far as you can? What kind of life is that? She'll get over it. I'm in the family business now. I want to be good at it. I cannot be good at it if I am limited. I know Father wants me to be great at what I do. I want to do everything Father does."

"Until that time comes, here are today's cases your father would like you to handle. He needs your full commitment on these while he and the men are off investigating those murders."

"Do you know who is funding this investigation?"

"I know what information you are looking for. Please, just take the files."

I took the files from her with disappointment and flipped through them. "I'm not challenged by these monotonous will disputes and inheritance ransom cases. It's time for me to graduate to something else—something more challenging."

"Do not forget these humdrum cases generate a lot of money for this office," she said with a sparkle in her eyes.

"Do you have copies of those unsolved murder files from other Asian countries yet?"

"Come on, Anjali, please. I have to be mindful and respectful of your father's requests."

"I thought I would ask. The worst thing you can say is no, right?"

She smiled and shook her head at my stubbornness. I could not help but be fascinated by a case that brought the Asian police forces from different countries together. They had gone all out for this. The victims must be daughters of well-to-do families or politicians even.

"You know if I—"

"I know your angle, Anjali. Please do not ask me again," she said, cutting me off.

"Hmm. That's all right."

She eyed me like I had something up my sleeve. Before I turned away to walk over to my combined office and file storage area and drown myself in the work she had just given me, the somber Esmé walked in. Madame Montha and I greeted her in accordance with custom. She looked beautiful as usual—thin, tall, and well put together—yet her countenance indicated she had been crying.

"May I please speak to you in private?" she asked with a quivering voice and look of anxiety in her eyes.

"Please follow me to the meeting room. I will catch up with you later regarding these files," I said to Madame Montha as I left them on her desk. I led Esmé down the hall on the west side. I opened up the French double doors to the conference room with broad windows overlooking palm, *pothi*, and *bane* trees. The sun threw a streak of light on the right wall of the room. Our suite sat on the top level of the six-story brick French-style office building. I closed the door behind us and offered her a seat while I walked to the other side of the table to open up the windows. The morning breeze gently caressed my face. I turned to walk to a seat next to her.

"What's wrong, Princess? I mean Esmé," I said, remembering she did not want me to refer to her as princess or use any other honorific titles.

Her sorrowful face turned into a sob. She pulled a handkerchief from her brown leather Boules bag with its golden handle.

"Oh Esmé, please do not cry. We can discuss and resolve whatever it is that is troubling you. Please don't cry." Feeling bad for her, I went to the credenza to pour her a glass of water. A month ago her eyes had shined with joy, and now they were drowned in sorrow. It must only mean one thing: Mith Sovann. "Please be strong and pull yourself together." I tried to calm her down as I would normally calm a distraught client. Besides, I could not understand her if she let her emotions overwhelm her so. "When you are good and ready," I assured her.

"It is my Papa..." She paused and began to sob.

"Your father? Is he all right?"

"No."

"What happened? Is he in danger?"

"No. He...he..."

"Did he hurt you?"

"Yes. With his cruel words and rules. He...he told me—us—that...Oh Anjali, it was awful." Her mind was all over the place. She did not know what she wanted to tell me first.

"Please calm yourself down. Take a deep breath. How about starting from the beginning?"

"He saw Mith and me at the Mahapanchasila Temple. We were with his grandparents, making alms offerings to the monks. He commanded his guard to remove me from the temple. He asked why I was spending my time with that family. I confessed that Mith and I were in love. I even revealed that Mith's grandparents, your parents, and your elder relatives were preparing to request for my hand in marriage to Mith. The news enraged him. He started to ramble about how Mith had 'dared to overstep. We are too high above him...'"

"Why?"

"He does not think he is a perfect match for me."

"Why not?" I replied. "He is highly educated, a physician who attended to the sick and wounded soldiers back in France, and financially well off." *Did I mention he is the dreamiest man on this planet? The Rama of our time?* "Granted, officially he is a peasant. Heck! I'm a peasant. Father is a peasant. The majority of the people—"

"True. He did not like it that I am socializing with peasants. He told me to stay away from your family as well. He said your father is respectable in the eyes of Khmer royalty and society, but not his."

"I do not know how to respond to that," I told her. She gave me an apologetic look. I felt the heat of fury coming from my face and body. It upset me to hear such a negative comment. But then I remembered what Father had said about arrogant and uppity men like Esmé's father. He said that people like him could not upset me without my permission. As with everything he told me, it was easier said than done. I had no idea how he dealt with arrogant men like the governor.

Esmé continued. "He...well, you know what he is like. But he is still my father. Nevertheless, I feel the need to apologize for his arrogant ways."

"I understand," I said. But I did *not* understand him.

Based on my few encounters with him, he appeared hard as granite. But that was just me, a native observing a Frenchman. We, as Khmers, accepted French and other groups of people as fellow human beings, but they saw us differently. Like most French people in our country, they displayed a superior attitude against the natives. To them that was normal and decent behavior.

"There's more to it," Esmé added.

"Which is?"

"He is..." she started, but she could not bring herself to say it.

"Are you suggesting your father thinks Mith is not a perfect match because he is neither French nor a Western man?"

"Yes."

"Does he acknowledge he himself is married to a Khmer woman?"

"Yes. He said his situation was different."

"Hmm."

"He said that it was out of his love and compassion for her that he married her. Moreover, he considered her the most beautiful woman he had ever seen in Asia. But..."

"But?"

"You know. He is not exactly well respected in his society due to his marriage to my mother."

"Based on that, I should think he would be more open-minded. He should accept Mith into your family."

"Unfortunately, Father's French family, relatives, and society never let him forget he married a *barbarian*, even if she is a princess and even if he married for love. He does not want my brother Alexandre or me to end up like him and Mother, being ridiculed on both sides of the gene pool. He has felt especially slighted and disrespected by

The Governor's Daughter

European and Western people. They never let him forget his sin against the Almighty God and his race. He hates it. He said I'm better off with a Frenchman. If I refuse to marry a French or Western man here, he will send me away. He said there are many Western suitors in town, one of whom he approves."

"Oh?"

"Furthermore, considering that I could pass as a white woman, he said he would send me to live in Paris and marry a Frenchman or a European man who did not know of Mother's ancestry. He knew he could never live in France being married to Mother."

"What about your mother?"

"What do you mean?"

"What does she think? What does she have to say about all of this?"

"Oh, she is devastated. She likes Mith. She saw goodness in him. And she does not want me to be sent away. She is already torn about my brother being away for such a long time. Her heart is conflicted. She thinks I'm better off with a Khmer man, as our society accepts mixed races, whereas French society would not be so accepting."

"Luckily for you Khmers generally love and value those who are of mixed ancestries. We tend to be open-minded toward outsiders, put them on a pedestal, prostrate and worship them while we become closed-minded against our own. In this country, you have the world at your feet. You can still live a meaningful life, especially with Mith. He has every means to provide you with a happy and wonderful life. What more does your father want?"

"Race. Class. Title. I just do not understand this world," she said, sobbing. "All I know is he does not want me to see Mith or come by your house anymore. He suggested I refrain from communicating with anyone connected to Mith. Oh Anjali, I do not know what to do without him. My feelings are deeply invested in him. Mith exudes gentleness, courteousness, and love. I feel loved, happy, safe, and protected when I'm with him. I wish I could describe these amazing feelings. But now all I feel is sorrow and heartache without him."

Welcome to my world!

"I could do nothing when Father pulled out his pistol, threatening Mith not to see me anymore."

"Pardon? When did this happen?

"When he came to my house to talk to Papa the next day."

"Your father did that?"

"He was only trying to scare him away, but still..."

"Is Mith okay?"

"Mother nicely told him to go home—that she would talk to my papa. But Father would have none of it. I don't know what to do, Anjali. I feel helpless...and hopeless."

"I am sorry you are going through this awful affair. I believe this is something the elders must settle among themselves. Don't worry too much about it. I'm sure Mith will consult Father. Father is a smart man. He will figure something out and have a talk with your parents about it. I would like to believe your papa is of sound mind. Father will reason with him." I had no idea how my father would deal with her father, considering the way her father looked down his nose at him, but I tried to calm her worrying heart as best as I could.

"Thank you, Anjali. You are a wonderful friend." She wiped her tears. "I better get going before he finds out where I am."

The Governor's Daughter 75

"He doesn't have people following you yet? How did you get away without being detected?"

"I told my parents I would like to stop by to visit the queen before I head to Le Beau Monde. They agreed as long as my maid Kolap accompanied me. She's waiting for me downstairs. Thank goodness I have her. I wouldn't know what to do without her. She's been with me since we were little. We're practically sisters. I trust her. I share my most intimate secrets with her," Esmé said, staring into nothingness as if she was in a world of her own.

Of course her parents would buy her lies since Le Beau Monde was a fashionable place for the bourgeoisie of Cambodge, which consisted mostly of French and other Europeans. It housed expensive shops, sophisticated restaurants, and other commercial edifices. It was like a separate town for the French bourgeoisie.

Esmé woke from her reverie as if she had just remembered something. She pulled a small sealed envelope and turned to me. "I know you dislike being a messenger, but can I count on you to give this letter to Mith?"

I was a bit hesitant. "Sure. It's the least I can do. I'll make sure he gets it," I told her with sincerity upon meeting her sad blue-gray eyes. "Don't worry too much. The elders will come to a compromise. They'll work things out."

"If you have any message from Mith, please be sure to let me know. You can pass it on to my maid, who always goes to the market first thing in the morning."

"I will."

"You're a true friend," she said. She looked at me like she did not know how she would repay me. I held and squeezed her hand to assure her that everything would be fine. She pulled herself together before we exited the conference room.

"I'm walking Mademoiselle Esmé to her car," I said to Madame Montha. She smiled and curtsied at the sad, distressed governor's daughter. Madame Montha looked at me with perplexity. She probably wondered what was going on with the governor's daughter.

We descended the stairs and exited out of the brick office building to find her maid standing on the curb and her driver sitting inside the dark Peugeot Landaulet, engrossed in a Khmer newspaper. The city was full of Asian and European people casually strolling on both sides of the street. Some were entering and exiting shops. Others sat outdoors, enjoying their coffee and other beverages. The huge, tall trees as far as the eyes could see on both sides of the clean road touched each other above our heads and served as a giant, shaded canopy over the passing pedestrians, pedicabs, *romork* (three-wheeled carriages), horse carriages, bicycles, and cars. The occasional breeze, which sounded like many cymbals struck glancingly, made the leaves dance, touching us gently. The air felt balanced and spiritually pure, fresh to the lungs. Cambodge was a laid-back, easy place to work and live. The harder one worked, the more a person could accumulate wealth. Even if a person did not put in much effort, he could live comfortably. Our beautiful Siem Reap, my birthplace, had always been an inviting place to those near or far. The atmosphere showed its radiance, contrary to what Esmé must have been feeling inside. Upon seeing us, Kolap approached us, and her driver put away his paper and rushed out to open the door for them. Just then a long-legged man ran across the street through the slow-moving traffic.

"Esmé, what are you doing in town? Your father told me you were either shopping at Le Beau Monde or at the summer palace, visiting the queen," said Andre Thomas, the man with the hawk-like nose. I remembered him from the day I nearly got ran over and the second time at Nagara Theater, when he was chasing after Esmé like a little puppy. Monsieur San Nuon had mentioned to us that Andre was an English merchant who owned an ivory business in Bangkok. Apparently, he had not left the country yet. Esmé turned to look at me. I wondered if he was one of the few Western men the governor was considering for his daughter. I studied him up and down.

"I'm on my way to visit the queen. I am just stopping by to see my good friend Anjali," she said with a smile. "You've met Anjali before." She stood shoulder to shoulder with me as if trying to get him to notice me.

He glanced at me, which was the closest I would ever get to being acknowledged, and then refocused on Esmé. Inside, I felt slighted by his arrogant demeanor, but outwardly I remained smiling and courteous.

"What are you doing here?" she asked.

With both hands at his back and rocking back and forth from his toes to his heels, he said, "Actually, I'm meeting my American friend, James Albertson. He's just come back to town from Burma a few days ago."

"Oh. He was here before?" asked Esmé.

"Yes. I'm showing him around town." He glanced over at the other side of the street. Our eyes followed his. Sitting at a table and waving from an outdoor cafe was a jolly-faced man with a double chin whose massive physical size probably put him somewhere around one hundred and thirty kilograms. His hair was straight and blond and combed back. He wore a dark suit and dark red bow tie. At a second look, his eyes conveyed mischievousness. I remembered him. He was one of the guys who accompanied the governor and Andre on that Friday morning when

I first met Mith. "Please come with me to say hello," said Andre.

"I'm sorry. Maybe some other time. I don't want to keep the queen waiting. Surely you understand," said Esmé.

Andre looked disappointed, but quickly composed himself, as if understanding that as *barbaric* as these Khmers were, they esteemed their kings and queens. Surely he would not keep the king and queen of England waiting for him. He felt obliged to let it be. "It's quite all right. We are having dinner tonight with your father and other French dignitaries and their families. We'll see you then."

"I suppose," Esmé responded, as if not looking forward to it. "Goodbye then," she said to Andre. She turned to me and said, "I will call on you. I need your opinion on Khmer clothes. I have always admired yours. Would you be available to go to the tailor with me?"

I told her that I would. Glee rose within me. This was my chance to peek into the new upscale tailor that had just recently set up shop in town. From passing by their windows I could see a variety of silks and saris that came from various countries, including our very own beautiful silks from the countryside. My parents, mostly Father, had often lectured us to be frugal when it came to accessorizing ourselves. With all the wealth we had acquired since my great-great-grandfather's days, one would think we would live and spend extravagantly, but no. Not Father. He did not believe in enriching others by exchanging our "hard earned money" for "unnecessary goods." This would be a perfect excuse, taking Esmé shopping. She was probably trying to show Mith and his grandparents her demure and beautiful Khmer side. I told Esmé about the new tailor.

"Good. I can't wait to go." She flashed me a smile of excitement.

The Governor's Daughter

After we exchanged our cheek-to-cheek kisses, the gentlemanly Andre helped Esmé into the seat in the back and closed her door. The maid hopped into the passenger side and closed her own door. The driver tipped his hat to me and I responded with a smile. Andre watched the car drive away before he carefully crossed back to his American friend.

6

TO CATCH A SERIAL KILLER

Father, his five associates, and an unfamiliar man about his age rounded the street corner as Esmé's car took off. The long-legged Andre Thomas crossed back to the cafe to sit with his American friend, James Albertson. He still never looked back or acknowledged me. I shrugged my shoulders and let it be. I turned and excitedly walked to meet Father and his associates. The stranger walking shoulder to shoulder with Father sported a decorated uniform while Father wore a two-piece suit, *kben*, long black socks, and dress shoes. He had on his top hat.

"Pouk!" I called out to Father in excitement. I curtsied at his associates, who walked past me. They acknowledged me with gentle smiles and went upstairs to the office. They all carried boxes of files. They would be burning the midnight oil.

"Anjali, I want you to meet Uncle Nadee Chao. He is the police chief of Bangkok. He will be staying with us for a few days before he and I take off to Bangkok," Father explained.

I raised my palms to my forehead and bowed as I normally greeted my elders.

"Very good. Very good. So you are the young sleuth of Siem Reap. Your father tells me you will be helping him out with minor mystery cases so he can focus on this international one. What a smart and beautiful young daughter you have here," Uncle Nadee said to Father in Khmer with a Siamese accent.

I found out later that he was of Khmer descent and that his ancestors had lived under Siam sovereignty when the dwindling Khmer Empire was being divided between Siam and Annam. He turned back to me and said, "You know, I have a few handsome sons myself. You can have your pick. It would be fantastic if we became in-laws. We would be a powerful combined force, now would we not, Detective Oum Chum Chinak?" He nudged and winked at Father.

Father chuckled good-naturedly. "You're making her blush. Let's head upstairs to discuss this case and make arrangements for our trips." They walked in front of me.

Trips? Father must be traveling to where the crimes took place. How exciting!

"Speaking of which, Father, may I be put on the case? You can sure use all the help you can get," I said from behind Father and Uncle Nadee as we ascended the marble stairs.

The police chief of Siam laughed with amusement. "Oh, little child. This is a very dangerous case. You're much too young to know the filth, violence, and gore in this case. The sheer magnitude of it sent our heads spinning. That's why we're all putting our differences aside to solve this one. We're here to seek your father's expertise since we came to a dead end."

"Uncle Nadee is right. This is not the type of case for a young woman," said Father.

"Considering this is my future career, isn't it time for me to learn every aspect of the business?"

"Oh child," said Father, "we'll discuss this some other time. Right now, we have deadlines to meet, places to go, and people to see."

I decided not to push my luck. "By the way, Pouk. There's another matter of great concern you must attend to immediately."

"Are you talking about Mith and Esmé?"

"How did you know?"

"I have spoken with Mith about it this morning, and not too long thereafter I received a barrage of verbal attacks from the provincial governor himself at the meeting," he said with a smile.

"Yes. I can attest to that," chimed in Uncle Nadee. "Boy, did your father get an earful of rage." They both chuckled as though it was amusing.

"The truth is," Father said, "the provincial governor is angry right now. His temper flares. I will request an audience with Princess Dhana. Maybe she has some kind of influence over him. It appears that she has a soft spot for Mith. Let's get back to our work, my dear Anjali. I understand you're a good friend of Esmé's, but don't concern yourself too much with their problem. Adults make the rules, so surely they can come up with a solution. We'll find a way to resolve it."

I pulled Esmé's letter from my dress pocket. "Since I won't see him anytime soon, do you mind passing this note to Mith?"

*A*s promised, before Father set off for Bangkok with Uncle Nadee, he visited the princess. She decided that everyone needed to cool down and agreed to reasonably work out this matter of the heart with her husband. Esmé was pleased with the outcome, as she revealed to me on our shopping and tailoring expeditions during my lunch hour. She had a positive outlook on life and could not wait to wear the beautiful ruby *kben* that I helped her picked out. Later that day, Mother and I stood on the side of the road near our house to see Father and Uncle Nadee off. They were loading the last luggage on the truck. Father's job required constant traveling, but Mother was never used to it. He and mother both looked at each other with sadness, worry, and love.

Uncle Nadee must have seen similar expressions in his wife because he turned to Mother and said, "Don't worry about your husband. I'll make sure to steer him away from all those beautiful women in Bangkok." He grinned upon seeing the reluctant smile on Mother's face.

Father waved to us. We watched as the truck drove out of sight before we returned home.

Considering how lonely Mother was, I tried to kill two birds with one stone by begging Madame Montha to leave her boys with Mother to keep her company late in the evening, which would keep her from overseeing me too strictly, as I was hoping to take a peek at the files that Father's associates were working on. They left Madame

Montha to work late and organize those files for them. I offered her my help so that she could make it home before her boys fell asleep. I did get my chance to sneak a peek at those files.

The first time I reviewed the photographs of the murder victims from those crime scenes, I did not know how to react. I stared, wide-eyed, at the pictures in silence. An onslaught of light-headedness and disorientation buzzed through my head. Suddenly I felt sick to my stomach. I lost count of my trips to the ladies room to vomit. The first few times, Madame Montha held my hair while my stomach emptied out what I ate that day. In between, I found myself crouching over the toilet crying as if someone had whipped me, for it seemed as though pain seared every inch of my body. My heart throbbed. At the same time, my head hurt as though someone had hammered it. I shivered. Many questions ran through my mind. Why would someone do something like this to defenseless women? What possessed someone to commit such atrocious acts? The images of these women, some curled up like a fetus and some on their backs lying in a pool of their own blood, burned into my mind. Some had clothes on but most did not. I could not help but think that those women could have been my friends, relatives, or even me.

"Oh my lord," said Madame Montha, pacing back and forth outside of the bathroom stall. "I pray I will not get in trouble for this. I wouldn't know where to find work if your father fired me. I shouldn't have let you see these crime photographs. Oh Lord Buddha, what have I done?"

I pulled myself together by sitting up and wiping my tears. After a few minutes, I was able to speak. "I'm sorry for scaring you like this. It's just...it's just mind-boggling that someone can do that to another person. I heard things, but to actually see these things, I'm shaken to the core. And these are just photographs. What if I'm faced with the real thing? What would I do then? Madame Montha, how could you get used to such gruesome scenes?"

She stopped pacing. I could feel her watching me. "The truth of the matter is you never get used to it, my dear Anjali."

I turned to look at her. She had a vacant look in her eyes. "But at least you're not constantly running into the bathroom throwing up and crying your eyes out," I said, feeling the urge to curl up in a corner and bawl like a baby.

"It's true that I have seen deaths—even that of my parents and my husband—but not as gruesome as what I see here. I found myself throwing up and crying just like you when I first came to work for your father. I had nightmares for many months. I thought about the suffering of the victims, the fear, the pain, and torture they went through before they breathed their last breath. Then I thought about my beloved husband. I thought about how much he must have suffered before he died. It was too much for me. I cried all the time. Misery and wretchedness haunted me day and night. I couldn't focus. I thought I couldn't perform this job. I panicked. I realized I had three boys to take care of, and because of them I stuck to it, even if it meant throwing up, crying, and facing nightmares. Your father knew. He pulled me into his office. He sat me down. He said to me, 'Montha, we'll never become desensitized by these crimes, but we must put our emotions and feelings aside to do our job. And our job is to find the killers for our victims and bring them to justice. We can't do our job effectively or efficiently if we let our emotions control us.' I learned that whatever compassion we have for our victims, we must channel it to finding their murderers and solving their deaths. That we give their spirits and loved ones closure. We must emotionally separate ourselves from the victims, otherwise we'll be emotional wrecks and will never get anything done. We won't be able to do our job and find justice for them. Do you understand, Anjali? I'm passing on the words of your father to you."

"I think so," I said, though the nausea and headache still lingered. "But you know, words are easy to say."

"Do you want to go home and rest?" Madame Montha asked.

"No. I must be brave if I'm going to help Father and our agency solve these crimes. I'm sorry. I don't mean to be a big baby about this."

"You're not. It's a normal reaction. You wouldn't be human if you reacted otherwise." I had always loved Madame Montha like a big sister. I grew up in a family with four brothers: two married and living in different provinces while the twins studied abroad in France. What she revealed to me incited great compassion in me. I felt closer to her, and with her around, I felt so much better. She made me a stronger person. What a great role model. She had three boys with no family and relatives to help, and she did whatever it took to survive.

We went back to the conference room to work. Madame Montha poured me a glass of water.

"Thank you," I said, having forgotten that I was dehydrated from all of the vomiting. Heaps of files were scattered all over the table, credenza, and floor.

I helped her to compile and organize those gruesome files. While Madame Montha put the reports in chronological order, I browsed through the ones she had already done. Anyone who worked on the case knew the serial killer had a type: Eurasian women. I could not help but think that this was such a high-profile case because it was Eurasian women who had been raped and killed, as opposed to just Asian women. Not only that, but they were daughters of dignitaries and wealthy people—the movers and shakers of our colonized society.

"I wonder why this killer—whoever he is—targeted Eurasian women? And they were not the average or plain types, but all of his victims were tall and stunningly beautiful." I found myself saying this out loud as I looked at their profiles and pictures taken when they were alive.

"I don't know. Maybe he was rejected by one of them and decided to wreak havoc on them all."

"Based on all these files, no one has a clue as to who the perpetrator is—whether he's Asian or European."

"Not one clue?"

"Oh my lord," I said, feeling light-headed and nauseated again.

"What is it?"

"According to these reports from the medical examiners, they were all raped with a foreign object." I flipped through all the reports that had been translated into Khmer and French. "No one found this foreign object," I continued. "What does that even mean?"

Madame Montha looked at me with confusion and horror. Details about this type of violence were brand new to me. My hands were shaking. My heart continued to throb painfully. I could not wrap my head around the idea of a woman being raped by a foreign object, I must admit. Father was right: I was not ready. Again, self-doubt crept into my mind. *What if I am not cut out to perform the job? What else am I good at if not solving mysteries?* As mature as Madame Montha was, she also had never heard about women being raped with a foreign object before. This was all new to her too.

"What kind of sick, twisted person is this? I hope your father finds who this killer is and catches him fast before he hurts other women," said Madame Montha.

"Well, we can be sure of one thing," I said.

"What is it, Anjali?"

"That this person is hateful and has an axe to grind."

"How do you figure?"

"His level of viciousness," I said, fanning out the crime photos for her to see. "At least that's what I've learned from Father, anyway." She cringed in fear and disgust. I briefly scanned them myself. It was too much. I wanted to toss everything aside and just give up. But I stared at the victims' faces. I thought about how much they suffered before they breathed their last dying breath. Why should I give up? Why should I let these women down? Madame Montha was right. These victims needed an advocate—someone who would find justice for them. I flipped through the report from each country. Every one of these women died from a ruptured bladder; hence, each investigation reporter concluded it was a foreign object. It confused me. How was this foreign object used? How could it break a woman's bladder? My stomach twisted and my heart throbbed for what I was about to ask for. I felt I couldn't stomach them but that I had to see them.

"Where are the autopsy photos?" I asked.

"Detective Duong Chea took them. He is consulting with Dr. Suriya Chandara at Mehta Hospital." Detective Chea was Father's most senior associate. He had been with the agency since he was a young man.

"I see. I guess I can work another angle for now.

However, I need to see those pictures to help me with the investigation."

"You're serious about this?"

"Yes."

"You're not officially on the case. Don't tell me you're going to defy your father's request. What about all those other cases he asked you to work on?"

"Don't worry about that. I've got it all covered. I can work on those cases with my hands tied behind my back. Father is not going to find out."

"I don't want any part of it."

"No worries. If he finds out, I will assure him it's not your fault—that you had no involvement in this."

"You've got that right. Just out of curiosity, how will you get your hands on those photos?"

"I'll find a way."

She shook her head at me. I continued to look at the reports and wrote down the dates of the murders. Suddenly a light flashed before me. Father probably had a clue. That was why he was traveling to Siam and other Asian countries. He probably had a type of suspect in mind. Excitement broke through.

"I know what Father is doing."

"What is it, Anjali?"

"No wonder they all thought that this was an act of one person, aside from the type of victims and how they died."

Madame Montha gave me a perplexed look. I went to Father's office and came back to the conference room with a map of Southeast Asia. I put it up on the wall. I used pins to mark the places where the murders took place.

I pointed out to her the dates of the crimes. "I don't know who he has in mind, in terms of suspects, but he is looking into a certain company that has satellite offices in all these areas. The evidence points to a businessman. He might not be a local businessman, but a foreign one. Father is going to the scenes of the crimes to match up schedules of businessmen traveling in those areas. And he's probably interviewing witnesses. I believe he has narrowed down the profile. Maybe this killer is closer to being identified than we thought."

I had difficulty sleeping that night. I kept seeing the haunting faces of the victims. Somewhere in between I no longer could tell if I was awake or sleeping. I felt the presence of spirits in my room. They even stood at the foot of my bed, pleading in a chorus for me to help them. They also appeared before me individually. Then I saw a familiar face among them. She sat, kneeling by the side of my bed as if waiting on me. Her presence became more solid. She was adorned in golden Khmer royal clothes and kneeled by my side with a demure smile on her face. I found it puzzling that the provincial governor's daughter would be kneeling by my bedside. "Esmé…Esmé…Esmé," I called out to her in my mind. I tried to get up, but I could not move. I tried again. Still I could not move. A strong force kept me from waking up. I struggled to move and scream. I saw myself lying in my bed with my eyes wide open, but I could not wake up. I panicked. I kept telling myself, *I must get up. I need to get up. Help. Somebody, please help me!* Then I did scream, but it sounded muffled. I tried harder to scream, from the top of my lungs, but only a whimper came out. I kept struggling to move my body, whimpering as loud as I could. The next thing I knew I heard loud knocks on my door. A gentle voice called out to me. "Anjali...Anjali...Are you all right, my child?"

Oh good. Mother is here. Mother. Mother. I'm in here. Please help me. But she just kept on knocking and asking if I was okay. *No. I'm not okay. Please come in. Help me, mother. Help me!*

7

BAD OMEN

*E*ven though I heard Mother's comforting voice I couldn't wake up. Then I felt a hand on me, causing me to sit up and scream so loudly that it gave Mother a good fright. My loud scream sent her jumping from the side of my bed. I found myself struggling to breathe.

"Anjali!" Mother found herself screaming as well.

"Mae!" I called out.

"What is wrong with you, dear?"

"I'm sorry, Mae. I did not mean to scare you. I had a nightmare. That was all."

"Must be some nightmare. You poor child. You're sweating raindrops." She wiped my face, especially my forehead, with her blue checkered *krama*.

"Mae, I'm fine. I don't mean to worry you." I moved her hand away from my forehead.

"What brought on this nightmare?" She raised one of her arched eyebrows at me. "Have you been reading your father's case files again? Have you been viewing those photographs too?"

I didn't look up at her.

"Oh Anjali! What have we told you about sneaking to look at those files, huh? You're too young. You're not ready for this job. Look what it did to you. It gave you nightmares."

"Oh Mae. It has nothing to do with that. It's hot in here and I have a heavy cover on. I was probably experiencing a heat stroke or something that made me feel like I was drowning...or something."

"Given the weather that we've been having, it's plausible. But I was not born yesterday, Anjali. And I'm not old enough to be senile. Goodness, child. How could you lie to me like that? I thought I raised you better than that. I know what you have been up to, working late and leaving Madame Montha's children with me—not that I mind that—but you're being sneaky. I don't like sneakiness."

"I'm sorry. You're not going to tell Pouk, are you?" I looked up at her.

"I have a good mind to pull you away from this job of yours once and for all."

"Oh, please, please, Mae. You can't do that to me. This is what I want to do in life, to help people. Didn't you say the most rewarding thing in life is to help people in need? I want to be in the business of helping people. Granted, they're dead people, but just like Pouk, I want to find justice for them, give them a voice. They can't defend themselves in court against their killers. Face it, Mae. You and Pouk made me think this way."

"Don't you throw that back at us," sputtered Mother, glowering. "Don't you ever use our teaching against us to get what you want."

I still gave her a pouty, pathetic look.

"Why can't you be like girls your age who are..."

"Prim, proper, and ready to take on a husband?"

She gave me a disapproving look.

I locked my left arm against her right arm and rested my head on her shoulder like a little girl. I looked up at her face. "I'm sorry, Mae. I was born into the Chinak family. I have a deep connection, passion, and duty to protect the trinity of king, people, and country. I know you love me. You want what's best for me. I think this is the best. Please, let me do this. I can't picture myself wanting to do anything else. Why can't I do something that I love?"

She thought long and hard, for I could see a vein appear by her temple. She gently tapped me on the arm. "All right, all right. If you're wholeheartedly into this, I can't stop you. I only ask that you wait until your father returns and after he has solved these cases, then we'll sit down and talk about this as a family. I'll not make my decision without him. After all, he's the head of this household. Surely you can understand that."

"Yes, I do, Mae."

A vague thrill ran through me as Mother and I came to an agreement. However, something dark still lingered within me. I was not the type to overanalyze a dream, but I had this strange and uneasy feeling. Something was not right. I could not wrap my head around the fact that Esmé had appeared before me, kneeling at the foot of my bed after the victims had begged me to find their killer. Normally, I would dismiss a dream as a manifestation of what I saw and thought during the day, but the frightening feeling in my gut told me otherwise. Esmé's Euro-Asian background could make her a target of the serial rapist and killer. Could my dream be telling me that the killer had arrived in Cambodge from another Asian country? I wished I could ask Father to which class or group of people he had narrowed him down. But that avenue was closed to me.

I suddenly had the urge to visit Esmé. She had become one of my few good friends after all.

The day he found out about Esmé and Mith, the provincial governor forbade her from stepping into our home because he thought our family had acted as matchmakers. But surely he wouldn't mind me visiting his home. Just to be safe, I telephoned the Laurent Manor to find out who was there. According to the head maid, Madame Sari, the governor had a morning meeting with the French authorities from Phnom Penh and Prey Nokor. Before I headed out to work on this cool morning, I stopped by the mansion.

After having finished my chores at home, which I made sure I had gotten up early for, I cleaned myself up nicely and rode my bicycle through the tree-lined road of the Golden Hill Village, which encompassed about 150 homes of wealthy people. My family had moved here after he left the Royal Calvary and opened his detective agency. In thirty minutes, I stopped before the front gate of the Laurent Manor.

"Hi, Miss Anjali," said the guard as he left his guard booth. He approached me from inside the metal gates. "You must be here to see Princess Esmè."

"Indeed, I am."

"Is she expecting you?"

"No. She doesn't know I'm visiting. However, I phoned the house. I spoke to Madame Sari. She said Princess Dhana approves the visit. Madame Sari said she would let you know and to add my name to the list."

"She did?" He scratched his head. He went inside the booth and picked up something. He strolled back out flipping his notes and said, "Ah. Here it is. Mademoiselle Anjali Chinak. I'm sorry about that. The previous guard didn't let me know. Indeed, she said you were coming."

"How many guards does the Laurent family have?" I said with a smile.

"Just two. Me and another guy." He opened up the gate.

"Thank you," I said as I walked my bicycle inside. He tipped his hat to me. After I left him, I hopped back on my bicycle and rode along the cobblestoned driveway of the Laurent Manor. It was immense. I followed the long driveway around the big fountain and parked my bike in front of the two-story, yellow colonial mansion with intricately designed archways, round columns, and mullioned windows.

Madame Sari greeted me at the white door as I ascended the three concrete steps. I put my palms together to greet her and she did likewise. She led me through the opulent, bright entranceway, with its high ceilings, French murals, and a huge crystal chandelier hovering over elegant staircases to the left and right sides that merged at the upper level. The stairs matched the white marble floor. Intricate red rugs randomly covered the floors. Below the landing, a carved and polished, round wooden Khmer table stood in the middle of the foyer with beautifully arranged and assorted flowers in a European vase. Two elegant armchairs and arranged flowers in vases on smaller, round end tables were artfully arranged next to them. In fact, flowers could be found in almost every corner of the room. The beautiful flowers emitted a light fragrance. The family had furnished the house with luxurious French furniture and gold-framed oil paintings of the French emperor Napoleon Bonaparte, the provincial governor's parents, the ruling Khmer King and Queen of Cambodge, and a family portrait of the Laurents.

The images of the Laurents burned in my mind. Even as I walked away, I could still see the thin, tall, mustached French governor standing with his arm resting on an ornate but elegant royal chair with gold frame and cream fabric on which sat his wife, Princess Dhana. Their son and daughter sat on the rug-covered floor with their heels to their buttocks on each side of the chair with their hands resting prim and proper on their laps. If Esmé was considered beautiful, her older brother Alexandre was surely found to be handsome, but not as handsome as Mith. No one could be as handsome as Mith Sovann, with his chiseled good looks and his remarkable physique.

My heart still skipped a beat whenever I thought about him. But I tried to forget him. He belonged to Esmé. I continued observing the many paintings as I passed by.

The portraiture gave the mansion a certain gravitas, an importance beyond its age. The morning sun shined through the floor-to-ceiling windows and the double-glass doors led to a grand evergreen topiary garden.

The maid led me to the large, arched threshold where we stood as she made the announcement of my arrival to the lady of the house. I entered, and Madame Sari walked away to attend to other duties.

Sitting in the middle of the room, in front of the arched,

curtained windows, was Princess Dhana, adorned in her traditional Khmer laced blouse sashed in blue *peanear* and wearing a blue *kben*. She was entertaining Princess Nakry, the widow of Prince Dara Vong, and her only son, Prince Phirun, Mith's blubbery and gluttonous half-brother who nearly ran me over on the intersection of Indara Devi Boulevard and Count of Vermandois Boulevard. It was no secret he had insatiable appetites for women, food, and cars —not necessarily in that order. He was one of those princes who, like his mother, would use his power to prey on the poor and weak.

No one was supposed to know he was Mith's half-brother. I wondered sometimes about men. If they didn't love the women they were with, how could they bear children with them? If Prince Dara Vong did not love Princess Nakry, how come he had a son with her? But my thoughts digressed.

Phirun wore a gray three-piece suit with a blue cravat. Traditionally, in a royal setting, blue was a designated color for Friday, if we were to wear Khmer attire. I, coincidentally, had on my angle-length light blue dress.

I kneeled down and prostrated myself on the floor, placed my palms clasped together on the floor and rested my forehead on them. "I prostrate before you in respect," I said.

Princess Dhana gently touched my hand in approval. Chills ran down my spine. I now had to turn and offer the same respect to Princess Nakry. I felt disgusted and annoyed having to bow before the woman who ordered the killing of another woman. I did not mind kneeling before a person of intelligence, grace, class, and benevolence, yet tradition could be a nuisance when I had to prostrate myself before a despicable person.

Since tradition and class level called for it, I put on my veneer of politeness and respect for her in accordance with Khmer tradition. I understood the feelings were mutual. Princess Nakry automatically loathed me because Father was the detective who revealed the crime she committed. Not only that, but Father took great care of the love child, Mith Sovann, who was the constant reminder of her husband's love for another and the role she played in having her killed and her body disposed of.

As demanded by custom, I also prostrated myself before Princess Nakry's son, Prince Phirun. He looked just like her, with his thin lips, triangular face, and prominent eyebrows. Though I did not raise my eyes to look at her face, which was considered rude, I could tell that Princess Nakry stared down at me as if she lusted for my blood. I remained demure and respectful.

"You must be here to see Esmé," said Princess Dhana.

"Yes, Princess," I said as I remained sitting upright with heels to buttocks on the floor.

"My husband will not like this, but seeing that you and my daughter are good friends, and knowing how unhappy she is at the moment, you would be a welcome face. She could really use a friend right now. I know she doesn't have a lot of friends."

"Who needs friends outside of our royal abode?" scoffed the evil Princess Nakry.

"That's not true," said Princess Dhana.

"Thank you, Majass," I said, with my clasped palms on my forehead, bowing my head.

"You know, I don't get you sometimes," said Princess Nakry to her cousin, Princess Dhana. "You allow your daughter to fall in love with a filthy peasant. Not only that, he has no mother nor father." She knew full well he had a mother and father. She had had his mother killed, and as a result drove his father to madness and death. "And on top of that she befriends such a low-class group of people," she said, as she looked down at me from the corner of her eyes with her mouth hanging in an expression of disgust. In my peripheral vision I could see the nice princess give me an apologetic look.

"My dear Princess Nakry, granted we're born into different titles, but we're all children of the earth."

"Well, there's a reason why we're born into different classes. Why must we act contrary to our birthrights? If we socialize with the filth and scum of the earth, they won't know their place."

My blood boiled. She may have been of royal blood, but she sure acted cheap and vindictive. I wanted so much to tell her that classes were human creations to make their purported members feel important and respected, but that respect should be earned, not forced upon others.

"Oh mother, you're such a direct and honest person," said her son, Phirun, as he laughed in a derisive manner.

If I had to sit here and listen to this venomous woman any longer I would give her a good slap and risk paying a fine, being imprisoned, or worse, being executed for disrespecting the royal family.

"Kolap," said Princess Dhana.

"Yes, Princess," answered Esmé's obedient maid. I did not know she had been sitting and waiting behind me to be called upon.

"Take Anjali to see the mistress."

"Yes, Princess," she said, as we both prostrated ourselves before the three royal figures and took off. My prostration was secretly only meant for Princess Dhana.

"This is despicable," mumbled the wretched Princess Nakry.

"Please be dignified," whispered Princess Dhana.

Miss Kolap led me to the corridor, up the grand stairs to the upper level of the house, turning to the corridor of the left wing. She knocked on the door at the far end. A soft voice called out, "Come in." Miss Kolap announced my presence. Her mistress nodded. She showed me in and left.

Esmé quickly stuffed a note she appeared to be reading into her dress pocket. The paper looked new and the red and black seal had just been broken. She must have received it today. Her face flushed pink. She got up from the armchair that was seated by tall French windows. I curtsied to her. She elegantly moved to where I stood and exchanged a cheek-to-cheek kiss with me. The note in her pocket must have sent her welcoming news, for her eyes twinkled and her cheeks were rosy. She offered me a seat in one of the chairs by the windows while she walked to her dresser drawer to tuck away the stack of letters sitting on top. They must have been letters she received from Mith.

"I'm so glad you're here," she said, excited. "Have you seen Mith? Has he changed?"

"No. Since the day your father forced you to sever all ties with him and our family, he has not come around. He had no reason to since you're no longer allowed to visit us. Or possibly, since you two were acquainted there, he felt guilty for putting our family at odds with your father. After all, we have to work together for the safety and prosperity of the province of Siem Reap."

"I'm sorry."

"It's not your fault."

"I know. I just feel awful about everything. I'm especially sorry for putting you and your family in the middle of it."

"That's okay. Love should be simple, right? Who knew things would turn out like this?"

"Yes," she said as she got up from her chair to pace around her room and fidget with her knickknacks. "It has been forever, so it seems, since I've seen him." She appeared suddenly sad and reflective.

I tried to lighten up the mood. "Thank goodness your mother is more gentle and understanding. She's on your side. She'll make everything all right."

"You're right. I'd go mad if weren't for my mother and..." She stopped short, staring at her drawer. Then she continued, "If it weren't for my mother, you, and your family, I wouldn't know how to deal with Father. He's being extremely unreasonable." I had no clue who she thought she was fooling, but I knew with certainty that it wasn't what she originally wanted to say. The letters she exchanged with Mith kept her from feeling completely separated and hopeless.

"Really?" I asked.

"Yes," she said, trying to sound sincere. She walked from her drawer to sit on the chair next to mine. She turned it around to face me. "Anjali, when Mith confessed how much he loved me and wanted to spend the rest of his life with me, I thought I was dreaming. I went weak in the knees. I turned to jelly upon his gentle touch."

"Oh?" I raised one of my eyebrows.

"Yes, his gentle touch of my hand," she said, feeling embarrassed. In Khmer culture, it was considered highly inappropriate for an unmarried man and an unmarried woman to be alone together, let alone touch one another. "Everything about him is so perfect. His coolness, his voice, his spirit, his soul. I love the way he loves me, gentle and caring. I wish I could describe to you how that feels."

"I'm sure I will find out one day," I said grudgingly.

"You're right. Why is love so complicated? Why can't two people who fall in love with each other so irrevocably just fall in love, get married, have children, and live happily ever after? Why must we go through this drama?" She looked at me. "I'm sorry to confess my feelings to you like this. You're young. You probably don't understand."

Little did she know that I understood everything—at least about the heartache part.

"I have some idea. Besides, I'm only a few years younger."

She smiled her pleasant smile. "You'll understand more when you meet and fall madly in love with the man of your dreams."

Oh, I have found him, but he is in love with you.

I said to Esmé, "You'll get your chance to live happily with each other. You're just bumping up against a little obstacle. The governor will realize how much you two love each other and he'll approve of you. He only needs to be reminded of his love for your mother. He defied his parents, his culture, and all the obstacles that your mother went through in Siam to rescue her and form a good looking and affluent family."

She looked at me with a genuine smile. "Sometimes I forget how mature and wise you are."

"You're too sweet."

I had a pleasant visit with Esmé. Thank goodness I did not run into the governor. I was not sure how I would react in front of him.

I rode to the office. I worked my normal hours, investigating missing valuables at the monastery and the museum. I had to tell the authorities of the monastery and the museum that their missing valuables were an inside job.

The Governor's Daughter

They did not believe me. I presented my case before them. I had plenty of evidence, time, and witnesses. I confronted the thieves themselves. Before I even finished, they confessed to having stolen valuable artifacts to sell to foreigners who were willing to pay huge sums of money for them. Stolen ancient Khmer jewelry, artifacts, and statues had been an issue since the French's domination of the region.

I wished Father would come home so we could discuss my involvement in more serious cases. Based on his telegram to his senior associate, Detective Duong Chea, he was knee deep in clues and feverishly working the evidence in Burma. I hoped the clues panned out.

8

MITH SOVANN'S ARREST

I woke up early the next morning to go to the market for meat and vegetables with Jorani. The earlier we went, the fresher we could get our meat and produce. Some people used money while others bartered their goods. We finished early and rode back home in her oxcart with her father, Samkol Sem, who had just come back from dropping off his four sons at the rice fields. Hard-working peasants like his family attended to their farm and rice fields fifteen hours a day, seven days a week. He had to return home to pick up some more food.

Now that it was the month of May, it was rice cultivating season. The village was devoid of people. Most were out in the fields. Whoever finished first would help the other villagers finish sowing their seeds. This common practice of exchanging labor, whether cultivating or harvesting, was called *bravass*. Jorani and her mother needed to make more food for her family and fellow villagers who were helping them in the rice fields. As for our acres and acres of rice fields, my parents' poorer relatives oversaw them for us. We reaped and shared the yield with them.

My paternal family had known the Sem family for generations. We had inhabited Siem Reap possibly since the reign of King Suryavarman II. Both of our families and ancestors always seemed to come back here, no matter where they went to study or work.

Monsieur Samkol Sem was a thin, tan, well-built man in his early fifties. He loved and cared for his family and was a devout Buddhist. He was neither poor nor rich, but we knew him to be an honest man and a hard worker.

Monsieur Sem gently tapped his two oxen to go faster, not paying attention or listening to us chatting in the back.

Jorani asked, "Say, Anjali, what's going on between the governor's daughter and Mith?"

"What do you mean?"

"Do you think her father will allow her to marry him?"

"I don't know."

"Well, rumor has it that he would either send her abroad or marry her off to one of these *Barangsess* here," she whispered. Khmer people did not like how the French treated our royalty, not to mention the regular people, so in their passive way, they referred to them as *sess*, which in Khmer means horse.

"Who told you that?"

"My sister Channi overheard one of the Laurents' maids talking."

"Who?"

"Not sure."

"Oh dear. She should be careful. The Laurents do not tolerate gossip. If they found out one of their maids was acting in an undignified manner they would surely fire her."

The Governor's Daughter

"Oh no. Please don't let them know. We don't want her to get into trouble with the Laurents."

"No. I won't say anything, but just be careful. Don't get caught up in these rumor mills, especially because of your curious sister, Channi. She's too young to be taking an interest in such things."

"I know. I should have known better than to participate in gossip. But sometimes you can't avoid all the talk."

"I understand."

"Well, I hope it works out for them. This town cannot take any more unfulfilled love."

"What do you know about unfulfilled love, Jorani? Do you have something to say about your fiancé, Kosal?" I said with a smile in my voice.

"Oh, stop teasing me about Kosal. I know you don't want to confirm this, but don't you think Mith looks exactly like Prince Dara Vong? May the Lord bless his soul!"

"I beg your pardon?"

"Come on. I know you know."

"I don't know what you're talking about."

"Oh, come now."

"I can't rely on things that can't be substantiated. Besides, it's none of our business."

"Really, Anjali. It doesn't take a detective to know Prince Dara Vong had a thing for a peasant girl in Beung Mealea. It was the talk of the town. The elders lamented how a killer brutally raped and murdered a young peasant woman up there, but the killer was swiftly brought to justice. Everyone knew your father investigated her death at the request of the Prince. Peasants seldom get swift justice..."

"That's not true. At Chinak & Associates we investigate the deaths of poor peasant folks, too."

"Really?"

"Yes."

She seemed unconvinced. "But this was a special request, with all of Prince Dara Vong's resources at his disposal. Though your father never disclosed the final report, word was that the prince or the Kambujastra royal family did not want the information revealed. It's kind of shameful and sad, really, that they hid this truth about their daughter-in-law, considering how their ancestors were known as the most honest and just monarchs. As a result of the injustice and his sorrow, the prince died from heartache."

"Correction. He died of an aortic aneurysm."

"Same thing. Anyway, they have a son together. Do you see the resemblance of the dead peasant woman and the Prince in Mith? What person would argue about that? Besides, Mith's grandparents, whose only daughter mysteriously died, used to live somewhere in Beung Mealea, and we know your father was best friends with the Prince. Why else would an orphan like Mith be well taken care of by your father?"

"You've got everything figured out, haven't you? You truly missed your calling. You should have become a detective."

"Perhaps. But then again I don't have concrete clues and the scientific method and solid evidence to prove my theory—as you often remind everyone whenever someone bases their conclusion on gossip and sees things through *untrained* eyes. Let's see, what's that adage that you often quote? Oh yes, that's right. *Things are not what they seem.*"

"Don't mock me," I said, as I gently elbowed her in the arm. She pretended to rub her arm in pain and gave out a gentle laugh.

"Whoa. What's going on at your house?" asked Jorani's father, suddenly breaking his silence.

Approaching my house, we could see the governor's car along with several police vehicles parked in our front driveway.

"What do you suppose is going on, Pouk?" asked Jorani.

"I don't know," said Monsieur Sem, "but I think it looks serious."

"You and me both," I said. "And from the sound of it, it's probably not good."

Jorani and her father looked scared. My nerves rattled and my heart raced upon hearing the fracas that was coming from my house.

"We'll come with you," said Monsieur Sem. I did not bother to gather my groceries.

We marched up the stairs to find the provincial governor of Siem Reap and his three armed men terrorizing Mother, our driver, and the grandparents of Mith Sovann. I noticed the corner of our driver's mouth was bleeding. He was on the floor with his left heel to his buttock and his palms together at his forehead. He was trembling while muttering desperately in broken French, "No, no. We don't know..." Suon used to be a kickboxer before he started working for Father, who taught him how to handle a gun and shoot. But this training did not matter because a stronger force had accosted him. He became as docile as a lamb with the gaping black hole of a rifle barrel leveled at his face. Oh, how I loathed men with power and prestige who eviscerated men of lower status. My heart beat like a big drum. My head spun with anger and frustration so much that I believe I could have knocked this governor to the ground.

"Where is he? Where is that bastard grandson of yours?

I will kill him!" The governor screamed and yelled in French at the scared elderly couple.

He had lived in Cambodge for over twenty years but had not bothered to learn one word of Khmer. From his perspective, we should all have learned his language, for it was the language of power, class, and prestige and we were considered subservient. Thus, in order for Khmer natives like us to succeed and be understood we must speak French and address each other as Madame, Monsieur, and Mademoiselle, otherwise they would find it utterly confusing and annoying that we referred to each other as grandfather, grandmother, uncle, aunt, sister, and brother even when we were not related to each other biologically. Not that I was anti-French nor against learning new languages and embracing new cultures, as our forefathers had often taught us to learn from outsiders and take in the positive aspects of their contributions. However, I abhorred the way they treated us native people. Mother, the driver, and Mith's grandparents huddled next to each other on our buffed wooden floor like frightened rabbits. They did not dare to raise their eyes at their interrogators.

"Who are you looking for, Governor?" I asked cordially. Deep down inside, I wanted to snatch one of their rifles and blow each one of their arrogant heads off.

"Good, someone who can speak French. Ask these two imbeciles where the spawn of their spawn is hiding." If he only knew that the only monster standing in this room was he.

"You do not need to be so disrespectful and volatile. What's this all about?"

"Do as I told you or I will have my men blow all your brains out. Damn barbarians." Half of his upper lip tightened upward. He was trouble.

The Governor's Daughter 113

I glared at him in defiance. "I implore you, as a governor and a gentleman, to be just and not barge into our house bent on terrorizing my elders who don't speak your language and don't have a clue as to your purpose."

His face turned crimson. His eyes widened in a fixed glare at me, as if deciding what to do with me. "Little girl, you're trying my patience. Tell me what I want to know, or you'll see a world of hurt." His furious countenance and tall frame faced me. I knew he was trying hard not to knock me senseless for making such a saucy remark and for daring to defy him. "Ask them the whereabouts of their grandson," he said through clenched teeth.

"Is there a reason why you're looking for him?"

"Just ask them!" he thundered.

I abided, hoping he would receive the answer he needed and leave us be. I relayed his message to the elder couple. They looked at me with bewilderment.

"He had an appointment with Dr. Alex Beauvis, at the restaurant at the Maharaja Hotel, to see about a job in Phnom Penh," said the grandfather.

I relayed the message.

He and his armed men stormed out of our house. Jorani and her father shook with fear, their eyes wide. They gathered their strength and composure to help the others, including Mother, from the floor. My heart raced and my entire body trembled. My boldness could have gotten me in serious trouble, but I could not allow an outsider to come into my home and threaten and disrespect my household as he had done. Anger ran through me. Father would not stand for this.

Just as I thought that, Mother said, "Please don't let your father know about how the governor barged into our house and threatened us with guns. He doesn't need to know the hostility that took place here, just that he came to inquire about his daughter. Are we in agreement?"

"Why not tell him?" I asked.

"I know your father. He'll confront the governor. He'll get himself into trouble with the French authorities. He has been walking a fine line with them as it is."

"Father's not afraid of them."

"Your father is not afraid of anyone, and I'm afraid that might get him into trouble one day."

"Oh Mother, that's not the way to look at things. Besides, the French pride themselves on law and civility. Surely what he has done just now is something he's not proud of."

"We're *savages* to them. They don't care how they treat us."

"That's the thing, Mother. We're not savages! We should show them that we're not. We have two eyes, a nose, lips, hands, feet, and we bleed red, just like them. We have a heart and a brain like them. We ran a rich and powerful empire at one time. Now we have become a kingdom of cowards, a docile group of people who act deaf, dumb, and mute just to survive. Will we ever rise up and fend for ourselves to live an enriched and just life?"

"They have sophisticated weapons. We don't."

I did not want to argue with my distressed mother.

"This is not good," said Mith's grandmother, who did not care about my politics and social issues. "Why is he looking for my grandson? Is he going to hurt my poor Mith?"

"Our grandson hasn't seen his daughter since he threatened us at the Mahapanchasila Pagoda," said Mith's grandfather.

Apparently, after the incident at Wat Mahapanchasila, according to what Esmé told me at the office, he and his wife did not know his grandson had gone to the governor's house to have a civilized talk with the governor himself only to be threatened by a rifle or that he had been secretly exchanging love letters with Esmé.

Mith's grandfather continued. "Mith has been crushed. He hasn't been eating or sleeping, but he has promised to stay away from Esmé until everything is resolved. Words of encouragement from detective Oum Chum Chinak reinvigorated him. That was why he went to interview with Dr. Beauvis. He sought a surgical position, hoping his title would impress the governor. He had hoped not only to provide for Esmé, but allow her to marry a doctor."

"It'll take more than being a doctor for the governor to accept Mith into his family," I said.

"Oh, my dear grandson," lamented Mith's grandmother. "He's better off marrying a nice peasant Khmer girl. We shouldn't have allowed him to reach for a high-class girl like the governor's daughter. We should know our place. We should have learned our lesson with our own daughter. The curse has struck our family once again. We try to reach too far up."

"Please don't think that." Suddenly I found myself quoting my teacher, Professor George H. Williams. "There's no such thing as a curse or anything too high to reach. If you set your mind to it, you can reach for anything. There'll be obstacles, but you shouldn't let it deter you."

Professor Williams was an American archeologist, anthropologist, and scientist. He happened to be the person responsible for stimulating my mind and showing me how far it could take me. While white people generally possessed a colonial mentality, he was progressive, ahead of his time. As my brothers had gotten to travel and study abroad, Father had worked something out with Professor

Williams to provide me with the best education he could offer. Then again, my education did not come cheap. The man had wanted something from my father, which he promised to give in return for my education. I found out from the professor, when I asked, why a man like him would be willing to impart his knowledge to me. He said Father had valuable information. However, he kept his lips tight when I asked what information he was seeking. I followed up with Father on this matter, but he said it was a secret. That was the thing about Father—his life was a maze of secrets. I made it my mission to uncover them.

"The governor's daughter could have gone shopping or stayed over at a cousin's house. This is what rich young girls do when they don't get what they want nowadays," said Monsieur Sem.

Jorani added, "Yes, Father is right. This is just all a misunderstanding. It's going to be all right. When the governor finds Esmé's not with Mith, he will leave him alone."

"No," said Mith's grandfather. "I must go to the Maharaja Hotel to make sure our grandson is okay."

"I'll come, too," said his distraught wife.

"No. You stay here. You're too weak to travel."

"But you'll be all alone, going to appeal to someone of a high class all by yourself." I was not sure what she could have done, but she must have thought that by being together they would be strong enough to face the elitists.

Peasants, as I had seen all of my young life, seldom had the courage to look into the eyes or frequent the fancy places of people of higher status, so to hear them wanting to go to such a place proved how strongly they felt about their grandson's safety and their love for him. Why shouldn't they be concerned about their grandson's safety when the governor had threatened to kill him? I hoped the governor's wife, Princess Dhana, or someone else would knock some sense into him.

"I'll come with you. I have my oxcart parked in the front," said Monsieur Sem.

"I'll telephone the police chief to meet you there. Just to be safe," I said.

"All right," said Monsieur Sem hesitantly. He was not sure if the police chief was on their side considering the authorities looked out for each other only. After I reassured him that the police chief respected Father and he would be a good person to diffuse the situation, if anything should get out of hand, I saw relief in his face. After all, as a peasant, he too felt uncomfortable and intimidated by the governor and the upper classes. I walked over to pick up our phone off the floor. I put the earpiece back on the cradle of the black candlestick phone. Then I picked it up again, asking the operator to connect me with the police station. She plugged in the number and hung up when the person at the other end answered. I asked for the police chief of Siem Reap, a good friend of Father's, to check in on Mith at the Maharaja Hotel. If a familiar face was there, the governor might not do anything drastic. I had no idea how Father dealt with power-tripping men of this town, but I felt grateful he taught me who to trust and who to guard myself against.

"I would like to come, too," insisted Mith's grandmother.

"Please stay here. We won't be long," said Monsieur Sem. "Jorani, stick around to help out here."

"Yes, Father."

I walked over to the door to watch them leave. Jorani turned to me and whispered, "I hope they don't elope. It'll be murder, I tell you." Jorani helped the elderly grandmother sit on our wooden loveseat, and then she straightened up our furniture and the Khmer pieces of art that had been knocked down by the governor and his henchmen.

I hope not, I said to myself, still eyeing my open front door. Strange and unwelcoming feelings of anger and frustration dominated me. *Where could Esmé possibly be?* It was unlike her to go anywhere without telling someone. She would have told her trusted maid or me. But then again, if she were secretly meeting the love of her life, she would keep silent. She had not even told me about the love letters she hid in her secret drawer when she thought I was not looking. If she was actually missing, I needed to retrace her footsteps. In the back of my mind I knew her family would not welcome me. I needed to talk to Princess Dhana or the servants at the Laurent Manor.

I turned to Mother to see her still shaken up as she sat next to Mith's grandmother, holding her shriveled hands.

"Are you all right, Mae?" I asked her.

"I'll be fine. It's Suon that needs help. Please go see if Dr. Lim is around." Dr. Nat Lim was a Sino-Khmer, of a Khmer mother and Chinese father, who lived on the opposite street from us.

"I'm fine, madame. I don't need to see a doctor," said Suon.

"No. You took a bad beating to protect us."

"If it's all the same to you, I would like to go there myself. I can walk." He appeared to be in more pain than he let on. He was trying to be brave, salvaging whatever manhood he had left.

"As you wish," Mother said with sympathetic eyes. Suon carefully reached for the wall to prop himself up to move across the floor to the front door. I tried to reach out to assist him, but he raised his hand to refuse. He made his way to the front door and descended the stairs. He held onto himself as if his body was about to fall to pieces. Mother walked over to stand by me in the doorway of our house on stilts, looking out to our almost empty road lined with *chankari* and other trees. I could see the limping Suon make his way across the street. His thick frame disappeared into the vegetation and trees as he got closer to the three-cornered house of Dr. Lim, which stood three houses away. At the same time, I could feel Mother's hands trembling as she held onto me.

"Oh Lord Brahma, how I wish my husband was home." She looked at me and wiped the sweat from my forehead. "You're such a brave child, brave just like your father. I hope he found what he's looking for and comes back home soon. I need him. His family needs him."

She wanted Father home not because she wanted to tell him what happened, but to feel protected. No one would dare to enter our house if Father, the man of the house, was home.

I placed my hand over Mother's hand. "Don't worry, Mother. I have a feeling he'll be home soon."

I walked her over to the chair by Mith's grandmother, who was crying in silence. I kneeled beside her.

"Please don't cry. Everything will be fine. I will make some tea for you and Mother." Somehow I felt tea would calm everyone down—at least it would soothe *my* nerves.

"I'll grab your groceries," said Jorani, still trembling. I had forgotten that Monsieur Sem had left the grocery baskets on our front porch. "I'll return to help you."

"The workers in the fields must be starving by now," I said. "I'll help you cook here now, Jorani."

"Oh. Good idea. By the time Father gets back it'll be done."

"Right. Thank you for being with us. You're a good

friend."

"Think nothing of it. You'd do the same for us." She descended our wooden stairs.

"My poor Mith," said his grandmother from her seat. "Do you know where the Hotel Maharaja is located, Anjali? Could you please take me there?" She still looked shaken up. "I can't just sit here and do nothing."

I felt for her. I wished I could do more, but Father had not trained me for something like this. "You're shaking and frightened. Please sit down and calm yourself," I said.

"That's right, aunty," said Mother. "You can't do anything anyway. Please sit here to wait with us. Let the authorities handle it.

"Yes, Mother is right. The governor won't dare do anything uncivilized in the eyes of his fellow Frenchmen. After all, they're here to 'civilize' us, and that won't sit well with his superiors. Besides, when he sees that Esmé is not with Mith, he'll leave Mith alone. Please don't worry too much about it. Be concerned with your health. I'll make you some tea and telephone Mademoiselle Kolap. Maybe she can tell me what's going on at the Laurent Manor. Please don't worry too much. Everything will be fine." I didn't believe what I had just said, but someone had to be positive.

I rushed to the kitchen with all sorts of bad feelings and confusion whirling through my mind. I broke and piled some small twigs into one of our three tripod stoves. I struck a match and lit it. I blew and fanned the flame with a palm fan in the shape of a *pothy* leaf. I added the charcoal pieces, one by one, as the twigs burned. My mind was busy thinking about what had just happened as my hands performed my task in the kitchen. I found it perplexing that the governor should bring his armed men and barge into our house looking for Mith. *Where could Esmé be, for her father to wreak havoc on all of us like he did? Was this in addition to the bad omen that chewed at me the night before? Where could she be?*

"Anjali, your fan is burning," Jorani said, pulling the fan from my hand. She scooped water with a silver decorative bowl from our *peang teuk* and poured it over the palm fan. "Are you all right?"

"I'm so careless. Thank you."

"Don't mention it. I will put the groceries away and make tea for you. Why don't you go out there," she said. "You seem to be distracted. You're thinking and analyzing something. I know that look. Go on, go out there and calm your mother and Mith's grandmother."

"Thank you."

I made my way to the receiving room to ask what had transpired that morning. Apparently, Mith's grandparents had brought over their first round of a variety of ripened fruit for my family from their farm from their first harvest of the year, as they had done every year. They did not know how to repay Father for his generosity in helping Mith gain a high-class education, so this was their way of saying thank you. Father did not want them to feel obligated to do anything of the sort for us, but he knew they wouldn't feel right if we denied them the one thing they could do.

"Mith's grandparents had not even comfortably sat down when the governor and his armed men forced their way into our house," said Mother. "Suon stood up to them, trying to protect the three of us, when one of the soldiers attacked him by punching him in the face and hitting him in the stomach and head with the butt of his rifle. He was even unconscious for a little while." That was why Mother sent him to see the doctor, to make sure he was not seriously injured.

"I'm very concerned about my grandson," said Mith's grandmother.

"We are too," said Mother, squeezing the elder woman's hand.

"When do you expect him back home?" I asked.

"He said he would be back for lunch."

"Well, it's only eight o'clock," I said, looking at the pendulum clock. "Excuse me. I would like to make a phone call."

"Who are you calling, dear?" asked Mother.

"I would like to give Madame Sari a call, just to check out the situation at the Laurents'." I walked up to the chair by the window next to a round wooden table.

"Do you think that's a good idea?" asked Mother.

"It'll be all right."

I proceeded to pick up the mouthpiece with my right hand and placed the receiver on my ear with my left hand. At the sound of the operator's voice, I asked for her to connect me to the Laurents' home. She plugged in the number. "Laurent residence," answered a somber voice.

"Madame Sari?"

"Urr. Anjali. You're...you're not allowed to call this household."

"I beg your pardon?"

"I'm sorry, but it's the order of the master," she said in a very low voice.

"Please, Madame Sari. I must know what's going on. Do you know anything about the unexpected disappearance of Princess Esmé?"

"We have just received tragic news. I must accompany the mistress. I can't talk to you now." Silence fell. My heart dropped. My entire body shook like an earthquake.

"What is it?" Mother asked.

"Something is not right. Something is not right," said Mith's grandmother as she looked at me.

"You're very pale. What is it?" Mother asked.

The teapot whistled. Then the sounds of heavy footsteps could be heard louder and louder as someone hiked up our stairs.

Mother went for the door. "Detective Chea," she said. She hadn't expected him.

Detective Duong Chea, who stood as tall as Mith Sovann, took off his flat tweed cap, which matched his two-piece light brown suit. He loved Western fashion and liked to stay current. In his early forties, he wore the same pomade hairstyle that was popular for men. His big, round and doleful eyes glanced back and forth between Mother and Mith's grandmother.

"There's trouble brewing in Siem Reap," he said, with a tone as somber as Madame Sari's.

We heard the sound of a teacup dropped against the wooden floor. It made us jump. Jorani ran in from the kitchen with her eyes wide as an owl's. "I'm sorry. I'm so sorry. I broke one of your porcelain teacups," she said, holding out her hands with the broken pieces.

We did not care. We turned back to Detective Chea.

"What is it?" asked Mother, as if bracing herself for the most tragic news in her life.

"The governor had ordered *le directeur général* to send his men to arrest Mith. He is in their custody now."

Mith's grandmother fell to the floor before Jorani could run to catch her. We all rushed to gather her up. "Aunty! Aunty, please wake up. Oh my lord. Aunty, please wake up!" implored Mother in a panic.

Jorani was at a loss as well. She did not know what to do. She paced back and forth as if she intended to get something or do something but could not remember what it was.

Mother said, "Could one of you girls grab a balm from my room, please?"

"Sure, I'll grab it," I said. "Jorani, why don't you get some water?"

I rushed to my parents' room, opened up her basket of medicine, and rushed back to her with the balm. She twisted open the metal jar and put it under the elder woman's nose so she could get a whiff of it. The strong menthol smell brought her to her senses.

"Please, take me to see my grandson," she said weakly. "I want to be there with my grandson. He needs me." She started to cry. In this day and age, she knew that her grandson, even with the amount of education he had received, would be no match for the system run by French authorities. If they were kind they would lock him up for the rest of his life—if they were cruel they would take his life. She started to hyperventilate at the prospects of his fate.

"No, you should rest, Aunty," said Mother.

"Yes, that's right," said Detective Chea. "This is just a misunderstanding. We don't actually know what took place. Please stay and rest. We'll get to the bottom of this and report back to you."

Mith's grandmother continued to cry since she knew we were all just trying to make her feel better. As uneducated as she was, she knew that the authorities had their own laws, which they could change to fit their agenda at any time. Meanwhile, we peasants were always prosecuted to the fullest extent of the law. Instead of being viewed as innocent until proven guilty, we were viewed as guilty until proven innocent, and sometimes they made it so that we could never be innocent—which was why Father created his detective agency, to find justice for all.

"If you don't mind, I would like to go with you to the police station," I said.

"Sure. You can ride with me."

Jorani brought some tea and water for Mother and Mith's grandmother, who would remain in the house until they received news from us.

"Don't worry," she said. "I'll be here to keep them company while I cook."

"Thank you. I'll send your father back. He can help bring food to the field workers. Also, I'll drop by your house to tell your mother where you and your father are so she does not worry about you," I said.

"Thanks, Anjali."

"Don't mention it."

Detective Chea and I arrived at the headquarters of *La Police Nationale*, in the heart of Siem Reap, about a fifteen-minute ride from my house. He pulled up to the sidewalk in front of the four-story white concrete building, which took up the entire block of Harshavarman Boulevard. Detective Chea led the way into the station. Meanwhile, in front of the station, Mith's grandfather and Monsieur Sem paced back and forth in front of the main entrance. Afraid of authorities, they were probably waiting for us. I rushed to them.

"Uncle," I said to Monsieur Sem, "we can take it from here. Please return to my home to pick up the food and take it to your helpers out in the field. Jorani has been cooking at my house."

"Okay. Please let me know if you need anything. I know your father is not here and—"

"Don't worry," said Detective Chea, "we are among friends at the station. We'll get to the bottom of this."

"Uncle," Monsieur Sem said to Mith's grandfather, who appeared to have been crying, "your grandson has a lot of people helping him. Don't worry too much, the truth will soon emerge."

"Thank you," said Mith's grandfather, although he did not seem convinced.

It was clear he was just skin and bones from working all his life so hard in the fields. Now, his exhaustion and fright revealed his weakness and frailty. I took his hand, and he held onto me for support. The three of us walked through the glass doors with two huge Greek columns to their left and right sides. I could imagine us looking like little ants going through the grand entrance of this massive building. Two granite lions—not the Asian species, but Western lions—stood guarding the stairs as if ready to devour unwanted people who passed by or entered.

"Detective Chea," said the young staff sergeant at the front desk.

"We understand Mith Sovann was brought here. Who was the arresting officer?" the detective asked.

"Yes, sir. He's here. Please take those seats while I fetch Lieutenant Sun Tan." He pointed to the seats in the waiting area across from his desk. During this worrisome time, we preferred to stand. We were anxious to find the cause of Mith's arrest. The staff sergeant saw our anxiety. "Very well then," he said to us.

Lieutenant Sun Tan descended the stairs located in the middle of the lobby. He was a Sino-Annamese man with light brown skin and in his early forties. He had a tense expression on his face. He invited us to his office before promising to take us to see Mith. I sat next to Mith's grandfather while Detective Chea spoke with Lieutenant Tan.

Lieutenant Tan had a slight Phnom Penh accent—a

combination of French, Chinese, and Annamese tones when it came to the pronunciation of Khmer words. Sometimes he seemed to catch himself, as if he did not want to sound like an illiterate and uneducated person, and would switch to proper Khmer. After all, he was well educated in the Khmer language, despite the fact that the French could care less because their language was first and used in the society that mattered. On occasion, he slipped into a lazy and slurred tone, as people were prone to do who had a hard time saying the "k" and rolling the "r" sounds. Certain city folks thought this was a fashionable way of speaking Khmer, so they started to mimic foreigners or immigrants.

"I'm sorry about this," he said, looking at Mith's grandfather. The elder man did not say anything.

"On what charge is Mith arrested?" inquired Detective Chea.

"Rape."

"Pardon?"

"He has been charged with rape. I was under direct orders from the top not to talk to you about this case, not even to Detective Oum Chum Chinak himself. Your father," he said, eyeing me, "has been working with the police for a long time, and Chinak & Associates has helped us solve many cases. So this is the least I can do. The truth of the matter is the governor ordered Mith's arrest and retained his own team of policemen and detectives to investigate the..." he paused and looked at the elder man. "The rape of his daughter, Esmé."

My hands rested over my heart, as if I was trying to hold onto it so that it would not leap out of my chest. The hollowness in my stomach made me feel nauseated. Suddenly everything in the room spun out of control. My friend had been raped and my other friend stood accused and arrested. Denial started to kick in. This could not be true. I could not help but wonder if I was dreaming, like I did some nights ago. I prayed I would wake up from it. Tragically, this was not a dream. Out of nowhere tears started to fill my eyes. I realized I was not as strong as I thought. I felt helpless. I pulled out a handkerchief from my dress pocket. A flood of bad and fearful thoughts entered my mind. My heart and head ached.

"This can't be," I said, finding myself thinking out loud.

"No. No. That is not possible," Mith's grandfather wailed like a man possessed. "My grandson is a loving, caring, and considerate young man. He is very much in love with that poor, poor young woman. He would not do that to her. No. He is not a monster. He is highly educated. We raised him better than that. He would never do that to her." He paused, overwhelmed by emotions. He found himself catching his breath. "Oh my lord, what has my family done wrong to deserve this? From mother to son. What did they do in their past lives? What have we done for the Lord Brahma to cast such darkness on our only daughter and now our only grandson?" He took the end of the blue *krama* that hung around his neck to wipe his tears. I held his hand, trying to comfort him.

"Has he already been charged?" asked Detective Chea.

The lieutenant nodded, with a look of reluctance.

"Based on what evidence is he charged? Do you know how all of this came about?"

"According to her mother and maids, Esmé did not come down for dinner last night. Her parents thought she was still upset with her father for rejecting her relationship with Mith. That same day, her father offered her hand in marriage to Andre Thomas."

"Andre Thomas?" asked Detective Chea.

"Yes. He's a young English man who runs an ivory export business in Bangkok."

"I see."

"Princess Dhana went up with the maid to bring her a tray of food, but found the door locked. She thought her daughter was being stubborn. She told her that her father would come to his senses. She did not hear anything from her, so she asked the maid to leave the tray of food on the table outside of her room. The maid went to see her this morning only to find the tray untouched. She went to the governor and the Princess. At this point, the governor was livid. He summoned the footman to get the spare key and found the room was empty. The bed had not been slept in. He looked in her closet and in her drawers to make sure she did not run away. In one of the drawers, he found a stack of love letters. They were written in Khmer, so he asked his wife to read them to him. The latest letter from Mith, which was written in French, asked her to meet him at the abandoned Sok San's Cottage—the cottage that Prince Dara Vong built for your family," he said, looking at the heartbroken elder man.

I turned to look at his downcast face.

"I'm sorry to bring that up, Uncle. I know you left for a reason."

Mith's grandfather could not speak. He stared down at the floor.

"Naturally, the governor ordered his men to find out where this abandoned cottage is located. In the meantime he went to your house, but no one was home. The neighbor who spoke French said that you went to Detective Chinak's house. He and his men went there in hopes of finding your grandson and his daughter. Obviously, he did not find either of them there. You told him that Mith was seeing someone at Maharaja Hotel about a job. On route to find Mith, he met one of his men driving with his daughter in it. She had been in and out of consciousness since they found her lying on a dirt road. Her clothes had been ripped apart and were soaked with blood. They determined she had been violently raped. She must have mustered every strength she had to stagger out of the forest of Beung Mealea. When she came to, she kept moaning Mith's name. The governor was shocked into a nearly debilitating fit of weakness, to have found his precious and beautiful daughter in such a tragic condition. He screamed, cursed, and cried. He rode in the car to Mehta Hospital with her. He comforted her as best a father could until she arrived at the hospital. While doctors and nurses attended to her injuries, he ordered one of the policemen who accompanied him to the hospital to summon the police chief and his lawyer to meet him immediately. He's dead set on making the man responsible for his daughter's suffering pay for it. The chief ordered my boss to arrest and charge your grandson. So this is where we are...awaiting *their* further orders."

"That makes no sense. Only a mentally ill person would do something like that. Besides, Mith has been at home. Isn't that right?" I said to Mith's grandfather. I found myself siding with Mith—something that Father would not do. He would consider everyone a suspect until he sifted through the evidence to exclude him. But then again, he knew Mith. Would he even consider him a suspect?

"That's right! He has been home with my wife and me," he said. "He could not possibly have committed such a heinous crime."

"No. No. That's not possible." I said, refusing to believe that a respectable, educated, and courteous man like him would commit such vicious act against a woman whom he loved dearly and who loved him.

"I'm sorry. My boss received an order from higher up. He ordered me to arrest Mith. My boss could not defy their order, and I could not defy his order. The governor has put his own men on the investigation. I've said too much already. I'll take you to see your grandson now."

Mith's grandfather's cried profusely. He was inconsolable. We could not do anything but be there for him. It was sad to see a grown man cry, but to see an elderly man weep was all the worse. After he composed himself, Lieutenant Tan took us to the top floor to the cellblock. We found Mith sitting in his jail cell, his head buried in his hands.

His grandfather walked up to the cell and held onto the bars. "What have you done, grandson?" asked the elder man, still in tears.

"Grandfather," said Mith, in extreme sadness. He got up to touch his grandfather's peasant hands. "They've accused me of raping the love of my life and leaving her for dead. I did not commit such monstrous acts. Please, you must believe me, Grandfather. I'm not capable of these acts. The last time I saw her was when I went to her house to speak to her parents. But the governor chased me out of his property with a rifle, and her mother said she would talk with her husband."

"After we begged you not to go?"

"I'm sorry. I needed to let her parents know we loved each other, that I was in love with her. I wanted them to know that I would be a good husband for her, that I was more than capable of providing for her."

"You should not have gone there."

"I'm sorry. I love her so much."

"You've given them a...a reason to..."

I knew what his grandfather was thinking. Granted he, his wife, and the villagers could vouch for Mith's whereabouts, but their words would prove meaningless against those of a French authority.

"I'm innocent. I've been with you and grandmother all night."

"They have found your letters. Why did you meet with her in secrecy? Your grandmother and I, told you the story of your parents. Have you learned nothing from their past?"

"No. None of my letters had asked her to meet me in secrecy. That is not true," said Mith.

"But they said they found your last letter asking her to meet you at our abandoned cottage in Beung Mealea. Did you take her there?"

"I did, but it was sometime during the beginning of the New Year back in April. Grandfather, you must believe me. I did not go anywhere with her in secrecy after her father found out about us. We were only guilty of exchanging love letters. I had not done anything inappropriate but touch her soft and gentle hand. I promise you, I did not rape her. You must believe me."

"Why did you take her to our old house?"

"It was before the governor found out about us, which was a few days after you and Detective Chinak told me about my parents. I told Esmé all about it. I wanted to share with her the history of my family. Like me, she was intrigued. She begged me to show her the place. Since we were not doing anything contrary to the law of an unmarried man and an unmarried woman, we did not think it was wrong to see the place together—our own sense of adventure. It was the place that was closest to the memory of my mother and father's happier times. Granted I'm a man of science, but passersby swore they saw her spirit wandering in that village. I wanted to feel her presence. I wanted Esmé to know her. Who she was and where she lived. We did not think it would hurt anyone if no one knew. We only met there, talked, and held hands."

"Did anyone else know about this? Did other people see you going there together? Detective Chea asked.

"Not that I know," he said.

"Do you have any enemies? Does Esmé? Do you know who would want to hurt her? And hurt you in the process?"

"I...I don't know. I barely know anyone in town. Esmé is a sweet and lovely girl. I can't imagine anyone would hate her that much as to commit such beastly harm against her," said Mith.

"It's formality. We just needed to cover all bases," said Detective Chea.

"Unless..." I found myself thinking out loud. Everyone turned to look at me.

"What is it?" asked Detective Chea.

"Oh, it's nothing. I am sorry. I did not mean to interrupt," I said.

While they continued to drill him with many questions, I thought about Princess Nakry Ang, the proper and legal wife of his father. She hated him because he was the constant reminder of the love her husband had for his mother. Would she have something to do with this? I would not put anything past her. She might be up to her old evil trick again. She hated his mother and hired a ruffian to kill her. I saw how venomous she acted toward me when I visited the Laurent Manor on Friday. Could she hate seeing the constant reminder of her husband's and his lover's offspring just as much, the constant reminder that her husband had no love for her? What if Mith Sovann was a threat to her son's should family members find out Mith was also a member of the royal family? Would this be a case of hatred, greed, and jealousy? Therefore, could she have hired someone to commit a violent act against her own niece to have him accused of the crime and be hung? Then again, Esmé was her blood, her first cousin's daughter. Why would she do something like that? Regardless, due to her crime against another woman, she was my number one suspect. I would have to check her whereabouts. I could start with her maids, verify where they have been.

Then I thought about her son, Prince Phirun, the womanizer and power abuser. Royal families were known to marry and fall in love with their own first cousins, which families encouraged to keep the crown or wealth within the family's lineage. Maybe his mother wanted him to settle down, stop chasing and lusting after loose women. Maybe she wanted to keep her wealth within the family. The day I saw them at the Laurent's house—that Friday morning—could the mother and son have been there to talk about bringing their lineage closer? What if Esmè refused? No woman ever said no to him. Would he have gone that far to indulge in his lust?

"No! No! No! Never in a million years would I hurt her. You must believe me, Grandfather. I did not commit rape and abandon her. I'm not capable of such a thing. The real rapist is out there. If they are focusing on me, they'll never catch him. What other proof does the governor have against me besides those love letters and her calling out my name?" he asked our detective and the lieutenant. "She called my name because she needed my protection. And I was not there for her." His face dropped, crestfallen. Tears formed in his eyes.

"Her calling your name is subject to many interpretations. The thing is, the governor is set out to destroy you," said Detective Chea. "He's not interested in finding anyone else. He believes wholeheartedly it is you who committed these atrocious acts against his daughter. It's our duty to find the truth."

Mith turned away from the bars and sat down on the bench with his head buried in his hands, weeping, not so much for himself, but for the brutal violation of his love and for not being there to protect her.

Curiously, with all of her maids and bodyguards, no one knew where she had disappeared to—unless she knew the person who committed the crime. Someone must have known where she went and was afraid of getting in trouble for allowing her to go there. Many scenarios and theories floated in my head like lanterns floating into the spacious sky. The evil Princess Nakry Ang and her son, Prince Phirun Vong, had become my two suspects. I would definitely look into their activities. The people they met and the places they went to. However, what if there was a third theory? Fear ran through me. It made my hair stand on end. I thought long and hard about it. Could this rape be coincidental, or had the serial rapist himself been there? But how did the killer lure her to such a place? How did he know about this special place she and Mith shared? I remembered the letter stuffed in her dress pocket yesterday morning when I visited her. I remembered how the victims of the serial rapist and murderer were beautifully stunning Eurasian women. He lured them to a secluded a place—a place of significance to them. Such information couldn't be coincidental. Yet, t serial rapist killed his victims. The fact that Esmè is alive might point to someone else. It could be someone she knows. It could be her relative. It could be the womanizing Prince Phirun Vong.

"So when was the last time you saw her?" asked Detective Chea.

"Like I said before, I saw her for the last time when I went to her house to try to reason with her father—when he pulled a rifle on me five days ago. Since we couldn't see each other, we began to pass notes to each other."

"And when was the last time you sent her a note?"

"On Thursday."

"Thursday? Then the last letter could not have been yours," I found myself saying out loud.

"What are you getting at?" asked Detective Chea while the others turned to look at me.

"I saw her stuff a newly received letter in her pocket yesterday morning. Based on the imprints I saw from the back, the letter had been typed, using the Roman alphabet."

"That was not my letter," Mith said, sounding excited about this piece of information that indicated another person had lured her to the place of significance to them. "All of my letters were handwritten and in Khmer."

"So her rapist could be an English- or French-speaking Asian, which the governor could still use to accuse you, or it could be an English- or French-speaking white person," I said.

"Good deduction, Anjali," said Detective Chea. "Now we have something to go on. We need access to all of the letters."

"Thank you," I said, feeling proud at this acknowledgment from Father's most senior associate.

"I did not write that last letter! I had always written to her in Khmer. She often raved about how beautiful my penmanship was," Mith said, falling into the sad and brooding look. "After all of that, why would I start to write her in English or French and type it? It makes no sense."

"Right. However, it's your word against your accusers. I am sure they will come up with their own answer to that," said Detective Chea.

It dawned on me again. Could the serial rapist and killer who had wreaked havoc across Southeast Asia have made his way to our kingdom now? I needed to find out what happened. I could not rely on my theories without sleuthing around. The first place to look was our office. I needed to get my hands on those cold case files from other Southeast Asian countries. However, I still had to look into the evil mother and son. Either one of them could have done it or they could have worked together. In any case, they both had motives. It would be a challenge, considering they were heavily guarded. And if they sensed I was snooping around, I would not hear the end of it and I could get into trouble for it. I must do it for the sake of justice. Maybe I could start out by making friendly conversation with their guards. After all, they could hear and see things. No one paid any attention to them and tended to say things in front of them without giving it a second thought.

"Is there anything you can do to save my grandson?" Mith's grandfather, still teary himself, asked Detective Chea.

"We'll do our best. Right now, I would like to discuss with the lieutenant how much time we have to conduct our own investigation. I will consult with lawyer Bora Nuon to see if he can defend your son and if we can obtain copies of their evidence. Do not worry, uncle. I know what to do. First and foremost, we need to get Mith the best defense attorney. I will either wire or leave a phone message for Detective Chinak to inform him of what is going on and keep him abreast of the situation."

Though Detective Chea was doing a good job, I wished Father had returned already. Mother was not the only person who needed him. Our world had turned upside down without him.

I walked up closer to the cell. "Don't worry, Mith," I said, holding the bars and looking at him with compassion. "We will do everything within our power to get you out of here. I believe you. I believe in your innocence. The governor is a powerful man, but he will not break the laws he has sworn to uphold in this civilized society. I understand Esmé is under the care of a doctor. She knows who did this to her and will clear you of any wrongdoing."

He looked up at me with teary eyes, then down at the floor as if his soul and spirit had left him. He must have felt the lowest he ever had in his life.

Mith's grandfather told him, "Stay strong, grandson. We will be seeing you again when they allow us in for the next visit."

"Yes. We will be seeing you again," said Detective Chea. "We will want to interview you and follow up with more questions as soon as we get the reports from the other side." To guard against my guilty conscious of being biased and wholeheartedly believing in Mith's innocence without proof, and considering I had not known him that long, I was happy to know that Detective Chea was undertaking the task of interviewing him and perhaps clearing him as a suspect. However, my guts said he was innocent. Father said I should not rely on my guts, but it felt so strong that I could not help feeling that way. We said our goodbye to Mith and asked him to remain strong.

I do not believe Mith heard anything he said, for he was thinking about Esmé's wellbeing.

9

A PRINCESS IN DISTRESS

The evil Princess Nakry and her son Prince Phirun dominated my mind as we exited the police station.

"Anjali, where do you think you are going? My car is this way. I'll drop you and uncle off," said Detective Chea.

"Actually, umm, I would like to head to...umm...I need to give someone a visit."

"You better not go to the hospital, Anjali."

"W...why not?"

"Now is not a good time."

"Uh...umm...sure. I understand." I did not sound convincing. "Honestly, I need to check on a lead in my missing heirloom case."

"Today?"

"Yes, while I am hot on a trail. Please let my mother know I will be fine and shall be home soon."

"Okay. Don't venture far."

"I won't," I said, feeling unsure if he bought my lie. As

soon as he left my sight, I called a *cyclo,* a three-wheel bicycle taxi.

"Where to, young lady?" asked the driver.

"Please drop me off at Mehta Hospital," I said. He nodded.

Mehta Hospital was busier than before. I saw random policemen—French and Khmer—huddled around talking and pointing in various directions. I entered the main entrance and asked the front desk person if I could see Mademoiselle Esmè Laurent.

"I'm sorry, Mademoiselle Anjali. Anyone related to Chinak & Associates and has a connection with Mith Sovann is not allowed anywhere near her room."

"But she's my friend. I would like to look in on her."

"No. I am sorry. We're under strict orders."

"Please?"

"Mademoiselle Anjali, I'm the lowest on the totem pole. They can fire me at the drop of a hat. I really need this job. Please don't make it hard on me," she pleaded with me.

"I understand." I walked away and lingered around the lobby, thinking about how I could obtain Esmè's room number. I moved about in the lobby. I walked around and stood at a corner, out of sight of the woman at the front desk. I glanced at my reflection in a large window and noticed I had wrapped one hand around my stomach and was tapping my chin with the other. I had the tendency to do this whenever I was in my thinking mode. Not long thereafter, I overheard a woman asking, "Hi, mademoiselle. My name is Lena. I'm one of the Laurents' maids." My ears perked up at her voice. I peered around the corner to the receptionist area. "I'm here to bring food to Princess Dhana," she said, lifting up the stacked silver containers.

The Governor's Daughter

The maid was young like me. I had never seen her before. I doubted she had ever seen me before either.

"Sure. You can go through this hallway to that double-glass door. It leads outside where you will see connected buildings. Building number three is on the right-hand side. You can enter through there to the receptionist area where someone will give you the room number."

"Thank you."

"Sure."

I rushed ahead of her to building number three. While waiting for the young maid to catch up, I stopped in a shop to buy a bouquet of flowers and a stuffed teddy bear at the lobby area. It was not Khmer custom to buy flowers for patients, but European culture dominated us now. I took my time and walked out at the moment when the young woman walked up to a man at the front desk. "Oh yes, Mademoiselle Laurent is in room 127, which is on your left-hand side." She went ahead of me. I blended in with all the other people going about their business—doctors, staff, patients, and other visitors. Once I was close to room 127, I stood still. A few policemen guarded the outside. One of them knocked on the door for the young maid to enter. Madam Sari, the head servant of Princess Dhana, opened the door. She let the young maid in and before she closed the door she saw me. She gave me a worried look.

"What is it, Sari?" I heard a venomous voice call from inside. I moved my legs to walk up to the room. Sari shook her head as if to tell me that it was not a good time for me to be there. Then the door swung wide open like a storm had blown it open. "It's you! How dare you show your face here," said Princess Nakry with her hands on her hip. "Because of you damn peasants my niece is in surgery for hours now.

We don't know whether or not she's going to make it. If she doesn't, there's going to be hell to pay."

I stood still, unable to utter a word.

"Who's out there?" Prince Dhana asked one of her maids. Madam Sari disappeared back in the room and then returned with Princess Dhana holding onto her. Only within one day she turned into an old lady who could not walk on her own. Her distress showed in her face and body. She looked at me with angry and disappointed eyes. She stopped at the doorway.

Princess Nakry darted toward me like a jaguar. She grabbed the bouquet of flowers from me and shook it in my face while yelling, "What are you bringing these flowers for? My niece is not dead! What are you bringing these flowers for?" The woman did not make any sense as she raged on against me. "You go tell that spawn of that dead peasant woman of Beung Mealea that his day will come soon. That monster will be hung for what he did to my beautiful and precious niece! Go! Get out of my face!" She thrashed the flowers against my face. Other people at the hospital stood to watch.

The pain of the bouquet hitting my face and the way the evil princess humiliated me could not be compared to what Princess Dhana was going through. I threw my sad and apologetic eyes at the princess who used to show me consideration and kindness. Instead, she gave me an unsympathetic look.

"You're not welcome here. Not here. Not at my home," said Prince Dhana in a cold and shrill voice.

In the corner of my eyes, I could see Princess Nakry giving me some seriously vicious side-eye. I walked away feeling frustrated and disappointed at the situation. I saw a little girl crying in her mother's arms. I handed the teddy bear to her.

"Oh, you're very nice. Thank you, young lady," said the mother.

I never felt so down in my entire life. Many thoughts entered my mind. *Did the evil Princess Nakry have anything to do with Esmè's rape? If she did, she really put up a good show just now.* She was dead set on destroying Mith. Her reference to a "dead peasant woman of Beung Mealea" suggested she still harbored hatred and jealousy against his mother, Kolthida Sovann.

I did not know where to start. My mind was clogged with negative thoughts. My head started to ache. I needed fresh air and someone who would make me feel better after the insult and assault I had just received.

I called for a *cyclo* and headed to my paternal grandmother's house. She loved me and pretty much let me do whatever I wanted. She often made me feel better whenever I felt upset or down.

"Anjali, what are you doing here?" asked my thirty-year-old aunt Sopheary. She and her husband lived with my paternal grandmother and took care of her ever since my grandfather passed away.

"Is grandmother home?" I asked.

"No. She's praying at the temple."

"You look pretty. Where are you going, auntie?"

"I have been invited by Princess Soma Devi to help her plan for Bon Pkha."

"The Money Flower Festival?" I repeated.

"Yes. She would like to raise money for Bo Pagoda."

I could feel my face light up like the sun. This was perfect. I had a chance to be in the palace of the Kambujasatra without having to come up with a pretense for being there. The evil Princess Nakry and her son resided within the compound of the Kambujasatra's palace. My chance to snoop had just increased.

"Do you mind if I come with you?" I asked.

"Don't you want to see grandma?"

"No. I hardly ever spend time with you. Do you mind?"

"My, my. What did I do to deserve having my young niece—who seldom has time for me—accompany me to help with what she used to describe as boring," she said. One of my aunt's not so endearing characteristics was her sarcasm. I wondered who she took after. "I don't know what you're working on but you better not get us into trouble. These are royal and elitist women. I like being in their circles. They're influential. Don't you do anything to jeopardize my relationship with them, you hear me, my dear niece?" She placed her hand around my jaw and gave it a playful squeeze. "I need them to open up their pocketbooks for when I need to host parties and fundraising events."

"I promise," I said. "I will behave." I said what she wanted to hear. "So may I tag along?"

She looked at me and thought about it for a moment. "All right. Come on. I would like to get there earlier than other women. I want them to think I have a good habit. Let them know that I am a good and respectable woman. Having other people wait around for me is rude and disrespectful."

"But you do have a good habit," I said.

"I said you can go. You don't need to kiss up to me."

"I wasn't trying to," I said with a smile.

My aunt was one of those rare women who embraced modernity. She did not think like other women. She liked to be independent. She liked fixing and driving cars. Other women admired and envied her tenacity. We got along beautifully since we both embraced free will and had independent spirits. Actually, Father's side of the family possessed independent thoughts and minds, thus courage, which was why Mother often clashed with Father's siblings, especially aunt Sopheary. Mother came from a traditionalist and conservative family that did not want to move with the times. They were afraid of change. They felt comfortable in their traditional ways.

Aunt Sopheary was driving her brand new blue Citroën when she suddenly realized something. "Oh, by the way, does your mother know you're here? If not, we need to stop by your house to tell her you're coming with me. After all, it's the weekend. We don't want her to worry."

"She already knows I am out visiting someone for my heirloom case. We don't need to stop by. Detective Chea already told her."

"Is that a fact?" She raised one of her thin and arched eyebrows.

"Yes." I knew if I were to go home, Mother would make me stay and not go anywhere else.

"All right. What other witnesses have you got to speak with? Didn't Madame Chantha tell you everything?"

"How did you know it's about Madame Chantha?"

"Silly girl. I was the one who recommended you to her. She doesn't believe in investigation. She says she already knows the culprit. However, I insisted she get a smart little sleuth if she wanted her husband to take her seriously—that is, if it is true that his niece stole it from her."

"Oh. Thank you for sending her my way," I said.

"So, have you got a suspect?"

"I'm sorry, I can't discuss my case with you," I said.

"She said her husband's niece sold it by now and you will never find it," she said. Occasionally, my aunt turned sideways to look at me.

"That's not true," I insisted.

"Oh?" She raised her right eyebrow.

"I can't discuss it," I said with my hands on my lap and my head straight. I could see fast moving trees and random houses from both sides of my peripheral vision.

My aunt was right. We were among four of the earliest ones there. Princess Soma did not want to start without the rest of the women, so when I asked her if I could view her garden she insisted upon it. "Thank you, princess." I prostrated before her before I left the royal hall. I took the long way to the garden and passed by the royal residence of the evil Princess Nakry. Two guards stood sentinel in front of the Khmer mythical lions flanked on each of the white concrete stairs.

"Hello," I said, not sure if they would respond to me, as they were under strict rules to not talk or move about.

"Hello," the one on the right responded. The one on the left gave him a disapproving look.

"You two must be new. I've never seen you around here before," I said. Actually, I had never been to this side of the palace. I was just making conversation.

"Yes..." said the one on the right before he was cut off by the one on the left.

"Mademoiselle, we are not allowed to converse with guests here. Unless you are looking for the princess, we are not allowed to carry a conversation with you."

"So is she at her royal residence?" I asked, as if I did not already know.

"Do you have permission to seek her audience?" the serious looking guard on the left asked me.

"I'm sorry?" I asked.

"Is she expecting you?" asked the guard on the left.

"I'd thought I would stop by to say hi since I'm in the neighborhood."

"I'm sorry, but if you don't have a royal audience with her highness, I cannot let you through," he said. "I thought you understood the palace's protocol since you made it this far."

I did not like his saucy remark, but I needed to put on my thick skin if I was going to crack this case.

"So she's here, at her royal abode?"

"No, mademoiselle. She has been out since Friday," the excitable guard on the right chimed in. The other guard gave him a dirty look.

"What about Prince Phirun? Has he been out too?"

"Yes..."

"Mademoiselle, we are not at liberty to inform you of her highness's and his highness's whereabouts unless you're the resident of this palace," said the serious looking guard who cut off the other guard. "It's none of our business. Please don't ask us any more about them. Good day, mademoiselle."

Disappointed, I turned to look at the guard on the right. His eyes widened as if he had something to tell me but turned to look at the other guard with caution. He eyed me before looking down and trying very hard to contain himself. Luckily for me, he could be a witness—a cooperative one at that. I knew I had to find him later when he had his break. I would definitely like to check on the evil mother and son's timeline and the people they met.

The voices of chatty and excitable women broke my train of thought. I turned around and saw many familiar faces of royal and aristocratic women. They all seemed genuinely upset. I followed them back to the royal hall. I walked quickly to catch up with the women who were already huddling and talking. "Oh my God! The poor lovely Esmè Laurent," said Princess Soma Devi as she gasped and reached for her chair. Some of the women blamed it on her relationship with Mith Sovann, not that they believed he committed such heinous act, but that he was cursed because of what happened to his mother. They believed he brought Esmè bad luck.

"I don't believe in that curse nonsense. All right, we have to put our Bon Pkhar on hold now," said Princess Soma.

"Yes," chimed in another.

"Who agrees that we should postpone arranging and preparing for Money Flower Festival?"

"I do," everyone said. The women then threw in their theories as to what happened to the governor's daughter.

"Who would do such a thing like that to her? She's such a gentle soul. She wouldn't hurt even a fly," said one woman.

While Princess Soma Devi sat on a chair, the rest of us sat on the floor facing her. "Do you think the case would go to Chinak & Associates?"

They all turned to look at my aunt and me.

"I don't know," my aunt said. "I haven't heard anything. Besides, my brother is out of town and I have no business knowing his business."

The women then turned to look at me. I could see eyes coming from the front and I could feel eyes coming at me from the back.

"I don't know. Father doesn't allow me to work on violent cases."

"That's too bad," said Princess Soma, "because you are very good at what you do. How can this case be any different from all the disappearances and thief cases you have worked on?"

"Her father feels she's not ready, and my dearest sister-in-law would not allow her to do anything dangerous, princess. She actually tries her hardest to get her to stay home to help out with domestic work. If she could have her way my niece would not be working with my brother," said my aunt. "However, he convinced her that their daughter would not be in harm's way. My brother reviews the cases before he assigns them to her. He knows in advance what case is dangerous and what case isn't."

"It's not fun being a girl, is it?" the eldest woman of the group who was sitting behind me said as she tapped me on my leg.

"No," I said. I was not sure if she was being serious or if she was mocking me for wanting to follow Father's footsteps.

"Well, if you ask me, all the boys and men of Siem Reap are suspects," said the wife of the Minister of Agriculture. "Whoever is handling the case has their work cut out for them."

"Didn't Prince Phirun show an interest in his fair cousin, Esmè, Princess Soma?" a woman of royal blood of a different lineage with lesser prestige chimed in. We all looked at her for daring to ask such a question.

"My nephew likes to have the best of everything: power, women, money, palaces, and cars. Yes. Esmè is the fairest young woman of Siem Reap. He is very much infatuated with her to the point of being obsessive. Whenever he is not frolicking and spending time with loose daughters of other elitist and aristocratic women, he pushes his mother to take him to the Laurent Manor two to three days a week. I overheard him pushing his mother to offer a proposal to his cousin. Personally, I find cousins marrying cousins disgusting, but elders like to keep their wealth within the family, their royal blood pure, and they don't see anything wrong with this union. They actually encourage it." She paused, then she took a long sigh. "I must admit the truth. My sister-in-law, Nakry, is an evil woman. We don't see eye to eye. I never got along with her. I am sure you all know her contempt for me, as I sided with my brother and wanted him to marry the woman he loved, Ms. Kolthida Sovann. May she rest in peace! Princess Nakry had committed the unthinkable when my brother was alive. Who knows if she put her son up to this, to destroy Esmè's womanly virtue so as to tarnish her from other men? What man would want her now that she has been damaged?" She looked at all of us and said, "Now, ladies, you must remember, what I share with you must be kept in the strictest confidence. Otherwise, our relationship and this womanhood society would not work."

"Womanhood Society?" I whispered to my aunt. "What have you brought me into?"

She blinked at me, telling me to not ask about it...at least, not now.

"And I shall practice what I preach as well. Are we in agreement with each other, ladies?" continued Princess Soma Devi.

"Yes, your royal highness," said the other ladies unanimously. I only trailed behind after my aunt had gently elbowed me. I had no idea what this womanhood society was, but I knew one thing: having as many eyes and ears as possible on my side was never a bad thing. Father was right. To be a good detective, one must listen to witnesses. Who else would be good witnesses than these ladies who come into contact with the evil princess and her son almost daily, especially Princess Soma? It would be in my interest to listen to what they had to say and follow whatever lead I could gain from our conversation.

"I would not be surprised if the son committed the crime and the mother is helping cover it up. Or they could be colluding. Whatever the case, I don't have any proof, but the mother and son are so secretive about their whereabouts and the people they communicate with. Their maids remain tightlipped about everything ever since the murder of Ms. Kholthida Sovann," said Princess Soma. "My sister-in-law is careful not to say anything in front of me or her servants. However, her guards probably know more about what's going on in her residence than anyone else. I mean, why else would she change them like she changes her clothes?" It was interesting to hear Princess Soma bringing up the guards. Maybe I should start with her new guard and work my way up to her old guards. *There goes a possible lead.* My aunt gave me a puzzled look. She must have saw giddiness in my face. I gave her a smile and she shook her head in amusement.

Aunt Sopheary dropped me off at home before the sun began to set. I did not discover anything concrete with the ladies of the court but pure speculation and suspicion. However, Princess Soma did give me the name of the door guard who seemed anxious to tell me things he did not get a chance to tell me due to the other guard. She even gave me his work schedule and home location. I would have to see if he had a lead for me.

10

A WOMAN OF UNTOLD MYSTERY

I met up with the door guardsman of the evil Princess Nakry early Sunday morning before he headed to the royal palace of the Kambujasatra's. He was a chatty fellow. He gave me a lot to go on and I hoped the information he gave me panned out. He said Princess Nakry owned a cottage in a secluded place, surrounded by deep forest, a manmade lake, and a hillside of Svay Thom Village. "Big and tall trees shroud the cottage. It's very secluded and private. She goes there every Saturday and Sunday," he said. I asked how he knew about the place. He said he heard about it from one of her two closest maids. Apparently, she and the guard had a thing for each other.

I felt nervous venturing to this place alone. With this murderous princess freely moving about my beautiful city of Siem Reap, I invited Jorani to ride on our bikes with me to the village of Svay Thom, about twenty kilometers away. We rode side by side through random villages and cut through the forest where the gentle sound of nature lolled us in the background. Jorani enjoyed the freedom of having her own transportation to take her to distant and faraway places. She let the breeze caress her face.

As if realizing something, she turned to me and asked me nervously, "Anjali, do you trust this guardsman? What if he told Princess Nakry that you had been snooping around her residence? What if she told him to give you false information to entrap you? What if she hires someone to wait for us and kill us?"

"Are you afraid?"

"Well, yes, I am. I don't want to die. I have a lot going for me. I plan on living a long life, dying of old age like my grandparents, their parents, and their ancestors. In case you have forgotten, that woman was responsible for hiring someone to murder Mith Sovann's mother. She took another person's life. It seems to come naturally to her. How would you feel about taking another person's life?"

"I don't ever intend on committing such an act. It would be against my natural instinct."

"Exactly. You and I are taught to respect life. We embrace life. She doesn't. She's royalty. She thinks she has the power to do whatever she wants, even take another person's life without worrying about suffering the consequences. And look what happens to her."

"What are you talking about? Nothing happens to her," I said.

"Exactly. Nothing happens to her. Her family, her society lets her get away with it, so nothing happens to her."

"Someone is socially conscious," I said.

"You are not taking this ride across town to be killed, are you?"

"Don't worry about it. No one suspects anything. I'm naturally stealthy," I said.

"That you are not. You're a sleuth. You're the daughter of

a well-known detective in town. People see you and they assume you're up to something."

"I don't think people outside of our town know who I am," I said.

"Let's hope so. So, what do you expect to find in Svay Thom Village? I don't think there's anything special about her having an extra home. Wealthy people, especially a royal like her, tend to have extra homes. It's not out of the ordinary for her to leave the city for calmness and relaxation out here," said Jorani to the sound of doves cooing and other birds chirping.

"Supposedly her son doesn't know about this place. No one knows about it. It must be more than a place of tranquility and relaxation if none of her family members know about it."

"Hmm. Do you think she's there right now, cooking up some evil plan to hurt someone? Mith?"

"I'm not sure. With the tragedy surrounding her niece, Esmè, she might still be with Princess Dhana at the hospital," I said.

"Speaking of which, if her son, Prince Phirun, did indeed commit...you know...that thing against Esmè...when she wakes up from surgery, wouldn't the truth come out? And how would the mother and son act?"

"When I was there, I did not see Prince Phirun."

Jorani turned to me with eyes wide as a cow. "You went to the hospital?"

"Yes, but they kicked me out before I got close."

"That's too bad." She turned to watch the dirt road ahead that had tall and big trees lining both sides.

"It is. I do want to witness Esmè's reaction to the presence of either Princess Nakry or her son. Better yet, I want to ask her personally who did that to her. I hope her parents think to ask her that without wholeheartedly believing they already know the answer."

"Say, do you know where we're going? It seems we have been riding for over an hour now."

"Sure. We don't have further to go. There should be pathway made by Princess Nakry's car up ahead on the left, but we won't be using that road. We'll have to go down a pathway into the forest." Just before the road, I swirled my bicycle into the forest. I was told it would be two to three kilometers deep into the forest. Just as the guardsman described to me, we found a stone cottage overlooking a big lake with the hill behind it. A golden boat was docked on the lake. From where Jorani and I stood, peering from an ancient tree that could be encircled by five people, the cottage was surrounded by giant trees of all types. We stood there for a while to take in the view.

"Wow. Rich people have all the luck and luxury. This woman hired a ruffian to kill another woman over love and she goes about life like nothing happened and remains in luxurious bliss. Is it fair? Those who had never done wrong to others live in poverty and misery while she lives in a palace, is waited on hand and foot, rides in a nice car, and has this abode to come to for rest and relaxation—rest and relaxation from what, I don't know. How lucky is she to be born into royalty, power, and wealth. Why can't I be born into richness like that?"

I turned to look at her. "Seriously? You would rather be born into it and not earn it all on your own merit? Besides, she may have all of that, but based on my encounter with her, she seemed wretched and miserable. All the wealth in the world can't buy her happiness and class. Do you really think she's lucky?" I asked Joranai with one of my eyebrows raised.

Jorani hesitated. She seemed to put a lot of value on a person with wealth and power. Come to think of it, so did the majority of the peasant population. Why else would they spend their hard earned money on lavishing the pagoda with food and monk robes for good merit? I could not blame her. The majority of the population sweated and exhausted themselves out in the fields to cultivate rice to pay burdensome taxes to the French who lived in opulent houses who in turn treated the natives like third class citizens. And our so-called leaders, consisting mostly of royalty, were no different. Many Khmer children grew up seeing this and wondering what they did to deserve their fate. They did not have many positive examples of people who worked hard and did well.

"Oh look! The door is open," she said excitably. I turned to see a tall and good-looking young man, probably a few years older than Mith. He was well built and muscular.

"I know who he is. He is one of her personal bodyguards," I said, hearing the sound of surprise in my own voice.

"She has a very good looking bodyguard," said Jorani, staring at the muscular man sipping from his cup. "He's so proper, elegant, and distinguished. Do you suppose she had him trained at some etiquette school?"

"I suppose so," I answered. We were both studying him and his movement. My eyes widened like an owl upon seeing a woman in an elegant French nightgown come from behind and wrap her slender arms around him. He placed his cup on the front porch's railing and turned to her as if to sweep her off her feet. He smiled at her, caressed her face, and then gently kissed her all over.

"Whoa. What kind of bodyguard is that?" asked Jorani.

"Oh my Lord Brahma! She has a lover."

"He's young enough to be her son! Besides, he is too good looking for her. What does he see in her?"

"Oh, I can think of a few things," I said. We both turned to look at each other and snickered like little girls. As we giggled and turned back to look at them, Princess Nakry's eyes squinted and she hovered her palm over her eyes and looked toward our direction. I glanced over at Jorani. She was wearing her golden bangles that her fiancé had given her. The sunray that pierced through the crevice of the thick forest hit the smooth surface of her bangles and bounced off of them. Princess Nakry must have seen them!

"Who's there?" Princess Nakry yelled out. We both ducked and hid behind the tree. I stealthily leered from behind the tree and saw her lover looking in our direction and gesturing for her to remain where she was while he moved forwarded to see what was lurking behind the trees.

"Hey! Who's out there?" he called.

"We need to get out of here," I said only to discover Jorani had already run off and beaten me to her bike.

"I'm way ahead of you," she said, stumbling and falling along the way. Her knees appeared wobbly and weak. The authoritative voice of the princess's bodyguard must have scared her like he scared me. She hopped on her bike and missed the pedals a few times. We heard a man's voice yelling from a distance behind us. I hopped on my bike. Jorani and I pedaled as fast as our shaky legs allowed us. My heart raced. Jorani made her way back to the pathway where we came from and turned left from where we entered, trying to make her way back to the main road.

Before I could finish yelling, "Jorani, don't go out to the main road!" she was already there.

I followed her and eventually caught up with her. "Jorani, we should not be on the main road," I shouted.

"Why not? It's faster out here. There's no obstruction of trees, rocks, or twigs," she said, as she worked her feet like a roadrunner bird. A roaring sound of a vehicle came from behind us.

"That is why," I pointed out to her.

Jorani's face turned pale and her legs suddenly lagged like a deer caught in a trap. I swung around her and accelerated in front of her in the hopes of finding the pathway on the other side of the forest I saw earlier when we made our way to the area. As the sound of the zooming car came closer, I found the foot entrance to the forest on the opposite side and pedaled to it. I heard Jorani following me from behind. We disappeared into the forest and kept on following the footpath made by farmers and hikers. At the same time, we could hear the car zooming on the main road. Jorani and I exchanged a frightened look. We could not see out, and he definitely could not see in. I counted on the thick forest to shield him from seeing us.

"What if he stops and enters the forest to chase after us on foot?" asked Jorani in a whisper.

"If that is the case, he would have to decide which side of the forest to enter. Besides, I doubt he would abandon the princess's precious car to chase after us on foot," I said. "Either way, we have an advantage."

"What if he's not alone?" asked Jorani.

"Then we're in trouble," I said. We pedaled until the sound of the car disappeared from our ears.

"What if he guesses which part of the forest we are in and he is going to wait for us at the next exit?" asked Jorani. I did not say anything. We kept on pedaling, hoping the bodyguard did not follow us or know our whereabouts. Just as we continued on the path, a shadowy figure lurked before us with something on his or her right shoulder.

Jorani and I instantaneously stopped short. She started to scream. Then I started to scream. And the man before us started to scream.

Realizing it was a just a man collecting vines and carrying them around his shoulder, I apologized. "We are sorry, uncle. We didn't mean to scare you."

"You girls almost gave me a heart attack. You must be from the city," he said.

"Oh. Do you see city people here often?"

"Yes. Royalty and rich people pushed the peasants to less desirable land so that they could build their second homes around here. Now that they dominate this area, they have been congregating and frolicking around here. This preserved forest is their playground," he said bitterly.

"I'm sorry," I said, understanding his bitterness.

"Oh, I'm fine. At least they gave my wife and me jobs," he said, suddenly looking on the bright side of things.

"So, this is their playground," said Jorani, looking around scared.

"Yes," he said.

"Do you know how we can get back to the city without using the main road?" I asked.

"You can continue going down this path," he said.

"Thank you," said Jorani. She took off ahead of me.

"Thank you, uncle," I said, catching up with my friend.

"We should get out of here and get back on the main road. It's hard to ride in here," said Jorani. "Besides, if this is the playground of the royalty and the wealthy, then they are more familiar with it than we are. Let's get out of here."

"Hold on. The bodyguard and who knows who else could still be waiting for us out there. Let's think this through and at least check to see if anyone is out there on the main road."

"That's fine by me."

The sounds of the jungle seemed to echo louder and louder as we made our way toward the forest that acted as the gate between the main road and us. We veered toward the pathway leading out to the road and peaked out before we pedaled for our dear lives. When we thought we were in the clear, we pedaled out of the forest like wild animals were chasing after us. Just then a car started coming toward us. I could hear my own heart beating like a drum.

"Oh no!" gasped Jorani. "Please don't tell me it's him. Please don't tell me it's him. Oh Lord Buddha, what have we gotten ourselves into? I don't want to die. I'm too young to die," she said.

"Just play it cool. He doesn't know we were in the forest watching him and Princess Nakry. Control yourself and follow my lead," I said.

The car raced down the road and stopped in front of us. A menacing looking man got out and glared at us.

"Sir, is there a reason why you are blocking the road?" I asked.

"You girls don't look familiar. Do you live around here?" he asked.

Jorani and I exchanged a look. He did not know who I was. I had no idea whether that was a good or bad thing.

"I'm sorry. We don't tell strangers where we live," I said.

"Oh, good one," Jorani turned to whisper at me.

"It's my business to know who lives around here, as I am the protector of this area."

"Oh really?" I asked.

"I've been assigned by the royal decree of King Sisowath himself to be the eyes and ears of this area."

"So you're a ranger," I said. Jorani let out a nervous laugh.

"You're being disrespectful to his majesty himself by laughing and making light of my title. I'll have to take the both of you in."

"We're not disrespecting his royal highness because I don't believe he hired you for anything. I know all of the royal employees," I said, standing my own grown.

"Oh, who are you?" he asked. I remained still. "I'll have to take you in for disrespecting the King of Cambodge."

"Wait a minute," I said. "No one here is disrespecting the king. You're using his name in vain."

"How dare you accuse me of such thing? You need to be taught some manners," he said, exiting his car and pulling out his gun.

"No. No. Please. Please. We didn't do anything wrong," said Jorani, shaking and shivering in fear.

My saucy attitude had turned this man into a volatile person. That was a bad move on my part. *Is it too late for me to apologize to him?* I wondered to myself. *Nah. I am not the type to apologize. I must find another way out of this mess.* Because he was a big and husky man with a gun, he was probably letting his guard down. After all, we were just fragile girls. I gave Jorani a look that told her not to get off her bicycle, to be at the ready to pedal for her life if I should knock his gun out of his hand. She looked at me with fright. The man moved closer to me. Before I moved to knock the gun out of his manly hand, a car raced from the direction of the bodyguard's car and we all turned to look at it. My shock at seeing familiar faces made me forget about disarming the bodyguard. The car stopped by our side.

"What's going on here?" asked Princess Soma Devi from the back seat of Father's car. Aunt Sopheary was with her and Suon was driving.

"Your royal highness," said the bodyguard, as he dropped down on his knees to show her respect.

"Princess. Aunty. Pu Suon," I said. I had never been more relieved to see their faces.

My friend and I also curtsied to greet and show respect to the princess.

"Why are you pulling out a gun at these young women?"

"Someone was entering a restricted area of this village, your royal highness. I was just asking these young ladies some questions."

"Must you ask them with a gun?" asked Princess Soma.

"I...I...I made a mistake, your royal highness."

"Now it's my turn to ask you some questions. What are you doing in this part of the village?"

"I...um...I was summoned to guard the cottage of Princess Nakry, your royal highness."

"I see. I did not know she had a house around here."

"Yes, your royal highness. She has just recently acquired the land and built it as a place of meditation and relaxation."

"All right. Do you still have questions for these two young ladies?"

"Uh...no. No, your royal highness." His eyes remained on the ground as he spoke to her.

"All right. Carry on. I'll take them home. In the future, I urge you not to treat young women with such a hostile manner. Do you understand?"

"Yes, your royal highness," said the bodyguard.

Suon got out to place our bicycles in the back of the car. Jorani and I rode on the passenger side. I could feel my best friend shivering, but I could not tell whether it was the sound of her heartbeat or mine I heard beating since my head was ringing from the adrenalin of being led away at gunpoint to God knows where. I was not sure if he intended to kill us or to scare us into admitting his suspicion. Or he might have tried to take us to Princess Nakry to have her decide our fate.

"How did you know we were here?" I asked my aunt. She looked at Princess Soma Devi.

"All right. I'll tell the story," the princess said. "Father and I had an argument over acknowledging Mith Sovann. After all, he's my dead brother's son. I have been bringing up this subject for a long time now, and Father has always shut me down. If he doesn't want to acknowledge him as our flesh and blood, I'll acknowledge him as our flesh and blood. And to find out he has been accused of such a terrible crime without any proof, I could not sit still. I believe in his innocence. It's heartbreaking to see him accused of a crime that makes no sense. As an aunt, I have an obligation to help him. I asked your aunt to come with me to see him in jail and to introduce me to him since he only knows your family and relatives. I do not know how much he knows about us."

"Not very much," I blurted out.

"I figured as much," said Princess Soma Devi. "Anyway, to make a long story short, as my car exited out the palace, your aunt and Suon here drove up to my gate."

"I stopped by your house this morning with grandma," my aunt explained, "after we returned from having made our morning alms at the temple. I asked where you were and your mother said you went over to Jorani's house. It so happened that we drove by her house and it was obvious that the two of you were not there since I didn't see your bicycles. You would not go anywhere without them. Your mother kept on mentioning her searing gut feeling that you were in danger. She wanted to go to Jorani's house to retrieve you, to ensure that you would not venture anywhere far and out of her sight. I know how much you love sleuthing, and if your mother finds out you were putting yourself in danger, she would make sure you do not set foot outside of the house again. Your mother doesn't understand. She's too old fashioned. Naturally, I told her not to worry and asked Suon to come with me to fetch you from Jorani's house. I knew you were speaking to Princess Nakry's chatty guard. I went to the royal palace and caught Princess Soma on her way out. She and I went to see the guard. He told us about Svay Thom Village," said my aunt.

"I'm thankful you rescued us in time," I said. "I wasn't sure what he would have done with us."

"So, what have you found out?" asked Princess Soma Devi.

Jorani and I looked at each other. "I don't know if we should report what we saw," I said.

"What is it? What have you found out?" asked my aunt.

"Um," I said, feeling conflicted about the whole thing.

"All right. I'll make this easy for you," said Princess Soma. "I'm hiring you to clear my nephew, Mith, of the rape charge."

My face lit up like a firefly. I had just been officially hired to work my first rape case. Then I realized Mother said that she and Father would discuss about me working on serious cases. I had agreed to do so when Father returned home. I felt conflicted. However, Princess Soma Devi had hired me. I was sure Father would not mind if he found out after the fact. To ensure that Mother did not find out I said, "Can we keep this between us? If Mother finds out she'll pull me out."

"We know," everyone chimed in.

"Perfect. Thank you. Well, we found out that Princess

Nakry and her bodyguard, the man who pulled a gun on us, are…"

"Yes, what is it?" the princess asked eagerly.

"…lovers," I said.

"Are you sure?" asked my aunt.

"We saw them kissing and feeling all over each other," said Jorani.

"Well, that confirms it," said Princess Soma.

"You knew?" I asked.

"Yes. It's the way they look at each other. She speaks to him tenderly. She has more than one bodyguard, but she takes him everywhere. They're always together. We didn't have any proof. We could only assume. She has often acted holier than thou and high and mighty. Now we have something over her. But then again, I understand it. She has been lonely. Even when my brother was alive, he would not go near her. A woman has her needs too, you know."

"If the late prince did not go near her, how did they end up with Prince Phirun?" I boldly asked.

"Anjali!" My aunt elbowed me from behind.

Princess Soma laughed and said, "According to her previous maid, she got him drunk one night and she dressed up as Mith Sovann's mother to lure him into bed. Naturally, it worked, because my late brother had been missing the love of his life like a crazy person. She occupied his mind all the time. Princess Nakry seized on it and took advantage of him. The whole thing is just sad, really."

We all sat quietly, in tune with our own thoughts.

"So are we going to the police station to see Mith," I said, breaking the silence.

"You aren't. The princess and I are going. You—the two of you—are going back home. If you want to continue working, you have to be stealthy. And you need time with your mother so that she is not suspicious. You'll have to learn how to divide your time between sleuthing and spending time with her."

"Fine," I said, feeling smothered by Mother even when she wasn't present. "Are you serious about hiring me to investigate the rape of Esmè and clearing Mith's name?" I asked, making sure that I was on the case.

"That is correct," said Princess Soma. "It's off the record. No one should know about it. But you must promise that you will be careful and call for backup if you should venture into dangerous places."

"Yes, your highness," I said, feeling excited about my job. If the princess did not hire me, I would have done it anyway, considering Mith and Esmè were my friends, but my agreement with Mother to not sleuth until Father returned would still linger. However, the princess had made it official. Excitement and sadness hit me at the same time. I felt excited at having been hired to work on my first dangerous case, but sad that it involved my friends. I had a lot of work to do. I still could not decipher if Princess Nakry had colluded with her son to rape his own cousin. He could have done it without his mother's knowledge. Or it could have been that he had nothing to do with it at all. If they were not responsible, I need to clear them while chasing other suspects. But then again, what about her lover, her bodyguard? He could have been her accomplice. If anything, he knew her whereabouts. After all, he was with her all the time.

"Princess."

"Yes, Anjali," said Princess Soma.

"Since Princess Nakry's personal bodyguard knows her whereabouts at all times, then he surly knows what she has been up to. He can either clear her name or confirm that she had something to do with Esmè's rape and Mith's incarceration," I said.

"True. What are you proposing?"

"Well. If I ask Detective Duong Chea to look into questioning Princess Nakry's bodyguard, he might not cooperate on an account that she will intervene. Plus, I don't want Detective Chea to know that I was up to something either, so I am wondering if you could…"

"Say no more. I will accompany Detective Chea and Lawyer Bora Nuon to meet with Lieutenant Sun Tan to bring him in for questioning." Before I could open my mouth, she said, "Don't worry. Princess Nakry will not know that I am responsible for bringing her lover in for questioning."

"How will…"

"You don't need to worry your pretty little head. I have learned a thing or two about underhandedness. I live among the minds of men and women who make this world goes round," she said.

"Thank you," I said.

"What an adventure! What a rush this has all been," said the princess. "I can see why you want to be a detective. To find out what people actually do underneath their exterior layer, it is just enlightening as to who we are as human beings, am I right?"

"Yes, your highness. Please don't forget we sleuth to help find justice for the victims."

"Right. From now on, I will use whatever power or influence I have to help you with your job. I know our society does not value women beyond our physical and domestic responsibilities. We will have to do whatever it takes, in a subtle way, to help each other rise out of this pigeon hole."

"Yes, your highness," I said.

11

PRINCE PHIRUN VONG AND THE UNDERGROUND

After thinking about what Princess Soma had offered, her power and influence, an idea popped in my head. "Your highness," I said to Princess Soma Devi, "do you think you can assist me with the investigation?"

"Do you have another role for me to play?" she asked with almost restrained excitement.

"Yes, your highness."

She exchanged looks with my aunt. "Of course I would be glad to help with this too." She rubbed her hands together. "I am knee deep in this now. What do you want me to do? How can I help?"

She did not like her sister-in-law, Princess Nakry, and wanted to clear Mith's name, but I still felt hesitant about asking her to do this one thing for me. It meant testing her allegiance between her fully acknowledged nephew Phirun, who was born from a proper and legal marriage, against another nephew whose mother had the unfortunate fate of being born into a peasant family. However, she did have one thing that Princess Nakry Ang envied: the love of Prince

Dara Vong. He only had eyes for her. He could not stop seeing her and wanting to be with her, and that action had cost the poor woman her life.

Prince Dara Vong's love for Kolthida Sovann came with a hefty price. It caused betrayal and jealousy. As a result, Princess Nakry hired a ruffian to murder his lover violently. Her fate was cruel. Maybe this event had turned Princess Soma Devi against her sister-in-law and her son. Moreover, the mother and son had not been a model princess and prince, abusing their power and prestige, so I was sure Princess Soma Devi resented them for tarnishing their family's good name. I was banking on her sentiment for goodness and decency in seeking her help. I treaded carefully when I tried to get her to spy on her nephew's activities and whereabouts.

"This is unconventional, but in order to clear Prince Phirun's name, I would like to, first of all, to know if he owns a typewriter."

"I am open-minded. Whatever is the case—guilty or not guilty—I do like to know the truth. To answer your question, yes, as a matter of fact, he does own a typewriter. I don't know why he bought one, but as a wealthy person, he likes to own anything the world has to offer," said the Princess.

"Perfect." My eyes sparkled. "I understand he's not home. Do you think you can get me into his office when we get back to town so that I can take a peek at his paper and the kind of typewriter it came from?"

"Are you sure you want to do this now? Didn't you almost get caught by Princess Nakry's lover?" said my aunt.

"Umm...if you don't mind, I would like to go home," said my friend Jorani, timidly.

"I understand. You've had enough excitement for one day," I said.

"We'll take you home," said my aunt.

"We'll take both of you home," said Princess Soma. "Anjali, you can do the snooping tomorrow afternoon. I know he won't be home. It'll give me a chance to grab something today, after your aunt and I visit Mith in Prison. Just come by tomorrow a bit before noon. I will let the guard know to let you in. Meet me at my residence."

"Thank you, Princess."

The next day, I peered around the corner of the side of the building to watch Princess Soma Devi talking to Prince Phirun's guards. Knowing how much her nephew loved new gadgets that were not owned by anyone else yet, she stopped by a French store to buy him the latest gadget and wrapped it nicely with a big red bow. I didn't ask what she had gotten him. "I want to surprise him with this present. I would like to get in and leave this on his desk," she said to the guard.

"Yes, your highness." One of them unlocked the door and let her in. As soon as she walked through the threshold, I ran to the back to wait for her by the window. She opened the window, and I climbed in. I followed her through the hallway.

She turned the doorknob to one of the rooms. "I hope

he keeps this door open," she said. To our relief it was not locked.

"Okay. You go do your thing while I keep an eye out for him or anyone else. Be quick though, I don't want them to wonder why it is taking me so long just to leave a present."

"Thank you, your highness. I shall be quick. I know what I am looking for, so it should not take long."

"Good. I'll leave you to it." She closed the door behind her. I darted straight toward the shiny oak desk by the floor to ceiling window. There sat a black Royal typewriter. Princess Soma said a business tycoon from Hartford, Connecticut presented it to him as a gift. He provided reams of special paper for him as well. The typewriter appeared to have been used recently. Next to it was a pile of that blank special paper. I took one to insert and typed out, "My Dearest Esmè Laurent..." I then realized that I did not get a good look at the letter to recognize the font type. Was it the same font type and the same paper? I wondered. It did not matter. I could still use it to compare against the last letter sent to the governor's daughter, if they should introduce it as evidence in court. The seal was different, but that made sense. Prince Phirun wouldn't use his royal seal because Esmè would know and would not be easily lured into his trap.

I studied my evidence carefully, wondering if the typewriter produced the same font type as the letter I saw in Esmè Laurent's hand. The paper appeared to be the same as well. The seal was different, though. My mind reverted to my original theory. Could Prince Phirun have tried to pin the rape of his own cousin, who is a niece of his mother, on his half-brother, who is an illegitimate son of his father? Does he actually know Mith is his half-brother? But then again, why would he use his own brand of typewriter and paper that were given to him as special gifts? Did he not think it would be traced back to him? This didn't make any sense. How many people in this town, Khmer or European alike, own a Royal typewriter? It's American made. The French use their own products more than American-made products when they can. Hmm. How many people know about the prince's typewriter? Who would have access to it besides the prince? But why would someone else try to frame him? I wouldn't put it past him to frame someone else, why should I put it past another? After all, he made enough enemies by abusing his power and with his womanizing ways. Should I follow this lead or should I be focusing on something else? I had no other lead but this one. But if I could sit and think things through, maybe I could come up with a different lead. I acted too much on my own impulses. My mind warred with itself, like counsel and opposing counsel, which prompted me to think that the indistinct voices coming from the hallway were voices in my head. Then they came closer and closer.

"To what do I owe this pleasure of you visiting my residence, my dear Aunt?" asked Prince Phirun, sounding very sarcastic. "You seldom step foot in here. You only come when you are forced to."

"No! Don't go in there!"

"How peculiar. What is it? What are you up to?"

I went into panic mode when I realized who had returned home. I folded the sheet of paper I was studying and my elbow accidentally knocked over the candlestick telephone.

"What was that noise?"

I picked it up and placed it back where it originally stood. My heart raced. My legs turned to vermicelli noodles. I stuffed the paper I typed with the Royal typewriter into my dress pocket. I ran back and forth between the window and the door like a chicken with its head cut off. I did not know where to go.

I went back to the window to try to open it while Princess Soma Devi tried to buy me some time. Unfortunately, it did not budge. It was sealed shut, possibly for show only. *Who does that?* My heart fluttered like a butterfly. My knees shook. I started panicking and hyperventilating. For a microsecond, I began to lose hope. My eyes surveyed the office. I ran around the room again, looking for a place to hide. I could not find any. I lost hope. Out of the blue my mind reverted to the time when my grandfather told me about how palaces had secret rooms for the royal family and few trusted ministers to enter and exit without anyone else being the wiser. I started to push and pull on books to see if one of them was the key to unlocking the door. I then proceeded to feel, rub, push, and pull the statues that were strategically placed on the shelves. None of them worked. Now I was really panicking. I inadvertently leaned my hand against a beautifully carved Apsara, the celestial nymph, and a bookshelf flew open! I stood in awe. This was unbelievable. My grandfather had mentioned that royal palaces have secret rooms, pathways, and tunnels. This must be one of the secret rooms he was talking about. How intriguing. I heard the knob turn and something inside kicked me. I guess it was my brain signaling me to get inside, so I did. The bookcase door closed in on me. It was pitch black. I wanted to push it back but was afraid it might open just as easily. I feared what would happen to me if I was caught. I wished I had brought my golden flashlight with me, which was given to me as a birthday gift by my American professor, Dr. George H. Williams. If I made it out of here, I would remember to carry it with me wherever I went. A girl just never knows where she might end up.

"What's this?" asked Prince Phirun.

"See. I was trying to surprise you by leaving it there on your desk, but you came home very early and caught me in the act," said Princess Soma Devi.

"Not to sound ungrateful, but why? Why have you bought this for me?"

"I know I haven't been fair to you and your mother. I want to do something nice for a change. It's time for us to patch things up. After all, we are family. People look up to us. Anyway, I passed by the gadget shop the other day and saw this and thought you would appreciate it. I hope you don't have anything like it."

"No. Actually, I don't. It's very nice. I greatly appreciate it. However, you did not have to spend money on me."

"Well, I wanted to. I thought it would be a good gesture. I want us to be able to look each other in the eyes. I don't want any awkwardness between us. After all, you are my brother's son, my nephew."

"All right. Thank you for the good gesture. I will see you out of here."

"Wait a minute. Is this how you're treating me?"

I sensed Prince Phirun was trying to get rid of his aunt. He probably sensed someone was in his office and found a way into his secret room.

"I would like to invite you to stay for tea. However, I have important things to do. I need to get to work."

"What is so important that you can't delay it a bit and talk to your aunt?"

"I'm sorry. It's work that women don't understand."

"Excuse me?"

"I'm sorry, I don't mean it like that. Please, it is important that I get to work. I have wasted enough time already."

I have to find a way out of here, I told myself. I would be in deep, deep trouble if he found me. In desperation, I felt my way around the dark secret room, hoping not to touch anything slimy and creepy. My knee hit an object. It was a table. I cried out and immediately slapped my hand over my mouth. Then I felt my way on the table, hoping to find something to illuminate the place. After all, if Prince Phirun used this place, he must have a kerosene lamp or something handy. However, I did not sense anything of the sort. I started to panic again. I slid my feet on the floor and my hands along the wall inch by inch. My senses told me the wall was made of brick. To my astonishment, one of the bricks could be pushed in. Since I had nothing to lose, I pressed it. A door, which looked like a wall, opened up. The next room, as big as a throne hall, was illuminated with special lights coming from the walls. I swirled around like Alice in Wonderland and stepped inside. Then the wall closed after me. I turned around to push it back, but it did not budge. I was locked in. However, I did not feel bothered by it too much as the room piqued my curiosity. What was this room? What purpose did it serve? Had the room always been here? Judging from its cleanliness and the illumination, this place had been utilized a lot.

The sound of the wall opening sent me jumping. I ran around the room frantically looking for a door or something that would lead me out of here before I was caught. I pushed all four corners of the walls, hoping they would open. I felt each wall and any objects for an opening device. Nothing happened. I promised myself I would not be in darkness again. I saw something that resembled a torch, but it was not. The light that came out of it was not a fire at all, but some kind of special light that I had never ever seen before. I wanted to bring it with me but it turned out to be a movable mechanism that opened the door to my left. Whoever built this underground place was a genius. Again, what was the builder's purpose in building this underground place? Was it used for secret meetings or to exit and enter without anyone else knowing? The clicking and clanking noises came closer. I would have loved to stand around and admire the craftiness and the ingenuity of this place, but I had to get out of there. I told myself.

I stepped into the next room only to find three more huge doors in a wide and spacious square, a meeting point of North, South, East, and West. Old Khmer inscriptions were etched above each door. I turned to look up at the inscription over the door that I had just stepped out of and it read The Lion's Den. Someone sure thought big of himself. So the door leading to Prince Phirun's library and residence is called The Lion's Den. Not that I would have a chance to come here again, but it was good to know. Meanwhile, my mind went into overdrive trying to decipher what the other three phrases meant and where each door would lead me. The sounds of a door opening and closing and the clicking of heavy footsteps came my way. I had three choices. Door number one was labeled Sacred Space, door number two was labeled Vishnu Temple, and door number three was labeled Lotus Pond.

By the process of elimination, I could surmise that Vishnu Temple must be referring to Angkor Wat. If the tunnel led me to the temple, which faced west, it would be too far for me to walk home from, but at least Prince Phirun would not know it was me who intruded on his royal residence. As for Lotus Pond, I had no idea what that meant. Could it be a literal translation of some profound name of some temple, monument, or place of great significance to the royal family or the people? It could be someone's pond or a lotus pond somewhere outside of the city for all I knew. The sound of footsteps inched closer and closer. I had to make my decision, fast! I darted to the door that read Sacred Space and pushed it open. I found myself running through a labyrinth of tunnels illuminated by some sort of special lighting. I could not help but wonder if Prince Dara Vong, Prince Phirun's father, had built the tunnels. Or could it have been his grandfather or his ancestors? The tunnels looked old, but they had been kept up, which meant either Prince Phirun or his grandfather, who was still alive, but elderly, had this place maintained.

I came at the end of the tunnel at a golden door. I must have arrived at the Sacred Place. My heart pounded like a drum as I opened the door. The feeling of the unknown was the source of my fear. That door could be leading me to a dangerous place or a safe place. *Since when did I become fearful of the unknown?* I asked myself. Nevertheless, I gently turned the knob and proceeded to gingerly pull the door outward. Much to my annoyance, another door stood in my way. Actually, it looked more like a wall than a door. I pushed it. It opened. I stepped out. The door automatically closed behind me. I turned around to see a wall of shelves containing books, statues—naked statues—and valuable artifacts displayed beautifully looking back at me. The books consisted of leather binding with good leaf ornamentation. There must have been hundreds of them. I fingered through the title of each book: *The Art of Love, Kama Sutra...Sacred Space.*

"Sacred Space?" I said out loud. I pulled it out. The cover had a beautiful woman sitting under a threshold of a decorative gate.

Inside it read,

What is the Sacred Space? Your yoni, your womb, represents your sacred space. It is a magical and powerful place from which life is conceived and from which we all come. It is a place of honor and wisdom.

"Honor? Wisdom? What? Someone dedicated an entire book to a woman's private part?" I said out loud.

"Excuse me. Who are you?" A female voice called out to me. My body jerked upon hearing her voice and my hands became so weak that I dropped the book on the wood-paneled floor.

12

THE MADAM OF THE SACRED SPACE

A woman with shoulder length hair, upswept eyes, and pale skin rushed over to pick up the book and place it back on the shelf. She fashioned herself in the latest western garb. The woman looked about in her mid-thirties, but youthful and beautiful. She garlanded herself with the finest jewelry. She sized me up.

"My goodness, you startled me," I said, brushing off the fact that she caught me in a room in which I did not belong. "May I ask who you are?" I spoke with a calm and steady voice.

"Excuse me? You're in my office. Who are you to ask who I am? I should be doing all the asking here. How did you get in here? I don't remember seeing you come into the front door. How dare you enter my private office? It's even off limits to my girls. Tell me now or I will call the authorities."

"There is no need for that," I said. My voice changed to a nervous laughter. I searched in my head to find some excuse to give her while trying very hard to maintain my composure. "Actually..."

"Actually, she is with me," said a familiar voice. I looked up and saw the well groomed Detective Duong Chea, who was holding his flat tweed cap in his hand, standing next to a young woman around my age. "I told you not to snoop around without talking to the lady of the house first."

"I'm sorry, Madam Rose, but Detective Chea is here to see you," said the young woman.

"Oh, Detective Chea!" she said, changing her tone to one that was flirty, sweet, and gentle. "I take it this young girl works at your agency. There's only one young woman who works there. She must be the daughter of Detective Oum Chum Chinak!" She grabbed hold of my jaw between her thumb and index finger and gave it a little squeeze. "She's a pretty little thing."

"Please don't get any ideas," said Detective Chea.

"Oh, I would not dream of it. She's the daughter of the greatest detective of Siem Reap. I would not dare dream of anything of that sort. After all, she has a future much brighter than this." She let out a naughty laugh. I turned to Detective Chea and searched his face for some explanation.

He looked at me. "Why don't you go and wait in the car, Anjali? I have some grown-up matters to talk to Madam Rose about. I'll talk to you later about your behavior," he said, pretending to admonish me. "Don't stray like you have done here. Be respectful and mindful of the people here."

"Oh, sure," I said hesitantly.

"I apologize on her behalf. She tends to not follow the rules."

"Most woman leaders don't," she said, winking at me. I did not know how to react to that. "Dary, please show Mademoiselle Anjali out."

"Yes, Madam Rose," said the young woman. "Mademoiselle Anjali." She walked before me and led me through the hallway and then up the stairs to the first level of the house where gentle laughter and chattering voices dominated the wide space.

"What is this place?" I asked quietly to myself as I walked to the foyer. Beautiful women were pairing up with all kinds of men, French, Asian, fat, skinny, middle age and older men, occupied the house. Some pairs were making their way up the stairs. They were talking and laughing, not paying any attention to anyone outside of their circles.

"Right this way, mademoiselle," Dary said, looking at me with her big round eyes.

"Oh my Lord! I'm in a brothel," I mumbled under my breath. Suddenly, my face felt hot.

"Excuse me?"

"Oh, nothing."

"By the way, how did you get in, mademoiselle? I don't remember seeing you enter this house. I saw Monsieur Duong Chea arrive, but I did not see you at all. Madame is going to question me. She relies on me to keep tabs on all the guests coming and going from here."

"Oh, I arrived before Detective Chea did." I looked around the room to find another entrance. As soon as I found it, I said, "Over there. See? Over there is how I got in."

"You came through the back door?"

"Yes! Yes, I did. I saw people were gathering and meandering around the back, so I went to see the guests. I thought I knew one of them, but it turned out I was mistaken."

"Oh? Why are you and Detective Chea here? Is something going on?" she asked me, genuinely concerned. "Why would a dignified young woman like you come to this place?"

"Why would a nice young woman like you work here?"

"I...I'm an orphan. Since I don't have beauty like the rest of them..." She looked to the beautiful women arming themselves with all types of men: short, tall, old, handsome, and ugly. "I work as the monitor here. Like I said, I monitor people coming in and out, and I did not see you." She gave me a sharp look.

"Yes. Yes, something is going on. We're here to question some people. Maybe you can answer a few questions."

"No. I don't know anything. I am only to monitor people coming in and out. I don't know anything else."

"As someone who watches people coming and going, you do know something. In fact, I can guarantee that you know a lot."

"No. No, I don't."

"I think you protest too much," I said. "You do know something."

"Mademoiselle Anjali, I am an orphan. Madam Rose brought me here to work for her. She provided me with a place to sleep and food to eat. All I do is to keep my eyes on guests who come and go here. Please don't get me in trouble. I don't know anything."

"My question is simple. Since you monitor people coming and going here, have you seen Prince Phirun?"

"Umm. Umm. I...I don't want to get into trouble," she said.

"Come on, please tell me. I won't reveal you as my source. All you need to do is confirm with a nod or shake your head."

"Umm. Well. I didn't actually see him come in or leave, same as I did not see you come in here. Please don't ask me any more questions. I don't know anything else. I do not want to get in trouble with Madam Rose."

"No worries. I can take it from here," I said slowly, without thinking, as my surveying eyes stopped to focus on a man—a portly man. This would be my third time seeing him. He whispered something into a woman's ear. She gently pushed him away and threw her head back, laughing at whatever he said. I had seen her before. She rode with Prince Phirun when his car nearly hit me. "That man. That woman. I believe I have seen them before. Isn't she an aristocratic daughter or something? And isn't that American a friend of Andre Thomas? Why does she hang out here?"

"You're right. They like to hang out here because they say this place gives them comfort and they can let lose without the prying eyes of our conservative and traditional society," said Dary.

"How often do they come here?"

"Mademoiselle Rani Somavathai has been coming here for a few years now. As for Mr. Alb...Albert...Mr. Albertson," said Dary, trying to pronounce his name, "he only started coming here a few weeks ago. I believe Mademoiselle Somavathai brought him here. She was trying to make Prince Phirun jealous because he had stopped paying attention to her."

"Really?"

"Yes, he has been with many girls. However, the one he wants to marry is his cousin on his mother's side, Mademoiselle Esmè Laurent. I accidentally overheard them arguing. Mademoiselle Somavathai said he had used all the women in this town, including her, but he would only marry his cousin."

"Did he deny or confirm it, that he loved his cousin?" I asked.

"No. He remained quiet and just let her talk, scream, and yell. So now she's trying to make him jealous with this *barang*." Although the word "barang" originally referred to the French, Cambodgeins generally used it to refer to all Western or white men and women.

"I guess she likes rich and portly men," I said.

"I don't want to comment, Mademoiselle Anjali."

"I understand."

It had been a long day. I wrote a note and asked a messenger to deliver it to Princess Soma Devi, telling her I was safe. She would want to know how I exited Prince Phirun's office. I told her I would explain when we met again. On the ride home, Detective Duong Chea lectured me like he was Father. Actually, as Father put him in charge of the office, he had the right to demand what I was doing there.

"First of all, what are you doing at a brothel?" he asked.

"That was a brothel?" I asked.

"Don't play innocent with me. Your mother will be furious. What will the people of Siem Reap say if they find out you went to such a place?"

"You went there."

"I was on a case. I had a few questions for Madam Rose. Wait a minute. This is not about me. I'm asking you."

"I had a lead. I wanted to check it out."

"What lead? What are you investigating, Anjali? You

better not be investigating Mith's case. You are not allowed. *We* are not allowed."

"Why would you assume that? I could be investigating the missing heirloom of Madame Chantha. A witness could have come forward and said they saw a young and beautiful woman at this establishment wearing that missing jewelry. Maybe her husband visited the place and gave it to a woman there."

"Don't deflect. Everyone knows Madame Chantha's husband is a morally good man. People respect him. He would not do that to his wife. I understand Mith and Esmè are your friends. You want to find evidence to prove Mith's innocence, and at the same time, you want to find justice for Esmè. You have good intentions. I don't deny that. However, you are putting yourself in serious danger. Your father did not teach you anything about homicide. I doubt he plans on doing so anytime soon."

"Why?"

"You are young. You are a...?"

"A what? What am I?"

"You're a young girl."

"What does that have to do with anything?"

"Being a detective is not easy. It's a dangerous job. This is coming from me, a man. There are dangerous and powerful men out there. You're not ready to see what we see. Deal with what we deal with. And you're...you're young and inexperienced."

"How am I supposed to have experience when no one gives me a chance?"

"Be that as it may, there is a matter of..."

"Of what? Of being a girl?"

"This world is not ready for a woman detective."

"Then I am just the person to break that barrier."

"Oh Anjali. Why must you be difficult?"

"I'm capable. I just want to be given a chance. I wish you, Mother, and society would be more open-minded about it. There should be more to life than household chores. I thought our society was founded by a matriarch. I thought Princess Soma ran this country before Khmer men or the French colonized our country. Of all people I thought you would be more understanding of my interest."

He smiled and shook his head. "I am. I'm just letting you know what you're up against."

"I know what I am up against."

"I don't think you do. There are powerful people at play here. It's hard enough for us men to deal with them, let alone a young girl. You're putting us all in danger if we must constantly come to your rescue."

"I resent that. I'm capable to taking care of myself."

"Oh really? What happened back there?"

"Well..."

"Well, indeed. You're lucky I came just in time."

"I'll just be careful next time."

"What I would like to know is how did you get into Madam Rose's office in the first place? I am sure she keeps the door locked. How did you get inside without anyone detecting you?"

"Wouldn't you like to know?" I said, looking at him sideways with my raised eyebrow.

"I'm serious."

"I am sorry. I can't tell you."

We both remained silent the rest of the way to my house, where he dropped me and then returned to whatever he was doing that day. I could not sleep that night, partly because my relatives came in and out of my house after they had heard what happened to us a few days before, when the governor and his men wreaked havoc on our home. Also, Mith's grandparents were staying at our home. It did not help when the faces of Esmè and the other murder victims were crying and screaming for help. This was the second time I had dreamed about my friend. Whatever I did or worry about during the day must have caught up with me during the nighttime.

13

IT'S MURDER!

An unusual morning crept up upon us. Darkness hovered over the city of Siem Reap like some kind of bad omen. Thunder roared after flashes of lightning. The swishing from nearby trees sounded violent. Anxiety loomed. It appeared as if the gods were crying and in mourning. Wind and rain hit the ground in full force, as if to wreak vengeance. With all the bad things that transpired in this town, the rain just sent me into a somber mood. I stood watching the rain and distant lightning from the windows of the receptionist area at my father's office as my mind got lost in worrisome thoughts.

No one in my household had been sleeping—at least, not well—for the past few days. Mith's grandparents, who had become suddenly old and frail, had been staying at our home. Mother would not have it any other way because they had no one to cook and look after them as they had no relatives. The grandmother was especially feeble, and the elderly couple needed our moral support. My paternal and maternal relatives had been coming in and out of our home just to be there for us in the midst of these worrisome times. Plus, they became protective of us ever since the governor and his men ransacked our home, threatened my mom and Mith's grandparents, and beat up on our driver. My paternal and maternal uncles were livid when they found out what happened.

"Do not stand too close to the window while lightning strikes the earth," said Madame Montha without looking up at me. Her bright eyes focused diligently on her work. I could see her reflection through the window as I stared out at the dark sky.

I walked away from the window to peek out into the hallway. I opened up our door and watched random workers strolling the hallways, but no one was heading our way, let alone delivering anything.

I asked Madame Montha, "Do you suppose the report will come by messenger or will Lieutenant Tan deliver it himself?"

"If you are referring to the investigation report of Esmè's rape, it does not matter because we are not part of it."

"I beg your pardon?" I asked.

"We're not to be involved in the investigation," said Madame Montha.

"Why not?"

"We are too close to this case. They have decided we would not be partial."

I felt a flush of indignation. "In other words we are not to be trusted, right? You know what I say to that? I say we do not believe his team of policemen and investigators will be partial either. Who knows? They want to satisfy the governor, so they will say and do anything to let him hear what he wants to hear and see what he wants to see, hoping to get in his good graces. They will cook up evidence so fast that..."

"Now, now, Anjali. We can't make that assumption. Besides, he governs our city, so..."

"So we do as he says?" I finished for her.

"In a matter of speaking, yes. Besides, we would like to give him the benefit of the doubt that he will follow the law of the land."

"The law he and his men created. We all know they have a different set of rules for us," I scoffed. "I cannot believe this unfairness. So who have they hired to help Mith?"

"Detective Chea suggested to Mith's grandfather that he should hire a gentleman from Phnom Penh. Your father knows him. He is competent."

"Competent is not good enough."

"Well, we have a shortlist of people who do not work for the governor. He is the best of the pick," Madame Montha said.

"Fair enough. If you need me, I will be in my cave," I said.

"By the way, how is your work coming along with regard to Madame Chantha's priceless heirloom? She's been anxious to hear your update."

"It's coming."

"With all the darkness looming over our town for the second time since the tragedy of Mith's mother, I understand everyone was preoccupied, and since they are your friends, I'm sure it's been hard on you. So I bought you some more time. But she insisted you reveal your findings this week. I'm sorry." She finally looked up from what she was doing and eyed me with sympathy.

"So her husband is back in town this week, huh?" I said.

"Pardon?"

"Nothing. That's fine. I will give her my findings."

At the moment, my thoughts shifted elsewhere. My two friends were going through a heart-breaking event in their young lives.

I was anxious to hear about the investigation report on Mith. Princess Soma Devi, his royal aunt, had hired me to clear his name. I intended to find the truth and do just that. I paced back and forth in the internal office that held none of the homicidal files and records. My hope of perusing the report that was supposed to be delivered to Detective Chea had shattered.

Unfortunately, I was not allowed to contact anyone at Laurent Manor. I could not even go to the hospital to see my friend. "You're not welcomed here," said the Princess when I went to visit Esmé at Mehta Hospital. It hurts when a person whom you once respected now despised the sight of you. She was the nice and reasonable one. If she told me I was not welcome anywhere near her family, I must obey. I was clueless and in the dark about everything. Granted, I had snooped on Princess Nakry and Prince Phirun, but I was no closer to the truth. I ended up with more questions than answers. I could not find tangible proof, except for the letter and paper I found in Prince Phirun's office. Even that could be circumstantial. I could not be sure that his typewriter and paper were the ones used to send Esmè her final letter until they are tested against the last letter to Esmè. However, I knew for sure the red seal did not belong to him as I was familiar with all of the seals of the royal families. Even if the letter came from his typewriter and paper, I needed to prove he actually typed it up and passed it to someone to deliver to Esmè directly. I needed to find a witness or a confession from him. I could not ask Detective Chea what clue he had on the matter that prompted him to make his appearance at the house of Madam Rose. I could not do that without him asking me what led me to the place and how I got into her office. I did not want to explain about the underground labyrinth of passageways to who knew where else. Besides, I did not want to tell him Princess Soma Devi hired me to investigate Mith's case. She acknowledged him as her nephew, although he did not know anything about her or about the investigation.

By eleven o'clock, anxious and worried voices outside my open door caught my ears. I stepped over the threshold of my door and stealthily crept around the corner to see Monsieur Bora Nuon, the son of Judge San Nuon, looking very flustered. The thin, tall, and swarthy man, a few years older than Mith, said to Madame Montha, "I need to see Detective Chea right away."

"I'll take your umbrella." I could hear her putting it in the bin with the other umbrellas. "Right this way, monsieur," she said. She led him down the hall just behind her desk and knocked on the first door on the right.

The door opened. "Good. You're here. We've been waiting for you," Detective Chea said. *We? Who else did he have in there with him?* The door closed after Monsieur Bora marched inside.

I walked up to Madame Month's desk. "What is going on?" I asked. "He looked serious."

"I'm not sure," she said.

Rain and thunder continued. The sound of silence crept in between these raucous sounds. Madame Montha jumped at the ringing of the telephone. Everyone appeared to be jumpy lately, for good reason. My stomach fluttered. Something provoked an intense nervous agitation within me. I looked down at my hands. They were shaking profusely. Bad omens winged all around me. It was as if my body knew something before I did. This must have been how my dog, Tony, felt when he sensed danger. I could not take this tension of bad feelings and of not knowing anymore. I lingered, pretending to finger through the stack of mail on Madame Montha's desk. I could not decipher their muffled voices. I stood there for no more than a few minutes before the detective's wooden door burst open, with everyone flying left and right to get where they were going.

"Anjali," said Detective Chea, "please stay and help out Madame Montha in the office. We are going to be out all day."

"What is going on?"

"Mith Sovann has been charged with rape and murder. Instead of months, we now have days to do our own investigation and help lawyer Bora Nuon prepare for trial. Lord of the universe, please help us all."

My heart dropped. My head spun like a top. Nauseating feelings overpowered me. "No. That cannot be. Esmé is dead?"

"Yes," confirmed lawyer Bora.

I looked at lawyer Bora, eyes wide open, as if I misheard him. "But...but that cannot be!" Even as I was forced to accept it, my thoughts turned to Mith, still alive but vulnerable. "No. Murder is punishable by a penalty of life imprisonment. Considering we're the bottom feeders in our own country, Mith will be shot or hung," I said to no one in particular.

Detective Chea sighed and said, "I'm sorry, Anjali. I know they're good friends of yours. I know this is hard. We received orders that no one besides me is allowed anywhere near the hospital or the Laurent Manor. Let his grandparents know that family members are not to see him until trial."

"You're allowed to work on the investigation?" I asked Detective Chea.

"Yes. Bora here, with the help of Princess Soma Devi, convinced our king to talk to the French authorities since the person we hired has mysteriously disappeared. I'm asking one of the detectives to look into his disappearance. I now have written permission from King Sisowath himself and will need to obtain permission from the high court to permit me to work with counsel on behalf of the defendant. I'll be able to see him and inform his family of his wellbeing. Third-class citizens or not, we will do everything to get him out if he's indeed innocent. From the Criminal Court justice, we will go to the justice of the Court of Appeals, and the Supreme Court justice. One of the many great things I learned from your father is that in the face of battle, you must not lose hope. You must face it head on, with confidence and bravery. It looks like we'll be working late these two days. You can either go home or stay and help Madame Montha manage the office. It's up to you," he said sympathetically.

"No. I'd like to stay and help out," I said, looking down at the floor as if my soul had jumped out of my body. I just stood there like a log while other detectives moved all around me to gather their things and give orders to Madame Montha before they headed out. I felt like everything was moving in slow motion. Everything was so unreal. In minutes, the office was practically empty. Silence ensued in the office once again; but it was not the good kind of silence, rather the kind that brought darkness and misery.

I returned to my office, closed the door, and with my back against it, slid down to the floor. I could not control myself. I wept like a child. It was a raw moment for me. I pulled out my monogrammed beige handkerchief from my dress pocket and wiped the tears away. I felt so helpless. I could not imagine what Mith and his grandparents were going through. All I knew was that the Laurents were heartbroken and angry, and they would make someone pay. I was sure they were also devastated, scared, and full of questions. Once I could muster myself and gain control of my senses, I had to race against time to find the underlying cause of all of this. I needed to find answers to questions that lingered in my head. Did Mith rape Esmé? An assault that eventually led to her death? If not he, then who would have done this to my good friend? Time was not on our side. We needed the answers fast. It was hard to think when the persons involved were close friends.

I could not prove Princess Nakry was involved. However, I still had a lead in the matter of her son, Prince Phirun. I needed to connect him to typing and passing the letter to Esmè. He also had a jilted lover. A smiling face of a woman suddenly appeared before me. The woman I saw riding with the prince when they nearly ran me over and again at the brothel flirting with Andre Thomas's friend, James Albertson. Dary, the young lady, who was supposed to keep her eyes on the people who came and went from that place said she was jealous of the prince falling in love with his own cousin. She was an aristocrat's daughter. She could be one of his many conquests. I should establish the timeline of Prince Phirun's whereabouts. She might know.

Loud knocking roused me. "Anjali? Anjali? Are you all right in there?" asked Madame Montha.

"Just a minute," I said, as I wiped away more tears and pulled myself together. I took a deep breath before I opened the door.

She must have noticed my weepy eyes. "Are you all right? Do you need to go home to be with your mother and

Mith's grandparents? I know Mith is a good friend of the family, and Esmé was one of your few friends. I'm sorry," she said. She looked at me with sympathetic eyes. "This is shocking to all of us."

"I need to work. Besides, it would not be fair to you. You would be all alone."

"That's okay. I don't mind one bit. I can get more work done while everyone is gone. Besides, if I am overwhelmed, your father said I could hire a temporary assistant to help."

"No. I'll help you."

She looked at me quizzically.

"I will be fine. What do you have there?" I asked, looking at some papers in her hand.

"This is a copy of the investigation report given to the law offices of Bora Nuon. We need to make multiple copies and return the originals to his office. We need to type up this request, as written by lawyer Nuon. Then take it to Judge René Chenot for his signature. Detective Chea and lawyer Nuon will be at the judge's chamber to sign theirs as well in two hours. Do you think you can handle that?"

"Of course. I'll handle both tasks," I said. This was the report I had been anxiously awaiting. I went into my office file room where we kept our Multigraph Printing Duplicators and Oliver Courier typewriters. I made multiple copies of the report, an extra for me, and typed up multiple copies of the written request for all parties to sign.

I left copies of the case report with Madame Montha, put the original in a folder along with three extra copies and copies of the written request in another folder, and I took them all with me. I descended the stairs and exited to the busy street of Prey Nokor Boulevard, where pedestrians, cars, ox-carts, and horse carriages filled the street. People hustled and bustled as usual on this wet, hot morning. The rain had stopped by now. Just as quickly as it came, it went away. A man on a bicycle *remork* who parked in front of our building asked if I needed transportation. "I'm fine, uncle. I am going to grab my bicycle from the back. Thank you, though." He smiled and waved me off. I rode down five blocks south of Prey Nokor Boulevard and stopped at the intersection of Youthathor Avenue, right in front of a beige concrete building that took over the block. A bronze statue of the blindfolded Lady Justice, in her flowing gown, balancing the scales in her right hand and wielding a sword in her left, stood majestically in the town square. I looked up to her. I had seen the statue of Lady Justice many times in my life since Father brought me to court I was a little girl for the first time.

"She personifies the moral force in our judicial system. See there? The scales represent truth and fairness while the sword symbolizes the power of reason and justice," said Father. I was five years old.

I hoped truth, fairness, and justice worked for all and were not reserved only for people of power. In this unfair colonial world, those of us lower on the social ladder had to work much harder and insist much more loudly for our rights.

It appeared to be a busy day for lawyers, politicians, and other people who were entering and exiting the court. There were also reporters snooping around, hoping to score a good headline. There were so many people that they jostled each other to get to their destinations. I parked my bicycle and walked in.

"Mademoiselle Anjali," said the cheerful guard in the grand lobby. "Messieurs Nuon and Chea are waiting for you upstairs."

"Thank you," I said. Seeing that I did not have anything

with me but the two folders when he peeked in my satchel, he waved me in to go up the marble stairs. I met the two men on the fifth floor in front of the chamber of Judge Chenot. The governor must have pulled some strings to get the most conservative and narrow-minded judge to preside over this case. I prayed Father would return home soon because he knew how to challenge these tough-minded, stone-hearted individuals.

"Perfect timing, Anjali," said Detective Chea as lawyer Nuon greeted me. The case was close to him too, as he had been a good friend to Mith since they met on a ship after they returned from studying abroad. "We'll get these signed," said the detective, taking the sheets from me.

I told the attorney that I had returned his original to his office and handed him and the detective copies in case they did not return to their offices right away.

They went inside. I remained behind in the hallway, waiting for them and hoping to go with them to see Mith after they were all done here. I needed to see him, to make sure he was holding it together. And considering his grandparents would not be able to see him until the trial, I wanted to reassure them he was being brave so they should be brave too. I found myself pacing back and forth while thinking about how I should go about doing some sleuthing on my own. However, I needed to read the case report and find out where Detective Chea and his team were so I could contribute. They needed more manpower—or in my case, womanpower. I knew they would not give me a chance because they thought it too dangerous and that I was too young. This would be a good opportunity. Because they were too busy working on the matter, they would not care or pay me any mind if I were to go sleuthing on my own.

I needed some fresh air. I wandered off to one of the

Khmer restaurants in the vicinity, hoping to get something good for Mith. Prison food was likely horrendous.

About ten minutes after I returned, the two men came back out. It was good timing. "He's so difficult to deal with. His blatant impartiality makes my blood boil. We need evidence that someone else did it. You must find the killer," said the lawyer Nuon.

"Anjali, you're still here," said the detective, looking away from the attorney. He gazed at my hand.

"I take it you would like to come with us to see Mith."

"If you don't mind," I said.

"I don't see why not," said the lawyer.

"I brought my bicycle. I can meet you there."

"All right then. See you there," said Detective Chea, showing a gentle smile as if he was proud of how hard I worked.

14

MITH'S LOVE LETTERS

There he sat, with his face buried in his hands, plunged deep into lonesome grief, as if he had not moved from that position since his grandfather and I had last left him. I could not imagine what floated in his mind. He just lost the love of his life, was now accused of her murder and rape, and must have been as anxious to find her true killer as we were. I had not known the man that long, but my experience, knowledge, and intuition all told me he could not have done this. I knew deep in my heart and guts that he would not do anything like that to her. He was a man of honor, courage, and integrity. She had expressed how safe she felt with him. Surely she had whispered his name because she needed him. From the way she described his love for her, he could not do such thing to her.

These were my biased feelings, however. According to Father, I could not rely on guts alone. I must follow the evidence and see where it led me. I intended to solve my friend's murder and if Mith was innocent, clear his name.

As soon as he heard us coming, Mith got up and rushed from his bench to the iron bars. He held onto them and looked at us through the spaces between. Even in his deepest sorrow and in a gaunt, scruffy, and emaciated state of being, he was still handsome.

"Where is she? Where are they placing her body? I must see her. I want to see her. Do you think you can make such an arrangement for me?" he asked his lawyer and the detective.

They looked at him with extreme sadness and shook their heads. Then he turned to me with those melancholy eyes. The poor man now stood utterly bereft of speech.

I told him I was guilty by association with him and was not allowed to see her even when she had still been alive in the hospital.

He walked back to his bed frame and sat down, brooding, staring into nothingness.

"I brought you some good food," I said, lifting up the silver container. He did not look up. "You need to maintain your health. Please be strong for the sake of your grandparents if nothing else."

As if he had forgotten about them, he looked up and asked, "How are my grandparents holding up?"

"Not well, but if you eat something and keep up your strength, it would help them tremendously," I said.

He did not say anything.

"Guard, do you mind letting us in? We need to talk to our client," said the attorney.

"Yes, sir," said the guard.

As we walked in, the guard said, "I'm sorry, mademoiselle, but you must leave. Only his lawyer and the detective are allowed."

The Governor's Daughter

We all looked at him with our arched brows and inquisitive eyes.

"I'm under strict orders that only his lawyer and Detective Chea are allowed to see him."

As disappointed as I felt, I handed the food container to Detective Chea and said, "I must return to the office anyway."

"Please tell my grandparents not to worry too much. I'm fine. I'll be fine. I did not do anything wrong," he said, still looking at the floor and staring into nothingness. He did not sound fine, nor did he look fine. He most certainly did not feel fine. He huddled, his hands holding tightly to the bench, and sank his head upon his chest. Anger, sadness, and grief dominated him.

"I will tell them," I said, finding myself sounding sad.

I turned on my heel and left the cellblock. Another police guard escorted me down the stairs until I reached the outside.

I hopped on my bicycle and took my time getting back to the office. I needed the fresh air—however stuffy it was—to ponder.

The day had gotten much hotter. A burnt and steamy smell dominated the atmosphere. The ride brought me to the office after a while. I shut myself in to study the investigation report done by the detective hired by the governor of Siem Reap himself.

My heart shattered upon reading the report. Not only had my friend died from a violent crime, but also, according to the report, the police department had already made up its mind about her boyfriend's guilt. All the evidence they found appeared to point to him.

While the final letter, which asked to meet Esmé at the

crime scene, appeared damaging to Mith, I found this evidence circumstantial. He claimed it was not his letter, but that his last letter to her was sent on Thursday. So who sent her that typed letter I saw on Friday morning? I remembered seeing the letter Esmè stuffed into her pocket and the stack of letters she hid in her drawers when she thought I was not looking. If the rape happened Friday evening or night, then it could not have been Mith. Someone else must have led her there. But who?

I was still unsure as to whether or not the mother and son had a role in the rape and now murder of Esmè Laurent. I wanted to go back to the underground tunnel that connected the prince's office to that of Madame Rose's office. I wondered what kind of relationship she and the prince had, and if they talked about my sudden appearance in her office. Would they be able to connect that I was in his office and made my way through their secret tunnel to the brothel? I shuddered to think how much trouble I would be in. Still, I wanted to go back. I need my answer. The tunnel connection intrigued me so much. It did lead me to the brothel, where I found out for sure that the prince had romantic feelings for his own cousin. Considering he often got what he wanted, could Esmè's denial of his love and her attachment to his half-brother have driven him to the edge of raping her and pinning the crime on Mith? But did he even know that Mith was his half-brother, or that his mother killed Mith's mother? What I had found out at Madame Rose's house brought me more questions than answers. There were two other passages I had not explored. I sure would like to know where they went. Those places might lead me to more clues. I wish Father were here so I could ask him. My mind wandered. *What could I possibly find down those passages?*

The Governor's Daughter

The double knock on my door woke me from my deep thoughts. Madame Montha pushed the door and reared her head in. "I don't know what's going on, but Princess Soma Devi is here to see you."

"She is?" I said with excitement. I could feel myself smiling. She was the answer to my prayer. *What do you know? Whenever I think hard about something a light shines my way.* "I hope she can get me into the tunnel again," I said.

"I beg your pardon?" said Madame Montha.

"Oh. Did I say that out loud?"

"What are you up to?"

"Oh, nothing. Let me find out why the princess is here."

"I left her in the conference room."

"Thank you."

As soon as I walked in, she said, "You can do away with the long greeting formality. Let's cut to the chase. I'm glad to see you are in one piece."

"Thank you, princess."

"Tell me what happened. All of it!"

"Before I tell, do you mind telling me what happened while I disappeared?"

"It was a close call. My nephew was looking around. He had a feeling that someone was in his room. I told him there was no else but me. He looked at his desk and bookshelves as if someone touched something. Something felt out of place to him."

"Was that him who tried to follow me to the secret room?"

"Secret room? What secret room? Was that where you had disappeared to? That was my brother's Prince Dara Vong's office before his son, my nephew, took over."

"So he doesn't know anything about the secret room that leads to the..."

"You must tell me all about this secret room."

"Are you sure he doesn't know anything about it? Then who was it chasing after me?" My heart started to beat uncontrollably. "There was someone else in that room."

"What? I am positively sure that he doesn't know anything about the secret room, otherwise he would have gone after you. I decided to stay all afternoon with him. The next morning, I went to see him. I asked his maid how much time he spends in that office library of his. She told me he hardly ever stayed there."

"Does she see him come in and out of his office?"

"She assures me so. But tell me about this secret room. You have me on the edge of my seat here."

I caught her up on what happened to me when I was in the secret room.

"So it leads to the brothel house?" she asked.

"Yes. I only went there due to the misleading sign. It said Sacred Space. How was I supposed to know that a woman's private area is known as such."

"Oh, you're so young. I forget that since you're grown up and wise in other areas. We all know what a sacred place is. My goodness, didn't your mother teach you that? Why do you suppose elder women tell you to save yourself for that special man?"

According to the book I picked up, it meant more than that. I wished I had gotten to read it more before Madame Rose interrupted me.

The princess let out a hysterical laugh. She clapped her palms together and placed it over her mouth while still laughing. "I can't wait to tell your aunt all about this. Speaking of the place, can you take me there? I want to see it for myself. Since we know where one of the tunnels leads to, I am curious to know where the other two tunnels lead. I

The Governor's Daughter

wonder if Father knows anything about it. My brother must have known about the underground as it was bestowed to him by our eldest uncle who passed away when we were young."

"I am as intrigued as you are. However, are you sure that Prince Phirun doesn't know anything about the place?"

"I can assure you. According to his maid, he has not touched that typewriter since it was presented to him as a gift, let alone does he spend time in that office reading or studying. She would not dare to lie to me. Besides, have you met my nephew? He isn't the studious kind. The library office is a complete a waste on him."

"Then someone else must have been in that office and used the typewriter. And that someone probably knew about the secret rooms and the secret tunnel."

"This is scary and fascinating. To think a stranger was among us, in our own home, is frightful. Now you must really get to the bottom of this."

"I need to speak to his maid."

"You don't need to. You would only be wasting your time. But if you must, I am throwing a fancy party to help you with your investigation. I am practically inviting all the movers and shakers in this town."

"You would do this for me?"

"You aunt is right. You do have a big head."

I gave her a blank look.

"I'm just teasing. This will be a win-win for all of us. You can find your suspect and I will gain a handsome, intelligent, and a morally good nephew.

"Your highness, if you don't mind me asking, in light of what happened, you still want to throw a fancy party?" I asked her.

"I know. It's inappropriate. However, it had already been

planned before all this happened. I'll address the situation. I'll think of something appropriate to say and keep it light," said Princess Soma.

---

*P*rincess Nakry and her son, Prince Phirun, had been to the Laurent's house three times a week. Could the mother and son have seen the activities of Esmè? The son could be acting alone or his mother could be helping him. I pulled out the paper with the sample typed letters that I typed using Prince Phirun's typewriter. I did not have access to those love letters, especially the last letter the governor's daughter received. It would be great if I could make the comparison. I must find another angle. I sat at my desk with one hand propped against my cheek and the other tapping a pencil against my side chin. My mind went to work, calculating what I had gathered and seen.

Right then, I knew I needed to find out how Esmé had been receiving those letters from Mith. There must have been a messenger. So who delivered that last letter? I was sure she had just received it that Friday morning. That was why she was so happy. The person who wrote the letter invited her to the place of significance for her and Mith, so the culprit definitely knew a lot about them. The mother and son knew about their relationship. Princess Nakry even made comments about how Princess Dhana allowed her daughter to socialize with peasants, though she could have been talking about me. If Detective Chea and lawyer Nuon were asking Mith this question, then I could help them out by inquiring about the messenger.

I stuffed my copy of the report in a folder and then into my satchel bag. I told Madame Montha I was going to question some people regarding the cases I was working on. She suggested I take a driver with me, just to have someone with me.

"It's not dangerous where I'm going," I said. "I can take my bicycle."

"I'd feel much better if you had a companion."

"Please. You sound like my mother."

"Is that a bad thing?"

"Yes. You both worry too much. And over nothing! How am I going to strengthen my wings if both of you don't let me learn how to fly on my own?"

"We care, that's all."

"I appreciate that. Thank you."

"Just be careful. Do you hear?" she yelled out after me as I rushed out the door.

"I'll be fine," I said without turning back.

There she stood among the crowd of people with a full basket in her arm as if she did not know where to go next. She was dressed in her mourning clothes of a black blouse and *sampot*. Her eyes were sad and puffy. I knew I could find her here in the upper market at this time. I parked and locked up my bike on the other side of the building and walked back to where she was standing. After looking around to make sure no one was paying any special attention to her or me, I stealthily walked up to her.

"Mademoiselle Kolap."

She turned around and practically jumped upon seeing me. She looked around as if to check for suspicious faces. She led me away from the crowd to one of the quiet alleyways. She spoke to me in a hoarse whisper.

"What are you doing here? I'm not supposed to be anywhere near you. If the governor and his men find out I'll..."

"Don't worry. I'll be quick about it. I'm wondering if I can ask you a few questions about your mistress."

She broke down and wept. "My poor mistress! My beautiful mistress. How could anyone do that to her?"

"Please, Mademoiselle Kolap. Can you tell me who had been acting as the messenger between Mith and Mademoiselle Esmé?"

"It's my fault. It's all my fault." She pulled out her handkerchief from her pocket and began to sob heavily into it.

"I'm sure it's not your fault." I put my hand on her arm, trying to calm her down.

"I was their messenger."

"You were? Then you are closer to this than anyone else."

"Yes. The governor fired me over it."

"He did?"

Upon seeing my furrowed eyebrows, she continued to explain herself. "He did, but the princess intervened. She told him it was not my fault. She said I was her daughter's maid and I could not help but follow her orders. She's a very fair lady. She's a great woman. She keeps me even though my mistress is no longer alive. She knows I'm an orphan. I don't know anyone. The Laurents are the only family I know, which is why I feel so ashamed of myself. I let my mistress down. I let everyone in the Laurent family down."

"When did you last see your mistress?"

"I've already told this to the investigator," she said.

"I just wanted to confirm what you told him."

"I saw her last Friday afternoon after your visit. Before dinner," she said.

"So you delivered all the messages from Mith, correct?"

"Yes."

"Even the last one, from before she disappeared—the one from Friday morning?"

"Y...no. No. The last message I delivered to Mistress Esmé was Thursday when...when the princess caught me. She scolded me and told me to stop. Out of respect I did. Oh my lord. So there was a message delivered to her on Friday? I don't know anything about that. But how? I was with her most of the time."

Her story matched with Mith's. He said the last letter he sent her was on Thursday.

"Normally, how did you receive and send messages between Mith and your mistress?"

"He would send a boy to meet me at the town square."

"The same boy or a different boy each time?"

"The same boy. He would run and play with other boys in the town square. I would walk by, pretending to buy something from the street vendor, and he would run by and drop a sealed note in my basket. Whenever the mistress had a message and the boy was not around at the time, I was to go grocery shopping and would leave it under a heart-shaped rock at the foot of an ancestral house at Reamker Park for Mith to pick up. He prayed for their love to succeed."

"Who's this boy? What's his name? What does he look like?"

"I...I do not know. He is thin, has brown skin and round eyes, straight hair, and stands at just about my chest." She described the majority of Khmer boys in the area.

"What's his name?"

"He goes by Vichet."

"What about his surname? What are his parents' names?" In Khmer society, people knew who was who by knowing parents' names or grandparents' even. If I knew his parents I could easily trace his village and his house.

"I'm sorry. I don't know."

"Do you recall him playing with any specific kids at the town square? And did you happen to catch their names as well?"

"No. I did not pay attention."

"Was he with the same group of boys?"

"No, I don't think so."

"All right. Can you remember anything about Vichet that stands out from the rest of the boys of Siem Reap?"

"I don't know. I didn't get a good look at him. He's a typical boy."

"Please think back to all those times you received and sent a letter through him."

She took a long pause as her eyes stared into nothingness "Yes. As a matter of fact there is."

"What is it?"

"He has a fresh injury on his right ankle." She began to make faces and shook her body in disgust as the memory came to her mind. "His skin, a flap of his skin, could be seen hanging loose through a glob of herbal leaves that was slapped on his ankle. It looked as if it had been ripped by something. Oh my goodness. That poor boy. But I did not think too much of it because if Mith saw him, he would patch him up."

"Hmm. He probably got injured while learning how to ride a bicycle."

"How do you know?"

"I had the same injury when I was about his age." I pointed to my ankle.

"Your scar is barely noticeable."

"Yes. A good doctor can do that."

"Mith is a good doctor." She started to cry into her handkerchief again. "My mistress said he could mend a broken bone with his magic hands."

We both heard voices calling out her name, one of which sounded like the head maid. Mademoiselle Kolap's panic-stricken face incited me to do something fast.

"Please calm yourself," I said. "Goodbye, and thank you for your help. You stay here, and I'll run out that way." I skipped to the opposite direction of the alleyway, where I had parked my bicycle.

Just as I got out of her sight, I heard the head maid ask, "What are you doing here in the alleyway?"

"I'm sorry, Mademoiselle Sari. I saw something that reminded me of the young mistress. I did not want people to see me weep, so I came here for a private moment to myself."

I smiled as I walked away. I knew she would not tell anyone about our encounter or our discussion. Considering that I had a lead now, I needed to find the boy who acted as the other messenger, Vichet.

"Are you looking for a pedicab, mademoiselle?" asked a middle-aged man.

"No. I have my bicycle. Thank you, uncle."

I found myself, sitting on my parked bicycle, in the middle of the town square where a statue of two French soldiers, in all their glory, stood on top of a round pillar, holding their rifles while carved images of Khmer monks and people who were half dressed bowed to them. The statue was to remind us that France acted in our best interests to protect us and to save us from the iron claws of Annam and Siam. The French had these statues erected throughout the country. Every chance they could, they reminded us that if it were not for them, we would not have any kingdom left. And we, as a people, would cease to exist. But I digress. My mind tended to wander.

I walked my bicycle around. My eyes scanned the square where boys ran around playing freely without a care in the world—rolling wheels, shooting marbles, spinning tops, and kicking *seys* (shuttlecocks or featherballs). Pin Peat music could be heard from the nearby town hall, as could monks chanting from nearby pagodas. Excitement filled the air. Children's laughter and adult chatter surrounded me. Everything appeared happy and lively in the outside world, but a cloud of darkness hovered over my family and me. I could not begin to fathom what it must have been like for the Laurents and the Sovanns. But the weight of the matter rested on us, Chinak & Associates and lawyer Bora Nuon, to find out the truth. I would do whatever I could to help. First, I had to find that boy named Vichet.

A boy bumped into me. "Pardon me, mademoiselle."

Before he walked past me I asked, "Young brother, may I ask you a question?"

"Sure."

"Do you know a boy named Vichet?"

He gave me a puzzled look. "I'm sorry, I don't know anyone by that name."

"That's okay. Thanks anyway."

"Sure thing." He ran off to play with his friends.

I stood around, observing people playing and going about their business around the town square. I wondered to myself if I should go around and randomly ask these boys if they knew a kid named Vichet, but reasoned it would not be a good use of my time. There were too many of them. Then I thought about going by the nearby pagodas to see if any worshippers had a son named Vichet with a bad wound on his ankle. Surely the monks and laymen there could shed some light on this mystery boy. Before I walked over to one of the pagodas, I looked around the town square for the last time to figure out who would have encountered and played with Vichet. I walked over to the street vendors where Mademoiselle Kolap would have been standing around and pretending to buy something. From that distance, I looked to the groups of boys playing around in that area. They looked so happy and free. A boy of six or seven caught my attention. He had on black shorts and white, short-sleeved shirt. He had curly hair and thin lips. His bright, dark round eyes met mine. He left his one friend to walk over in my direction. I stood still, waiting for his arrival.

"Bonjour, mademoiselle," he said in French.

"Hi," I said to him in Khmer. "What's your name?"

"Nak."

"Nak. Who are your parents?"

"I'm the third son of Pheap and Ran."

"Well, Nak, son of Pheap and Ran, it's nice to meet you. I'm Anjali."

"Anjali Chinak, the daughter of the great detective Oum Chum Chinak!" His eyes grew wide. "Wow. I can't believe it."

"You know who we are?"

"Who doesn't?"

"Interesting."

"I noticed you were looking for someone."

"As a matter of fact, I am." I had the feeling he was about to tell me something I wanted to hear.

"Are you looking for Vichet?"

"Yes. Yes, I am," I said with enthusiasm. "Do you know him?"

"Well," he said, scratching his head, "I don't actually know him. I don't believe he is from around here. But I used to see him around, playing with those kids over there. Then all of sudden he disappeared."

"Really?"

"Yes. I remember he was a nice kid."

"How so?"

"Other boys were being mean to me, and he was the one to tell them to leave me alone. I admired him for being nice to me. No one is nice to me...well, except for that kid over there. Other kids bully him too. We became good friends. I'm glad you are looking for Vichet."

"How do you know I am looking for him?"

"Well, you were craning your neck and your eyes were scanning at boys only. And he has not been around for a few days now, so I just assumed...well, I was hoping you were looking for him."

"You're very observant."

"Plus, I'm too afraid to ask those boys where he is because they were the ones who bullied me."

"I see. Can you take me to the group of boys you were referring to, the ones who know Vichet?"

He hesitated at first. I extended my hand to him. He led me across the square to a small group of boys. He let go of my hand and stood behind me when we came close to them. The boys let out laughter and obscene noises. They bantered with each other. They were challenging each other to a game of Top, to see who could leave it twirling the longest. One of the boys looked up.

"Can we help you?" he said.

"Oh, look, it's the little baby Nak," another boy said, pointing.

"I'm not a baby," said Nak, lurking behind me.

"Do you boys know Vichet?" I asked.

"Yes, we do. What's it to you?" said the second boy.

"Hey, man. Haven't your parents taught you manners?" said the first boy. He had to be the leader of this pack. "You can't speak to an older person that way. She could be your sister."

I smiled. "I have a pressing matter to talk to Vichet about. Do you know where I could find him?"

"No. He has not been here a few days now, but it is just as well. He no longer fits in with our group."

"Why is that?"

"He has been bragging about making a lot of money as a messenger boy. He used his money to buy a bicycle and other fancy toys. He's too rich for us now. Maybe he thinks he is too good for us. Maybe that's why he has not been coming around here."

"Do you know who his parents are?"

"No."

"What about his village?"

"No. He didn't tell and we didn't ask."

"Do you know anything else that would be helpful to me?"

The boys looked at each other with pensive faces. "He was bragging about how he has been such a good messenger that a Barang—Frenchman—hired him to deliver a message."

"A Frenchman? Are you sure? Did he describe this man?"

"No. You know they all look the same to us."

"I gather they think the same about us. Anyway, do you recall if he is tall? Skinny? Fat? Bald? Straight hair? Curly hair? Brown hair? Yellow hair? Did he give you a name?"

"Mademoiselle, if he did, we would not remember. It would be too foreign for us to pronounce. It's bad enough we have to learn the language of Barang." The boys turned to each other and laughed. "We cannot tell if he is short or tall, thin or fat, because we never saw him. Vichet never described him to us. We're sorry. That's all we know. He said he was not supposed to tell us any of this anyway. The man told him it is a secret. He can keep his secret. We are not interested in any of it." They continued with their game of Top.

Interesting. This changes everything. A foreign person hired Vichet to be a messenger. Does that mean Princess Nakry and Prince Phirun are off the hook? Who could this foreign person be?

"All right. Thank you for your time."

I left the boys and the town square. I proceeded to meander with my bicycle along the neighboring houses and pagodas. I had no idea where I was going nor where I wanted to go. I just kept moving. Many thoughts occupied my mind. Theories emerged, one of which included Andre. He loved Esmé. Her father had promised her to him. But she must have refused him. Men—unlearned and unrestrained men—had a hard time accepting no for an answer. Could he have raped her in a fit of jealousy and rage? Could he have given in to his inner beast? Could his ego not withstand Esmé's rejection and drive him mad?

The boy said a Frenchman hired Vichet to act as a messenger, but since the boy could not tell the difference between one white man and another—French, English, or American—the Englishman Andre still stood as a possibility. Could he have hired Vichet as the messenger? Did he lure Esmé out to the cottage in Beung Mealea? How did he know about their special meeting place? I ended up having more questions than I had before. Whatever the case, I needed tangible evidence. I still needed to find Vichet and then get access to those letters that supposedly proved Mith's guilt. After all, I had only read the cited version.

I came across a big sign that read Reamker Park. Mademoiselle Kolap had said she would leave the message under a heart-shaped rock whenever she did not see the boy. Many ancestor houses were erected in front of many homes. Those were private ancestor houses. There must have been a public one around here somewhere. My eyes caught the golden and orange house erected not far from the statue of Ram from the Hindi Ramayana myth. Tall, ancient trees shrouded over it as if to protect it. I rushed to look for the heart-shaped rock among other rocks of various shapes.

When I found it and looked closer, I saw it was beautifully engraved with the phrase "Mith loves Esmé." A sense of sadness overcame me. I felt hot tears run down my cheeks. I pulled myself together and looked at other rocks and noticed other carvings by those who professed their love to one another. My eyes reverted back to Mith and Esmé's rock. I wondered how Mademoiselle Kolap would have placed Esmé's love letters there. She said she had put it under the rock. I tried to lift it up, but it did not budge. I felt around it. To my great surprise, there was a button. How clever! Mith must have built it himself. I pushed on it and the rock elevated itself. I could not believe it. I wondered if other rocks had the same trick. No. They were simple rocks with simple etchings, unlike that of Mith's and Esmé's. I had always admired his intelligence. The space beneath the rock was empty, to my disappointment. I didn't know why I expected something to be there.

Loud and hysterical screams disrupted my thoughts. I turned around to see women and men, boys and girls running in the direction of the Tonle Sap basin. I pushed the rock back down and got up to walk over to the gathering crowd. Local monks also rushed to the scene.

"Uncle, what's going on?" I asked one of the men outside of the circle.

"A boy drowned," he said. "Poor soul."

"Is he dead?"

"He is," he said sadly.

I decided to take a look for myself. This would be my first dead body in the flesh. I braced myself and made my way through the crowd to get a look. Someone had pulled his body out of the water and placed him on an old reed mat. It was a young boy of five or six years old. He had straight hair. On his right ankle, I could see a shriveled flap of skin. My heart dropped. I almost cried. He must be Vichet, the messenger boy.

How did he end up here? Someone must have closed his eyes for him. I could hear people expressing their sympathy and praying for his soul to be taken to heaven. Meanwhile, others found comfort in praying for him to have a better life in his next reincarnation. I tuned them out and focused on the body even though I was shaking terribly. There was this sense of fear, curiosity, and compassion all wrapped up. I almost felt sick, but I was able to put it all aside, as Madame Montha had taught me. I focused on his body, trying to determine the cause of death.

The boy had no shirt on but he wore new shorts. I recalled Father telling his associate about a case involving a drowning victim. He said in a drowning fatality an autopsy would reveal bruises and ruptured muscles, especially in the shoulders, chest and neck, indicating that the victim was alive in the water at the time of his demise. Something told me his body needed to be autopsied. This was too much of a coincidence. I needed to know if he was already dead when he was placed in the water.

Someone asked, "Whose child is that?" They all looked at each other cluelessly.

"I've seen him around, but I don't know who he is," said a middle-aged female.

"Whoever this child is, we must take him to the temple to provide him a proper prayer and burial," another voice said aloud.

"Look!" said a teenager. "It's the Abbot of Wat Mahapan-chasila. He's bringing the authorities."

I turned around to find an elderly monk rushing to the scene along with, to my greatest relief, the police and Detective Chea.

"Ms. Anjali, what are you doing here?" he asked.

"I...I was on an errand, and I came upon..." My voice rattled. I suddenly realized I was about to burst into tears, but I tried very hard to control my emotions.

"And what are you doing here?" I pretended to ask. He

probably was on the same hunt as me. Mith must have told him about the boy whom he had asked to be his messenger, to corroborate his story.

"I think you should not be here," Detective Chea told me. "Please go home or return to the office. You're much too young to be looking into things like this."

"But what about them?" My eyes scanned the young boys and girls standing close to the body.

"I'll tell them to leave the scene as well."

"Whatever you do, please take his body to be autopsied. I don't believe he drowned. He's very important to Mith's case."

"How do you know? Anjali, have you been sleuthing around on your own?"

"I...I...well." I bounced back as fast as I stuttered. "Can I help now that I know more than you do?"

"We'll talk about it back at the office. I know what we need to do. Now go on." He shooed me off like a pigeon. I hesitantly walked away with my bicycle and hopped on it to ride away as the policeman told the crowd to disperse while they worked the scene.

Before I made my way out of sight, I turned back to see what they were doing. I could see the Abbot, with his palms up to his chest, moving his lips to offer his prayers to the young soul. I walked away feeling empty and angry. Who could have done this to Vichet?

My mind must have been going a hundred and sixty kilometers a minute because I came close to being trampled by a pair of horses at the intersection of Sisowath Quay and Raja Devi Boulevard. I stopped short with my heart in my throat.

"Hey, barbarian girl, watch where you're going!" a man yelled out in English from the window of the small carriage.

I looked up to find the chubby-faced friend of Andre Thomas. It was his American friend, James Albertson. Andre lifted his downcast face. He stared out the window, apparently surprised to see me on my bike in front of their carriage. It was just the two of them. As the hackney rolled away, I continued to eye them and they, me.

15

THE PRIME SUSPECT

The French were careful to protect the status of the king's power and his reign as a means of ensuring order in the kingdom. Thus, at the request of King Sisowath, the French authorities granted Mith his due process. However, it took the head Brahman of Siem Reap to urge the king to make such a request. Otherwise the French would have declared Mith guilty and ordered him to be executed by a firing squad by now. We all knew they would find a way to execute him, but everyone worked steadfastly against time to prove his innocence. We all figured that if the French authorities did not acknowledge our evidence, we would bear witness to the truth and all the people of Siem Reap—indeed, the entire country—would know Mith Sovann was not the rapist and murderer of his beloved Esmé.

I sat in the file room—my temporary office—studying the other side's investigation report and autopsy, of which I secretly made copies. About ten minutes into reviewing and analyzing these reports something struck me: Esmé's injuries were consistent with all the other beautiful Eurasian women from all the other Asian countries. They were all lured by means of love letters to meet at places of significance to them.

"Oh my lord!" I found myself saying out loud. "The serial rapist and killer is in our kingdom!"

My friend Jorani would appreciate this piece of information. If ever the general population of Siem Reap learned that a serial killer used love letters to lure love-stricken and vulnerable young women to their death, they would definitely bar girls from learning how to read and write. As soon as I heard footsteps coming my way, I tucked the homicide reports under the humdrum case files I was supposed to have been working on. Detective Chea still refused to let me officially work on Mith's case.

Madame Montha gave a tap on my door and asked if she could enter.

"Please come in," I said.

She opened the door slowly and looked at the file room with me sitting in it to do my work. "Are you all right?"

"I am. Why?"

"You've been quiet. I'm just checking to see how you are doing," said Madame Montha

"I just wanted to be left alone to dive into my work."

"I understand. I should have known better. You're still upset about your friends. I'm sorry."

"That's okay."

"Everyone is working through lunch. I will be heading out to order something from a street vendor. What would you like?"

"I need to finish up a few things here. Besides, I have interviews with a few witnesses on my cases. I can grab lunch before I head out to see them."

"You can call the driver to take you."

"No. I'll be fine. They are locals." Besides, she knew I didn't go anywhere without my bicycle.

"All right. As you wish." She turned away, then spun her body back to face me. "Anjali."

"Yes," I said, looking up at her.

"Do not overwork yourself. And do not think too much. Everyone is doing their best. Everything will be fine in the end. You will see." I had no idea if she was lying to me or herself.

Nevertheless, I said, "I know. Thank you." She looked at me one last time before she exited. She closed the door behind her.

I returned to the investigation report on Esmé's death. The similarities of her rape and death to the victims of the other Eurasian women jumped out at me. Based on their photographs, they were all stunning Eurasian women, they were lured to places that meant something to them, and according to their autopsy reports, some died from "a ruptured bladder, complicated by acute peritonitis" and others just from the ruptured bladder. I was not sure what all that meant. The reports pointed to a foreign object that caused the bladder to explode. I wrote everything down in my notebook. I needed a doctor who was not on the governor's payroll to help me decipher all of this medical jargon.

Dr. Nat Lim sprung to mind. He was my neighbor who lived three houses east of my house and who attended to my driver Suon's injury when the governor and his henchmen wreaked havoc at my home. Dr. Lim could explain to me what all these medical terms meant. I needed him to explain to me how a bladder could be ruptured. How would a foreign object do such a thing?

I made a call to his office. A woman with a sultry voice

answered. She informed me that he had gone out to lunch. I think I knew where he could be. His mother, who often talked to my mother, packed his lunch every day. They were frugal people. On several occasions I had seen him sitting by the Tonle Sap basin to eat his lunch while staring engagingly across the basin where the street vendors set up.

I stuffed all my notes and copies of the reports into my satchel and ran out the door. I almost knocked down one of Father's detectives, nearly causing the files in his hand to fly across the room.

"Where are you off to, Mademoiselle Anjali?"

"I'm sorry. I can't talk. I must attend to my duty." I sensed he was shaking his head in amusement as he continued perusing his files.

There sat Dr. Lim on a wooden bench in a peaceful garden by the basin of Tonle Sap, munching on his lunch—just where I suspected he would be. The sallow-faced, thirty-year-old man had fallen madly in love with a young Chinese woman whose parents had immigrated to Cambodge during their country's revolution of 1911. In a little stall across the basin she sold fruits and vegetables that she bought cheaply from farmers in the countryside. Too afraid to express his feelings or ask his parents to seek her hand in marriage, he would come to this very spot during his free time to admire her from afar.

"What are you doing, Dr. Lim?"

The Governor's Daughter

He nearly jumped from the bench. "Oh, Anjali. I'm just enjoying my lunch outside."

"I bet."

"Whatever do you mean?"

"Oh, nothing."

"What are you doing on this side of town?" he said as his gaze shifted from across the basin to me.

"I need your help."

"Does it have anything to do with your friends?"

"Yes."

"I'm sorry to hear about what happened to them, but if you do not mind, I don't want to get involved. If the governor finds out, my business would be in ruins. It's a small practice as it is, and I do not want..."

"If you are truly sorry about my friend's death then you should help me. You would not be involved per se. I just need your medical expertise on a matter for me to pursue a lead."

"You're much too young to involve yourself in this. Besides, you're...you're a..."

"What? A girl?"

"Um. I understand from your mother that you are not supposed to be working on dangerous cases."

"Well. Actually..."

"Just as I thought. Whatever you have on the matter you should tell your father's senior detective."

"Who? Detective Chea?"

He nodded.

"I can't at the moment. I need to pursue it on my own. Please don't tell anyone. Please. Will you help me?"

"I don't want to get into trouble with your father or mother. Or the governor, for that matter."

"Oh, don't make me taunt you with a white feather.

Have courage and help me. They will not find out. The governor would not find out about it either."

"I don't feel right about this."

"Please. Do you not want me to solve the rape and murder of a fellow human being? Are you not in the business of taking care of people's health and saving their lives?"

"You're walking into dangerous territory here. From what I hear, even the higher-ups are not sure they will solve this, and if they do, it's not likely they will set Mith free."

"Must you be negative? I promise no one will know. I just need some confirmation. I'll owe you. Maybe I can return the favor when everything is clear." I looked over across the basin at a pretty young light-skinned woman with small eyes who appeared to be a few years older than me.

Dr. Lim stood with one hand on his hip and with the other he dug into his wavy hair, revealing his embarrassment. "I don't know what you are referring to."

"It's obvious how you feel about Sopheap Meng." Some Chinese immigrants, like her parents, chose to name their children in Khmer to assimilate into our society. Hence, they named her Sopheap, likening her to the feminine quality of gentleness.

"Obvious?" he said, glancing about like a man caught with his hand in a cookie jar. I did not want to tease him too much more.

"So can you help me?"

"All right. What do you have for me?" We both sat down on the bench. I pulled out the report from my folder and handed it to him.

"Here it is. Please turn to page seven and read this part about the foreign object. A few reports say the victims died of a ruptured bladder, complicated by acute peritonitis, but most simply say these victims died as a result of a ruptured bladder. What does acute peritonitis mean?"

"I haven't seen many cases involving peritonitis or a ruptured bladder, but according to medical textbooks, peritonitis is inflammation of a silk-like membrane that lines your inner abdominal wall and covers the organs within your abdomen. The inflammation is usually due to a bacterial or fungal infection."

"Infection, huh?"

"Yes."

"Can a violent rape cause that bacterial infection?"

He looked uncomfortable with the subject matter, as a young woman like me should not be discussing delicate matters such as this with a man. But he would have to get over it. I was trying to solve a murder...*multiple* murders. "It could," he answered.

"Can a foreign object rupture a person's bladder?"

"Yes, it's possible."

"However, they never found this foreign object."

"Hmm. Bladders don't just rupture like a balloon."

"So what else can cause a bladder to explode?"

"Well. Illness..."

"Illness? What kind of illness?"

"Illness that prevents a person from urinating."

"Hmm. We can rule that out. Unless—"

"Other causes of a ruptured bladder are an overindulgence of alcohol, a vehicle accident, a fall, or a strong kick in the gut or other assault."

"Um...so a good amount of force must be involved, right?"

"Right."

"What about a massive weight? Say, for instance, a one hundred and forty kilogram man?"

"I suppose," he said, scratching his head. "What are you getting at?"

Suddenly, an image of a heavy-set man grinding Esmé to a pulp with his large body while her bloodcurdling scream echoed from the abandoned cottage through the forest village of Beung Mealea set my body shivering in fear and disgust. I nearly screamed right then and there myself.

"What's wrong?" Dr. Lim asked.

"I've figured it out. I know who the killer is."

"What? Who is it?"

"I can't tell you now. I have to prove it first. Thank you, Dr. Lim. I greatly appreciate it."

I gathered the reports and my notes to put back in my satchel.

I rode back to town, buoyant with my discovery. I made it back to our office building at 777 Nokor Boulevard. I parked my bicycle on the sidewalk next to a line of trees with benches encircled around them. Before I entered the office, I decided to cross over to the cafe across from us that was flanked by a shop that sold French wine on the left and shop that sold sweets on the right. Mostly high-class Asians and Europeans frequented shops in this area. I looked around, observing the shop's patrons. They all seemed occupied with their personal affairs. Lonely ones just sipped their tea or coffee and stared into nothingness. No one familiar to me came. "Well, hello, Anjali. What can I get you today?" asked the cheerful son of the cafe's owner.

"Hello, Voeun. I would like some hot tea and butter cookies, please."

"Sure." He yelled out my order to his staff. "Would you like to sit inside or outside?" Since not too many people were sitting inside, I chose to sit inside, hoping to have some privacy and to ask Voeun some questions. Considering foreigners frequented this place and he liked listening to people gossip, he might know something.

"May I ask you a few questions?"

"Sure," said Voeun.

"Can you keep it between us?"

"Is this related to Madame Chantha's heirloom?"

"Oh my goodness! Does everyone know about her missing heirloom?" I said.

"It's a small town. Women gossip."

I gave him a disapproving look. "Anyway, do you know the English gentleman who happens to be good friends with the governor?"

"Oh, the governor," he said, clicking his tongue and shaking his head. "It's a shame what happened to his daughter."

"Yes. Do..."

"She was such a beautiful, elegant, and sweet young woman. I just saw her the other day and now she's gone. It's as if she was a figment of my imagination...such a beautiful and poised young woman. I heard that no good peasant..."

"Watch it," I said to him, giving him a sharp look. Realizing that he offended my peasant background, he backed off.

"I'm sorry. It's just that...that she should have not associated herself with him."

"Why is that?"

"Do any of us really know who he is? I mean, come on. All of a sudden he appears in our town. Who is he? What is he? How does a peasant like him have money to study in the most prestigious school in Paris? Where did he get all that money? Here he is, waltzing into our town and acting like he is somebody special. All the girls were swooning over him, and he thinks he can reach for the governor's daughter. Her father saw through him and he would not let him near his beautiful and fair Esmè. I totally agree with him."

Somebody sure sounded jealous. "How do you know all of this?" I asked.

"People talk," he said.

"Of course. People talk and you listen, huh? Can we get back to my question?"

"Are you investigating her death? Are you trying to clear his name?"

"No. I'm not working on this case."

"You shouldn't anyway because you would be too biased. After all, he's a family friend, is he not?"

"We don't operate like that. Besides, you know my parents don't allow me to work on dangerous or homicide cases."

"Good. What is it you want to know? Oh, yes, that's right, the English gentleman who hangs around the governor. He is not good for Esmè either. He's too leggy, thin, and sickly looking."

"No one is good enough for her, huh?"

"She's your friend. Of all people, you should be pickier for her."

"You would be the perfect man for her, right?"

"Wait a minute. If you are not working on the case then why are you asking about someone the governor knows?"

"Trust me. It's not related to Esmè's case," I said. He furrowed his eyebrows at me. "Now, about the English gentleman. Do you see him around here often?" I continued.

"He came here a few times," he replied. "But he mostly hangs out at the tavern around the corner more. You know how Europeans like their wines."

"During those times you saw him. Did you see him alone or with a companion?"

"Sometimes alone, sometimes with different companions."

"Were they..."

"They were white men. Scratch that. I did see him and his fat friend. I think he's American. They both speak English but with different accents. Anyway, I saw them with those loose Asian women."

Voeun was judgmental and opinionated. But he was giving me a lot of information, so I let him be. "Do you happen to know their names?"

"I do. They receive phone calls here sometime. Also, when one shows up first he would say, 'Please tell Andre Thomas I am next door getting some sweets,' or, 'Please tell James Albertson I am heading around the corner to grab some cigars.' You know, stuff like that. That's how I learn their names."

"Interesting. Do you recognize any of those so-called loose women?"

"I think one of them is a cousin—probably a distant cousin—of one of those royal lineages. I think Soryavong. Ah, yes, the Soryavong lineage. I think her name is Bopha Soryavong."

"I see," I said as information and more questions floated in my head.

"Why?"

"Hmm?"

"Why do you ask about these foreign men?"

"I rather not say."

"You're up to something, aren't you?"

"Oh look, my tea and butter cookies are here." A waiter placed my teapot, cup, and cookies before me.

"I know you're up to something."

"Am I that transparent?"

"All I know is stealth is not your strongest suit," he said in a singing voice before he walked over to attend to a patron who flagged him down.

With my fingers tapping my barely noticeable dimpled chin, I thought about one of the acquaintances of the governor. He now had become my prime suspect. However, I needed to prove it. I need to move on it before it was too late. In fact, I had been mulling over for some time now that I needed to see the crime scene: Sok San's Cottage. I heard so much about it. The governor's men found Esmè on the main road of Beung Mealea village. I wondered how far from the cottage they had found her and if they picked clean the place yet of any evidence of the perpetrator. Secondly, I did not know how she got there in the first place. Could she have sought out a cyclo driver or did her personal driver take her there? I needed to question her driver. But first, I needed to get to the crime scene. Maybe I would know how she got there from looking at the scene and then I wouldn't need to talk to the driver after all.

After I was done having my afternoon tea, I crossed the street and walked over to my bicycle to bring it inside. I love my means of transportation. It was liberating to ride it. It took me where I wanted to go and where I wanted to be. I would eventually upgrade to a car, but for now, my bike was my freedom. Strangely, someone had placed something on the cargo rack of my bicycle. I removed a large rock that sat on top of a white envelope. I picked it up and noticed my name written with nice penmanship: *Mademoiselle Anjali Chinak*. I turned around every which way to look for the person who had left the letter. The streets were bustling with people from all walks of life. The sounds of chatter and transportation filled the hot and humid air. Western men with their top hats and women with their lacy white umbrellas and fans complained about the scorching temperature while other Khmers, in their *kben* and *sampot*, haggled over the prices of goods with local vendors. No one suspicious popped out at me. I glanced over to the cafe. Nothing appeared to be out of the ordinary. I opened the letter right away. It was written in English.

Dear Miss Anjali Chinak,

We have met on a few occasions, but regrettably, we never spoke. I hope this letter will change this awkwardness between us. My name is Andre Thomas. I am a friend of the Laurents. My father did business with the governor and he has been looking out for me during my trips to Asia.

I regret I am not able to write this letter in a happy spirit. I am sure you understand why. You and I share a friendship with a gentle soul, the fair maiden Miss Esmé Laurent. I am sure you know how much I loved and adored her. Regrettably, the feeling was not mutual.

You probably think I blame your friend Mith Sovann for the violation of her body. At first, I thought he did it, but now, it could not be further from the truth. I have come across ample evidence that says otherwise.

I know the authorities will not look for the culprit because the governor wholeheartedly believes your friend Mith is the person who committed this barbaric crime against his only daughter. I understand that while your father is working on unsolved rape and murder cases from Burma, Laos, Siam, and Annam, his detectives are working feverishly to prove Mith's innocence in this high-profile rape and murder in Cambodge of the governor's daughter. I know you want to help him as well.

As a person who believes in truth, honor, and morality, I

cannot sit idly by and let the real killer of my beloved Esmé go free—regardless of the fact that she never showed the slightest interest in me.

The governor has not looked into this new evidence. He has even tossed certain pieces into the trash. He nearly threw me out of his house for suggesting someone else was responsible for the death of my beloved Esmé, the most beautiful maiden I have ever seen.

The governor is like a father to me. Surely you understand I cannot openly defy him. Hence, I am writing you this letter. I know who the killer is. I regret ever considering him a friend.

You have probably figured out who he is too. I noticed a scratch on his left wrist and when I asked what happened, he said a prostitute was playing rough. Furthermore, he lost his engraved eighteen carat gold pocket watch. I know he is a rambling drunk, so naturally, I indulged him with plenty of alcohol. Of course, as expected, his drunken rambling revealed he lured Esmé to the cottage in Beung Mealea. He took her to the smallest room on the second floor, and probably lost the watch there. I am sure you will find it since the other investigators did not.

Also, I know the killer shall not go there ever again. A clever murderer like him tends to not return to the scene of a crime. I can assure you he has moved on and is scouting for his next victim. Before it is too late, you must do whatever you can to remove this person from civilized society. Lock him up and throw away the key. I have handed you the evidence—it is up to you to seize it.

I am sure you know the place to which I am referring, Miss Anjali.

Sincerely,
Andre Thomas

P. S. I hope to make your acquaintance again, and then we shall properly speak.

"Sok San's Cottage," I said aloud. "I must go there." I was hoping the letter would offer more clues about the person I suspected of raping and killing Esmé, but it divulged no such thing. Though the letter was too good to be true, something did not add up.

16

THE SERIAL KILLER

I have the tendency to act on impulse. This time was no different. Before I could put any more thought into it, I found myself pedaling like a maniac, hoping to get to my destination to do my sleuthing and make it back home before the sun went down. I took a peak of the map my father's associate drew of the location of the area, so I knew how to get to Beung Mealea and Sok San's Cottage. Therefore, I would not be wasting precious time. I did not believe Detective Chea and his team had ventured there yet, so that was another reason why I needed to get there first. I pedaled out of the city of Siem Reap, past rice fields as far as the eyes could see, before I came to a forested area. I turned onto the road where the governor's men supposedly found Esmè. Upon entering it, I kept my eyes peeled for any evidence that would help me with the case. I could see footprints and tire impressions, which I committed to my memory for later usage. I veered off the main road and went along a dirt road until I came across an abandoned wooden house, larger than the others. The three-cornered house on stilts had a corrugated clay roof that was wrapped in vines. Wild trees grew all through and around it. Grass and weeds grew as high as my knees. Within a stone's throw there stood more dilapidated and abandoned houses that once made up this village called Beung Mealea. Gone were the chatter, the laughter, and the energetic spirits of the people who had lived here. It had become a ghost town, its houses withering away through time. Only the sounds of birds and other wild animals could be heard.

It was in much better condition than I expected. The two-level stone cottage, with its big glass windows, chimney, and limestone exterior walls, had the look of a medieval French structure. Not that I had been there, but I had heard and read enough about the French countryside. The prince had exquisite French taste. It was not surprising that he shared his good fortune, experience, and taste for all things French with his lover.

I turned on my flashlight by pushing the switch to the first click with my thumb. I stepped with one foot inside the creaking wooden door full of cracks and chipped paint. Before I made my way inside, I looked outside into the forest to make sure no one had followed me. If I took into account what Andre Thomas had said in the letter, I figured I would run up the stairs to the smallest room to find the gold pocket watch and then pedal my bike back to town. Then I realized that if I removed the watch, no one would believe I found it there. Somehow I let this logic slip away from me as I rushed to the cottage.

Red-orange light from the setting sun glimmered around the high ceiling. I shined my flashlight back and forth to check out the darkening interior. Curtainless, arched glass windows with worn out white paint on their frames surrounded me. The walls appeared to be all cracked, chipped, and peeling. The entrance door opened to a wide, open-spaced foyer where a wooden staircase started in the middle of the room and curved to the landing on the right. Though covered with dust and cobwebs, it remained beautiful and intact.

The first floor consisted of rooms and a hallway stretching to the back, and I wished I had time to explore this cottage as it intrigued me with all its glory, tragedy, and mystery. But the letter specifically stated that the perpetrator had attacked Esmé on the second floor.

Though the evening light glowed through the windows from the west side of the building, I left my flashlight on to help guide me. As I set foot on the first step, it squeaked. I stopped myself and shined my flashlight down to the wooden steps, thinking that mites might have chewed on the stairs. Looks could be deceiving. I slowly tested out the sturdiness of each stair. I continued to step up slowly and softly like a cat, hoping I wouldn't fall through the rotten or broken staircase. I smelled dampness and mildew throughout the cottage. It stank like dried cow dung due to the lack of fresh air. The squeaking of the stairs and some strange rattling in the walls spooked me. Fear and doubt began to gnaw at me, but I told myself to focus and not be scared. This cottage had been abandoned for many years, so squeaks and rattles were expected.

I arrived on the landing of the second floor more quickly than I expected. The elongated landing encircled the top floor, with many rooms all around it. I could not see clearly through the darkness but the house seemed to have more rooms than I anticipated. I did not understand why the prince had built a house in such a way. Perhaps it was to confuse intruders. The prince must have entertained many of his closest friends and trusted soldiers here. I wondered how many times Father had been to this place. What must it have been like during its heyday, furnished with fancy furniture and curtains? There must have been plenty of entertainment when the prince occupied this space with his darling.

But during this critical moment, these rooms presented a challenge to me. I had no way of knowing which was the smallest one without looking inside each one. I started out by opening the door to the first room on the right, across from the stairs leading up to the landing. I scanned it with my flashlight to take in the size of the room. Its emptiness haunted me. I made my way to the next room on the right, then the next room, and then more until I almost made my way back to the staircase. They were all bigger than the first room and had been picked clean. Like other areas of the house, only dust and cobwebs covered and frosted the rooms.

I walked back to the hallway. I stood with my flashlight pointing in every direction. I studied the layout. The landing gave access to the entire second floor. There were only two more rooms to peek into, but something caught my eye. I had not noticed it before. One of the corners of the left-hand side had a hallway that possibly led to other rooms.

At the same time, I wondered why the killer chose to take Esmé to the smallest room on the second floor. Was it so that she could not escape due to the tight space? Another nagging question emerged. I wracked my brains to understand why Andre Thomas had sent me that letter. He had never acknowledged me before. Would he have remembered me as Esmé's friend? Furthermore, why couldn't he just go to the authorities himself? My heart raced. My nerves consumed me. Maybe it was not Andre Thomas who sent the letter. Clarity started to set in. Suddenly a tidal wave of anxiety swept through me.

"I've been had!" I said aloud. I tried to dash to the staircase but heard a door swing open and thumping footsteps rushing out from one of the first rooms of the hallway on the left. A massive body blocked me from making it to the staircase, so close yet so far. I pointed my flashlight at the person's face.

"It's you!" I blurted out. My body froze.

"That's right," said the voice of James Albertson, that menacing and burly man. He squinted as he covered his eyes to block the flashlight's beam with his left hand. "You should have trusted your instincts, but here you are. I could not be happier. That was the plan all along—to get you here. I understand you are one curious young girl, but I can't believe how easy it was. I thought you would be more careful. I guess curiosity got the best of you. Little girl, you should never stick your nose where it does not belong. But hey, I am not complaining. It has worked out in my favor."

My heart raced, beating like a drum with my understanding how dire my situation had become. *This must be how a rabbit feels when cornered by a cobra.* My stomach twisted in knots. My mind whirled as my eyes scanned left and right, looking for a way out. I gripped my flashlight tightly and kept on shining it at the man's face. It occurred to me I could knock him on the head with it, but then it was already too late as he pulled out a handgun from his waist and pointed it at me. His fat finger was ready to pull the trigger. My knees went weak and my right hand went so limp that I needed to hold my flashlight with both hands. I still intended to swing it at him.

"Don't get any funny ideas, little girl."

My natural instinct was to raise my hands to let him know that I would not attempt any mischief. But my survival instinct told me to fight—a risk that might cost me my life.

He brought down his left arm as his eyes adjusted to the bright light. In his right hand he held the gun aimed at me, ready to shoot. He laughed an evil laugh, made a tongue-smacking sound, and said, "You girls are all alike. You are just one curious bunch, and easily tempted, I might add. One sweet word and I can lure you anywhere. Is it worth the risk—the risk of being raped and murdered—to satisfy your curiosity? Huh, Anjali Chinak?" He waved his gun up and down at me with a menacing look on his fat face. "Since you've come all this way for me, I should have a little fun with you before I send you to your death." He laughed again, a maniacal laugh. "Hmm. I admit, I never had a girl like you before." He began to leer at me, up and down. "You know what? You are not bad looking. Not bad at all. In fact, you're as attractive as those half-breeds. Too bad you are not going to live past your teenage years. It's no one's fault but your own."

I realized my flashlight was no match for his revolver, but my will to live had grown so strong that I was ready to fight him. I figured it was time to put all those self-defense classes Father had paid for to the test. I thought about distracting him by hitting him in the head with my flashlight, twisting his wrist and wrestling for his gun, and kicking him in his groin with all my might. Then when he was stunned I would push him off the second-floor landing. I knew that the rail right behind him could never support his weight. Then the naysayer in me kicked in as I stared at his thick and meaty arms.

"I know what you are thinking. My victims, they all tried

to escape. There is no way you will survive this. I made a mistake with Esmé by letting her live briefly, but I will not make that mistake with you. I will make sure you will die with no trace of my involvement."

"Why?" I asked.

"Why?" he repeated my question.

"Why are you doing this?" I asked, trying to buy some time. I wanted to do something, but had no idea what yet.

"You girls ask the same question. 'Why are you doing this to poor little old me?'" he mocked in a woman's voice. "Perfectly understandable. I guess I can grant you your last dying wish as I generously obliged the other women before they died their appropriate deaths." He laughed, as though his victims deserved to be mocked and ridiculed.

I realized he had a narcissistic nature. Sure, he tried not to leave clues that might get him caught, but I had a feeling he was dying to tell someone about his nefarious adventures. He seemed to enjoy it. While he bragged, my mind went to work to measure the room and the distance between where I stood and the staircase. I would shatter my bones if I decided to jump from the landing. There would be nothing there to break my fall.

Meanwhile, he was holding the gun steady with his hand, pointing it at me. I measured my agility against his slow reflexes. I was but several steps away from the stairs. I needed to make a run for it. But first, I needed to disarm him. Both of my arms, however, were getting weaker from holding the flashlight so long. And the flashlight beam was growing dimmer.

"All I was doing was trying to talk to them, those half-breeds. They think they are so much better than I am. They laughed and mocked me in their heathen tongues for trying to talk to them. It was not enough they rejected me. They had to mock me."

"You take your aggression too far."

"Shut up! I'm talking."

I tried not to look directly into his eyes in defiance, as it might set him off quicker than I wanted. I needed to buy time.

"Who are they to reject me?" he continued, staring down at me. "They should be lucky I gave them the time of day. They think they are better than me," he scoffed in laughter. "They are nothing but half-breed barbarians. I had to show them—all of them—who is the man. I *am* the man!"

His logic astounded me. I did not understand how raping and killing women showed his manliness, unless violence and ruthlessness defined what it meant to be a man.

"And you, you just had to stick your nose where it does not belong."

My heart jumped. He waved his pistol at me. I cowered.

"You had to be a sleuth! Now it is time for you to pay for that nosiness of yours. Get in there." He waved the gun at me to go into the hallway that led to other rooms. I had no idea of the layout of that area. He knew this house, as he had been here a few times before. At least where we stood I had a chance of escaping down the wooden stairs and out the door. If I followed him to a tight space, I would not have a chance to defend myself.

"Wait. Please wait a moment. I need to know something. How did you know about Esmè? I...I mean, how did you know about her relationship with Mith? That...that they had met here?"

"If you must know, her father used to throw lavish

parties." He smirked. "He only invited people of the upper crust to attend. I met her at one of the parties and my companion and I visited her every chance we could, almost every day. She hardly ever came out to greet us. Only when her parents forced her to, then she came out. Even then her mind was somewhere else. She would not give us the time of day. No one ignores me. I knew I would teach her a lesson in manners. So I followed her. I saw her meeting with that monkey who thinks he is Westernized and sophisticated just because he studied in Paris. I figured she could do better than him. I kept my eyes on her when she was at home. She was close with her servant. They were always whispering and acting in secrecy. So one day I followed her servant to see what she was up to, and sure enough, I found her picking and dropping off mail. They had a little boy acting as a messenger. I followed that boy to where he lived. He was an orphan living with an elderly couple in a rundown shack. I befriended him. It was easy. I gave him some money and he told me everything. Money brings out the worst features of Cambodgein society. They'll sell their souls and that of their countrymen. It's too bad I had to kill him. Oh well. His life did not mean much anyway."

My blood boiled having to hear his hateful ranting, but I had to give him his moment.

He began to lick his lips. It seemed his body had not gotten used to the scorching temperature of Cambodge. I could see sweat flowing down from his forehead into his eyes. I gauged the distance between us and judged how fast he could aim and fire his gun. The next time he moved a hand to wipe away the sweat, I could swing my flashlight against his forehead. And when he tilted backward I would kick him hard between his legs. As I stood rehearsing this scenario in my mind, the flashlight dimmed.

Again, to make him feel like he had the upper hand and to tell him I would not try anything funny, I remained still and asked him another question. "How did you find this place," I asked.

He laughed. "If you have to ask that, then you have a lot to learn about sleuthing, little peasant girl. We Westerners invented sleuthing. If you must know—though you will have no use for any of the information—that is where all those loose royal women come in. They had nothing better to do but to shop, throw lavish parties, and gossip. Their tongues dance without much coaxing from me. They passed by the main road leading to the village a few times, but no one dared to stop, as the dead peasant mistress supposedly meandered and haunted the place. You barbarians and your superstitious beliefs! You'll never amount to anything with superstition. Now come on, get moving! No more questions."

I had to do something. But then my flashlight went out! I panicked. I felt him moving close to grab me. He let his guard down, only for a moment, and I slapped the gun out of his hand and elbowed him in the nose with all my might. He tilted back and I made a run for it.

He howled, "Ow! You piece of shit! Oh no. You're not getting away from me." Before I made it to the landing, he pulled me by my hair and slung me around. He stood with his back to the landing. I hit him in the head with my flashlight over his left temple. Then I kicked him in his groin with all the force I could muster. He fell back and rolled down the stairs. After the final thud of his body hitting the floor below, everything went dark and quiet. My body shook. A sense of relief also hit me. I was safe. He could not harm me anymore. Then something else hit me.

Fear and curiosity consumed me. I must face it. I quite

possibly had just killed another human being. I went from a girl who vomited at the sight of a dead body to possibly killing someone. I fought against my subconscious over the impact of taking another person's life. Suddenly, my conversation with Jorani surfaced. What would she think of me if she found out I had killed someone? But I did not set out to kill anyone. I was only protecting myself. I felt bad about it. My head fought with itself. It got me nowhere. I decided to file it in the back of my brain to work out at some other time. At this moment, I needed to get out of here and report the incident to the authorities. I was in a world of trouble—if not with them, then with Mother.

I gingerly descended the stairs, directing my flashlight to the first floor, to see where the body had landed. There he lay, unmoving, at the bottom of the stairs. I shuddered to think about having to clamber across his massive body to get to the door.

At least he's dead. Or unconscious.

The sunset revealed its last glimmering light through the opened shutters by the door. I stepped over his body, opened up the squeaking door and put one foot outside. Then I aimed my light all around the first floor one last time before I went to fetch the authorities.

Something caught my eye. *Why did I not see this before?* Footprints. Stains. The attack did not happen on the second floor. It happened on the first floor, in the back.

I studied the multiple sets of footprints and followed them. I noticed droplets of dried blood—which could have been from when Esmé regained consciousness and gathered all the strength she had to exit this abandoned house. The footprints and bloodstains appeared to come from the sunroom, where the family must have sat to look to the garden in the back and enjoy refreshments. Just as I thought, an old pool of blood stained the middle of the room. I realized this was the scene of the crime where this portly man had brought Esmé Laurent. The room was empty, except for pieces of cloth from her clothes and the dried blood.

I stood frozen at the threshold of the room by the site of such a vicious crime. Tears cascaded from my eyes. The sound of weeping echoed through the empty place and soon I realized that the sound was coming from me. My body shook in fear at nearly being attacked. I could not imagine the emotional and physical pain and suffering she experienced before, during, and after it all.

Without warning, I felt two thick hands grabbing at my feet, knocking me off balance. My flashlight went flying and I hit the floor with full force. I felt a punch to my face. Everything went dark.

Next thing I knew, I heard a muffled voice say, "Leave my daughter alone before I blow your head off."

I saw images of men come rushing through the door. I did not get a clear view of them, as everything was a blur. But one thing I remember saying was, "Pouk, I'm glad you're back home."

Instinctively I felt my legs and body, to make sure I was not compromised.

"You're all right, my child. He did not violate you. We arrived in the nick of time," Father said. I know I felt relief, but I cannot remember anything else. I must have collapsed into his warm and protective arms.

I woke up to a room full of smiling people who were waving at me. I was back home. Upon seeing the faces of my tearful mother and cheerful father, I breathlessly told Father that Andre Thomas's friend was the serial rapist and murder. "His name is James Albertson. He came from New York."

"Anjali," said Father, trying to interrupt me.

"His family is involved in the ivory trade business. He is a mental case..."

"Anjali," insisted Mother. "Listen to your father."

"...who..."

"Anjali, dear. We know. You've solved all the cases," said Father as Detective Chea, Madame Montha, and my relatives looked on with amusement.

"Well," I said, "did you know the foreign object everyone was looking for that caused fatal internal injuries to those women was not really a foreign object after all—except in that he is foreign?"

"Yes."

"It was his weight. His one hundred and forty kilogram weight ruptured his victims' bladders during those violent sexual attacks."

"Anjali! You're a young lady. Don't be so descriptive and direct like that," said Mother.

"Come on, Neak," said aunt Sopheary, referring to Mother as sister-in-law. "Don't mind her. She's just doing her job."

"See what you turned her into," said Mother, looking directly at Father and his sister.

"He stalked and hunted down his prey, Pouk," I continued.

"Yes, we all know," said Father.

"Just like when she was little. She cannot stop talking. We cannot get her to stop," said Mother's older sister to the other people in the room. They all laughed.

"You still have a lot of explaining to do, young lady, running off to an abandoned place all alone like that. You scared me to death," said Mother. "But we will not talk about it now. I am just glad you are back in one piece. But these bruises! They will take weeks to heal. I just do not understand why you put yourself in danger like this." Mother leaned in to lightly kiss me on the forehead.

"I'm sorry," I said to her. Then I turned to Father and Detective Chea and asked, "What happened? What have I missed?" They turned to look at each other. I continued to look at Father and others in the room. Mother threw her hands up in the air, as if giving up on wanting me to learn my lesson. She probably thought the traumatic experience would have been enough.

"Do you have to hear all about this now?" asked Mother, looking flabbergasted.

"Why not, Mother, while it is still fresh on everybody's mind? Plus, if I'm going to be a full-time sleuth, Father might as well evaluate what I did wrong and what I did right. Is that not correct, Pouk?"

He smiled his proud smile. "That's my girl."

"I am not going to listen to this. Come, Vanny, please help me prepare lunch for everyone." Mother and her sister left the room. Feeling obligated to help out, Father's sister and Madame Montha also left the room.

"Oh Pouk! My flashlight."

"It's in a safe place."

"Did I break it?"

"No. It is not badly damaged. I will fix it and make it brighter than before for you."

"Thank you, Pouk. Now that I will be working with you, shouldn't I be carrying a weapon?"

"Hold on. You're not in the clear yet. We have to get your mother comfortable with the idea of you working in the field of homicide. We'll talk about your self-defense training and weapon when the time comes."

"We caught the bad guy. So what happened after I was out cold, Pouk? What happened? Is he going to be brought to justice?"

"I'll explain everything."

I could feel myself lighting up with a sense of wonder and excitement.

"You're the strangest young lady," said Detective Chea upon seeing the excitement in my eyes. "You really are committed to this job. I don't think we should stop her if this is what she is set out to do, boss."

"I agree," said Father. I could smile all day upon hearing their agreement, but since my cheeks and entire face and entire body still ached, I tried not to smile much.

While Mother and her sister prepared lunch, Father and Detective Chea filled me in on what happened after he left to go to Bangkok.

According to Father, his initial studies of the investigation reports and autopsies from the victims in Annam, Burma, Laos, and Siam showed him a pattern, from which he confirmed that one person committed these crimes. The vicinity of each murder all had one thing in common: it was not far from a company called Emporium Export & Import Ltd, which was involved in the ivory trade. The company was wheeling and dealing with local authorities and influential people who were either colonial authorities who intermarried with locals, or in the case of Siam, local elitists intermarried with foreigners from Portugal, England, and other European countries.

Father decided to make his way to Siam, Laos, Burma, and Annam to interview witnesses and get traveling records of the one suspect he had in mind, the son of the owner of Emporium Export & Import Ltd. He fit the profile. The brutality of the rapes and murders suggested the man had an axe to grind. Father and his team of investigators traced his background all the way to his birthplace in New York City. They sent a telegram to the authorities in New York. None of them responded. However, a private detective who had gotten a whiff of their inquiry did reply to them.

Father made contact with the man and realized they were looking for the same man. James Albertson had a checkered past. His crime stemmed from his childhood abandonment, the alienation of love and affection from his parents, especially from his mother. He felt he never amounted to anything in her eyes. Sadly, she pitted him against his slender and handsome younger brother. His father was always too busy with his business in New York and around the world to be involved in the lives of his children, but when he came home, his attention went toward the younger brother.

The private investigator described James as a loner. Boys picked on him. Girls did not pay him any mind—not until his early college days when he met a nice, beautiful young lady with auburn hair. He fell deeply in love with her. She was only interested in him in a platonic sense. It hurt his ego, but when he found out the young woman's father was a quadroon, a quarter black, he felt enraged. He accused her of deceiving him. He snapped. She became his first rape victim. Three days later, she died of peritonitis from a ruptured bladder. Her family could not bring charges without revealing to their influential high society the truth of their mixed heritage.

This success spurred James to seek out other victims whose welfare was not fairly protected by the law of the land. Due to America's system of injustice against non-whites, and James Albertson's family's wealth and influence, he was acquitted and dismissed of any charges. In total, he raped and killed ten women until he made a terrible mistake of raping a full-blooded white woman whose family was as well positioned as his. His father found the solution—he took him out of the country to work with him in Asia, and this was where James found his Eurasian victims.

After Father had chased all of his leads and compiled enough evidence, he sought the help of local authorities to bring James in for questioning. Unfortunately, the higher echelons would not have it. His family was too influential and too powerfully connected with local authorities. Besides, they considered these "half-breed" women's lives not worth worrying about compared to the millions of dollars these businesses and families brought in every year. However, there was still a warrant out for his arrest if he should happen to make his way back to New York.

"So that is where things stand right now," said Detective Chea. "Due to what happened here, his father has summoned him to live in Europe. We have no jurisdiction or authority to arrest him. We have turned our findings over to the authorities in New York City who are still investigating him for the rape and murder of the one white woman. Since we cannot prosecute him here, maybe their highest authority can extradite and prosecute in the United Sates. Maybe the death of that one white woman can lead to his arrest and imprisonment, or even the death penalty."

Pain, hurt, and disappointment all hit me at once. I felt sick to my stomach. It was a bitter pill, but what could I, or anyone else here, do when the world turned on the whims of men with clever and conniving minds, money, and destructive weaponry.

"What about Mith?" I wanted to know.

Everyone looked at each other.

"What?" I asked. "What is it, Pouk?"

"Mith is fine. He has a job offer in Phnom Penh. He and his grandparents are moving there. They really want to be as far away from this place as possible. I do not blame him."

"How long have I been out? When are they leaving? Can I say goodbye to them, Pouk?" I felt as if my heart had been ripped out of me again, losing two friends so quickly.

Everyone laughed.

"You will have plenty of time to say goodbye. They will be leaving at the end of the month," said Father.

"Yes, right after Princess Esmè's royal funeral procession. He wants to be there," said Detective Chea.

"Does that mean all of the charges have been dropped against him?"

"Yes," said Father.

"So how are the princess and the governor? I mean...are they still holding a grudge against Mith?"

"Princess Dhana is more open-hearted and forgiving. As for the governor, he is still bitter and angry. I don't blame him. He needs time to heal. They all need time," said Father.

"They need a lot of love, prayer, and support," said Detective Chea. "The community is rallying to provide them these things, as the princess is a beloved royal."

17

THREE MEN ENTERED TOWN, THREE MEN LEFT TOWN

Not until I stood there, among her loved ones and special guests, watching her body lying in a coffin did I realize that Esmé Laurent, the object of many men's love and affection, was gone. Her father would not allow her to have a traditional Khmer funeral, one in which her body would have been burned, but insisted she be buried the Christian way. Soft and loud cries surrounded me. Practically everyone in town attended her funeral. Villagers could only stand from afar to say their goodbyes to the gentle and sweet young woman who offered them a smile when she saw them. She treated everyone like a human being. She brought light to their hearts in a world of suppression, repression, and mean-spirited beings.

I glanced over to find Mith Sovann, flanked by his grandfather and grandmother, shedding his own tears among the crowd of ordinary people who came to show Esmè their love and respect.

The end of the month came so quickly. A stranger had entered our town and wreaked havoc on our community. It was the story of our lives. Painfully, he would not be brought to justice despite all the blood on his hands.

I let out a long sigh as I stood at the dock of the Tonle Sap River with Mother for Mith Sovann's departure. His bright eyes flashed upon mine. He said something to Father and his grandparents and then walked over to me.

"May I have a word with your daughter?" he asked Mother.

"Sure," she said with a pleasant smile. She walked over to join Father and his grandparents.

"I never got a chance to properly thank you. Thank you, Anjali. Thank you for risking your life to save mine and to find justice for my beloved Esmé. I'll forever be grateful. You have been a great friend to me and my Esmé."

"Think nothing of it. That is what friends do for each other, right?" I said.

Though she was no longer with him physically, they belonged with each other in spirit. She loved him. In fact, she called out for him and asked for him with her last breath. Mith Sovann belonged to Esmé Laurent. Esmé Laurent belonged to Mith Sovann. They loved each other. I had accepted that, and I was fine with it. I came to realize I was a silly girl with a silly crush on an older man. I would probably look back on it one day and feel ashamed of myself.

Mith let out a gentle laugh and smiled his handsome smile. It had been a long time since he showed those pearly whites of his. His smile displayed both joy and pain. I gave him a quick and dry smile, feeling utterly sad that he and his grandparents had to leave us.

"We'll miss you," I said.

"And we, you. Take care."

"Bye. Good luck."

"Thank you. You'll make a great sleuth."

"Thank you."

"There he goes. He came into our lives and left just as quickly," I said softly to no one in particular.

My teary mother, walking back and standing next to me, heard what I said. She wrapped her right arm around me and leaned her head against mine. "People come and go in our lives. It's natural. You must learn to let go. Otherwise, you will walk around feeling lonely and depressed all the time. Just be thankful they come into your life, that you know them."

"I guess," I said.

We said our goodbyes to Mith and his grandparents as they boarded the boat bound for Phnom Penh. They had left their village of Beung Mealea behind, and now they were leaving the great town of Siem Reap entirely. They hoped to go about their daily lives without being reminded of the tragic events that had transpired in this historic town.

I joined my parents. Mith Sovann and his grandparents walked up the bridge into the first-class cabin and settled themselves. A few minutes later, after almost everyone boarded the boat, I saw Andre Thomas getting ready to board the same boat heading to Prey Nokor, where he would board a ship back to his country, England. I found it curious a wealthy Westerner like him would lower himself to sit in coach with a mixture of different classes and groups of people from all around the world. He turned to catch my eye. It was the first time ever that our eyes had locked on one another. I did not look away. He did not either. We stood looking at each other, wanting to say something, but our eyes had said what we needed to say. I regretted having thought he wanted to do harm to Esmé Laurent, and for classifying him among those arrogant and snobbish Westerners. Maybe he regretted ever looking down his nose at me and thinking of my people and me as savages. He tipped his white straw fedora at me and smiled. I found myself smiling at him, too. He climbed the bridge and disappeared among the other passengers.

A sinister and familiar laughter sent chills down my spine. My heart jumped. My stomach dropped. Everything rushed through me like a flood. I turned around to find the repugnant and smug James Albertson looking our way as he led an entourage of Western men. Before they marched on to their first-class cabin, they stopped. Mother held onto me tightly. Father and Detective Chea huddled together with us. The nonchalant serial killer and rapist pulled his cigar from his mouth. He wore a white straw hat and held a polished wooden walking cane. He glared at me up and down with his evil eye.

"Goodbye, little savage girl. Until we meet again. I will not forget what happened. You will pay for what you did. You will get yours. Just you wait. Just when you least expect it...boom!" He made an explosive sound. He guffawed all the way to the boat.

The three of them are on the same boat: Mith Sovann, Andre Thomas, and James Albertson! I thought. My mind whirled, wondering if they would spot each other. What would happen if they did? Would they duel? Would they kill each other before the boat made it to Phnom Penh? We slowly walked away as my head turned back to get a good look at the serial rapist and killer. Somehow I was not afraid of his threats against me, but the chaos he and his men would cause on the boat. Poor Mith and his grandparents. They could not catch a break. While thinking about them, I forgot about my own poor mother. I could feel her trembling with anger and fright. I wondered if she held onto to me for comfort or to keep from sliding to the ground.

"This doesn't look good," said Detective Chea.

"No. No, it doesn't," said Father.

"We need to do something."

"We'll have to get him off the boat. Convince him to take the next one."

"Then his trip will be delayed."

"True. However, it's better to be delayed for a few days then to be caught in another incident that could be avoided. It's not too late to change course. Besides, if he has to get there on time to do his job at Phnom Penh's Hospital, then my family and I can make a trip out of it and take him to Phnom Penh with our own car."

I stopped to watch as Father and Detective Chea went over to talk to the purser, who then went to the first mate and then the captain. Moments later, Mith and his grandparents emerged with perplex and concerned looks. Their brows knitted. Their forehead creased. A crewmember brought their suitcases off for them. Father said something to the elderly couple and their grandson. Their mouths curved into smiles. They showed a sigh of relief. It put a smile on my face. I felt a sense of relief too. An incident had been adverted. Just then, a roaring truck that could easily fit five people in it made its way past Mother and me. It appeared to be empty with only the driver in it. A man with a curled mustache drove up to where Father and the rest of them stood. He got out to talk to them. Mith seemed to know the man. He first *sompheas* to him and then extended his arm for a firm handshake. He then introduced the man to Father and the rest of the group. They put their belongings on the rail of the roof of the truck and fastened them with a rope. Then they got in and the stranger drove off as they waved goodbye to Father and Detective Chea.

"I wonder who that is?" I asked out loud.

"I don't know. I've never seen him before," Mother replied.

Father and Detective Chea walked over to us laughing. "Well, a catastrophe is avoided," Father said.

"And it saves you the gas and mileage," said Detective Chea, chuckling good-naturedly.

"What happened, Pouk? Who was that man?"

"Oh, that was Dr. Suriya Chandara at Mehta Hospital. He heard Mith was leaving today to Phnom Penh. Since he was driving up there himself, he needed some company on the long road. See, everything works out wonderfully, my dear Anjali."

My heart smiled upon hearing the good news. Father, Mother, Detective Chea, and I stood to watch as the truck drove off. We could see hands reaching out to wave at us. We stood smiling and waving them off. We watched on as the truck become smaller and smaller until it completely disappeared from our view. I prayed to the universe for Mith and his grandparents to have a better life.

Blood curling screams broke my reverie. All of us turned around. Before Mother could yell, "Anjali!" I had already hit the ground like a jaguar toward the cacophony. The steamboat had barely made its way out of the pier. I saw a heavyset man clutching his manhood, with blood oozing through his hands and soaking his pants. He stumbled out of the lower deck and fell into the river. People looked on from the upper to the lower deck in horror. Some closed their children's eyes or turned them away from it. My eyes surveyed the scene and stopped upon Andre Thomas's expressionless face. His eyes gazed down and away. His lips shrunk. He was standing next to the rail on the lower deck. In the middle of all the commotion one of James Albertson's companions dove into the water to retrieve him. A few more who appeared to have run down from the upper deck yelled out, "What happened? Who did this?"

A small boat from the pier went to rescue the diver and James. A security guard pedaled his bicycle as fast as his legs allowed him. He was probably asked to fetch the police or a doctor. The authorities at the pier cleared all people from crowding around. The captain directed his pilot to steer his steamboat back. We walked over to the docked boat carrying James and his rescuer, whose mouth curved down with his eyebrows knotting, creating a vertical furrow. He was indeed upset.

The owner of the pier, a French-Khmer, approached us. "Detective Chinak. Detective Chea. I'm glad you're still here," he said to them. He acknowledged me with his eyes. "This is bad for business. You need to find what happened to this man."

"That's our intention," said Father.

The entourage, boat rower, and a few other men helped to haul the heavy James Albertson onto the dock. Father felt his pulse.

"What do you think you're doing?" asked Albertson's companion with the bovine eyes.

"If you don't mind, I would like to feel his pulse," said Father in a calm, cooled, and collected manner. He felt James's pulse. He shook his head and said, "Unfortunately, this young man here is dead."

"What are you, a doctor?" he asked.

"No. I'm a detective."

"A detective?"

"This is Detective Oum Chum Chinak and his associate. He's the best. Don't worry. He'll get to the bottom of this," said the owner of the pier.

"Oh no. No, you don't! I know who you are. You're not working on this case—not if I have anything to do with it," said the companion. His nose snarled. His eyebrows became lower, knotted, and more furrowed.

Father and I exchanged looks. "There he is, Monsieur." I turned around to find the pier's security guard leading none other than Lieutenant Sun Tan and his team of men to the victim.

"Detective Chinak. Detective Chea," said Lieutenant Tan. "What happened here?"

"I don't want him or his people on the case," said the companion.

"And you are?" asked Lieutenant Tan.

"It's Steve. Steve Madden."

"Mr. Madden. Detective Chinak is the best detective in this corner of the world."

"I don't care."

"But..."

"No, no. Don't worry about it," said Father to the lieutenant. "We'll be on our way. If you need to ask us questions as witnesses, you know where to find us. We would be happy to cooperate."

"Yes. Thank you, detectives," said Lieutenant Tan.

As we walked away, the steamboat made it back to the pier. Lieutenant Tan and his men, who by this time had shown up in throngs, cleared the scene and set up the area for questioning the witnesses inside the boat. Lots of men and women glared at the authorities. Some appeared worried and scared. I completely understood their fear, concern, and frustration. It was bad enough they had to make long trips to their destinations, now someone decided to murder a man. His death had become an inconvenience for them.

Father drove away from the pier.

"That man protests too much," I said.

Father and Detective Chea, who sat up front on the passenger side, exchanged smiles.

"I take it you know what happened," said Father.

"Subject to verification, but that man definitely had something to hide."

"How do you know it wasn't Andre Thomas? He looked just as guilty and he was on the lower deck," asked Detective Chea.

"No. He did not do it. His guilt stems from possibly not doing anything when his former friend was attacked. I know for sure that the man who dove in to rescue him had something to do with it," I said.

"How do you figure," said Detective Chea.

"Before James fell into the water, though I could not see it clearly, there was something long and shiny stuck to his private area."

"Oh Lord Buddha," Mother said, as if she did not want to hear any of it. She stayed back by the car when we ran to the scene. She did not want to hear any of the discussion about the blood and gore of homicide. She made a painful grimace, turned away, and tried her hardest to tune us out.

"He fell face forward into the water. After Steve Madden dove in and dragged James Albertson's body to the surface... that was when his blood gushed out and squirted with great force."

"Maybe the knife," said Detective Chea, as if he was testing me.

"No. I don't think so. Someone or something had to pull the knife out for that gush and squirt to happen. Mr. Madden probably stabbed the victim many times, as we saw multiple lacerations. He thinks no one would be wiser as he acted as the rescuer. Possibly, upon realizing the knife, if it is unique, could probably trace back to him. Therefore, he probably pulled it out and to drop it into the river. If we find the knife, we could trace it back to the killer. And he could be the killer."

"How did you know it was a knife?" asked Detective Chea.

"It was definitely a knife based on how the cup of his pants was cut and the multiple lacerations in a shape what could be concluded as a knife. I believe it was a fighting knife."

"A fighting knife, huh?"

"Yes. I noticed there was a cut on Mr. Madden's left hand. He probably doesn't think anyone saw it."

"That's right, Anjali. Under the untrained eye, no one would have noticed that. Plus, in a brief and a quick moment like that, people would be too fearful and in a panic to make such an acute observation," said Detective Chea.

"What do you suppose was his motive is for killing James Albertson, Anjali," asked Father.

"That type of killing can only mean one thing—revenge," I said, feeling very sure of myself.

"What type of revenge?" asked Father.

"Judging from what James had done to women across the globe, I'd say the man's motive is revenge, possibly for his sister, because he appears to be younger looking than Mr. Albertson. The most obvious thing is his manhood. If it was robbery or any other motive, I don't think the perpetrator would go after his groin."

"If the person is on a defensive, he or she would go after area. After all, it is one of the deadliest areas of a man's body."

"That's true, Father, but the level of viciousness in that area suggested that it was not self-defense. It was intentional. That can only mean one thing. Yes, it's definitely revenge for a sister."

"I'm impressed," said Detective Chea.

"You're learning. Good observation and deduction, my dear daughter."

"I'm curious to know who he is though. How did he come about to be hired by James Albertson's father? What..."

"No. That door is closed on us," said Father.

"So what does this mean, Pouk?" I asked. "Aren't we going to..."

"No. Nothing. It means nothing. We're told not get involved. We won't get involved. And I mean it, Anjali. I don't want you to go snooping around. Let it take its course without involvement."

All I heard were "get involved" and "snooping around." So, okay, Father said no. However, there was no way I could let this go. Granted, in my mind, I solved the case, but I still wanted tangible proof and a confession from the man himself.

"Now let's talk about something else before your mother faints."

Father, Detective Chea, and I laughed while Mother gave us a dirty, yet playful, look.

THE END

ABOUT THE AUTHOR

Sambath Meas was born in Pailin, Cambodia at a time of civil war between the Khmer Rouge and the Khmer Republic. Having survived the effects of the Vietnam War, the Khmer Civil War, and the Khmer Rouge regime, her parents decided not to stick around for another phase of mass killings. As Democratic Kampuchea and its former ally, communist Vietnam, fought each other bitterly, her family, like thousands of other Khmers, fled to the Cambodian-Thai border. There, her father worked feverishly to write letters to First World countries to sponsor them, to give them a chance to survive. After being displaced in the refugee camps for two years, her family departed for Chicago on a cold night in September 1981.

Meas graduated from Loyola University of Chicago with a bachelor's degree in political science. She has worked in the legal industry for over 19 years now. She also continues to improve herself by contributing to the richness that is Chicago literature. She loves reading history, mystery, supernatural, and science-fiction books. She is currently attending Northwestern University in Chicago to hone her writing skills and obtain her master's degree in creative nonfiction.

Sambath is currently working on three books: the second series to Mysteries of Colonial Cambodia, a science fiction novel, and a children's fantasy book. In her spare time, she helps novice writers to get started with their stories.

www.sambathmeas.com
https://www.facebook.com/sambath.meas1
https://twitter.com/TreasureGold

ABOUT THE PUBLISHER

VISIT OUR WEBSITE
TO SEE ALL OF OUR HIGH QUALITY BOOKS:

http://www.redempresspublishing.com

Quality trade paperbacks, downloads, audio books, and books in foreign languages in genres such as historical, romance, mystery, and fantasy.

Made in the USA
Middletown, DE
31 July 2017